Beloved Enemy

About the Author

Elizabeth Whitaker is a pen name for Kate Merrill.

Kate is a longtime art gallery owner who lives with her wife, two cats, and a dog on a lake in North Carolina. When she's not writing, she enjoys swimming, kayaking, and allowing her strong-willed golden retriever to take her for a walk.

Beloved Enemy

Elizabeth Whitaker

BELLA
BOOKS

2023

Bella Books, Inc.
P.O. Box 10543
Tallahassee, FL 32302

Printed in the United States of America on acid-free paper.

First Edition - 2023

Editor: Kay Grey
Cover Designer: Heather Honeywell

ISBN: 978-1-64247-377-3

Acknowledgment

Muchas gracias
to the crew at Bella Books and to my superb editor, Kay Grey. Without her, my Spanish would have been garbled and unrecognizable. Her sensitivity to the plot, the characters, and the culture of Puerto Rico was vital to the final product.

In loving memory
of

Mary and Enid

who introduced me
to
their beloved Puerto Rico

CHAPTER ONE

A little turbulence...

Ellie leaned against the jet window and gazed out at the lightning bolts. They fluttered like the butterflies romping in her stomach and flashed through a fabric of dirty gray clouds. With a little luck, when the pilot curved in over the harbor, leaving the ocean behind, San Juan would emerge as clear and sunny as advertised in those brochures she'd been studying for the past few months.

"If the storm scares you, ma'am, why not pull down the shade?" The deep, honey-smooth voice startled her.

An exceedingly tall guy hovered in the aisle, his elbow braced against the headrest of the empty seat beside her.

"Rocky ride." He stated the obvious, almost losing his balance. "Mind if I sit down till I get my sea legs?"

Those butterflies in her stomach started flapping like caged crows. What made this unwelcome stranger think he could invade her private space and make himself at home? This never would have happened a few years ago, during COVID-19, when jerks like him were masked up and isolated two rows away. Her mama hadn't raised her up rude, yet she was royally pissed when the man hefted up her personal briefcase, which occupied the vacant seat to discourage such ignorant behavior.

She lunged to repossess her property, but as they tussled, the unlatched case popped open, spilling its contents everywhere. "Shit!" This time even Mama's ghost couldn't control her rage.

"Aw jeez, I'm sorry, ma'am."

His arrogant grin did not remotely suggest an apology as he toppled down and planted his rump beside her. At the same time, his large hands began gathering up her papers. In the process, he bumped parts of her anatomy that were strictly off-limits.

She pushed his hands away. Was it her imagination, or was he actually reading her proposal? She snatched it and stuffed it, along with her other papers, into the case. She twisted the lock, shoved everything under her seat.

"Smart move." He smiled. "We are required to stow our belongings under our seats in this kind of turbulence." The nutcase fastened a seatbelt across his lap, like he intended to stay.

"Beg your pardon, but these seats were guaranteed to be vacant when I booked this flight, and I have work to do before we land."

"Hey, lady, the pilot just turned on the warning sign. We're supposed to stay seated till further notice."

"So how come you're roaming the aisles?"

"Call of nature?" He winked.

She sighed. *Dear Lord, why me?* She had noticed this man boarding at the last minute. Who could miss him? He was at least six feet, four inches tall and wore an old-fashioned, crisply ironed white shirt, unbuttoned to expose a little chest hair and a gold chain. He was somewhat attractive, if one liked straight guys, but a wicked scar running down the right side of his face from just under his ear to below his jutting jaw, made him less handsome, more sinister. She figured he was in his late thirties, ten years older than she.

"So, do you live in Atlantic City?" he asked as his knees pummeled the backside of the forward seat, awakening the infant passenger cradled there, who immediately began to cry.

"Yes, I live in Atlantic City," she informed him in her best dry ice voice, praying he'd go away. Something about him sent a sharp chill down her breastbone.

"I'm from Philly, but I was there on vacation," he said. "I like to gamble, and I like to win."

Was she supposed to ask how much he won? *In his dreams.* The intruder had a slight Spanish accent, though he claimed to live in Philly. Maybe he had family in San Juan.

Over the years, she'd worked hard to disguise her own accent. She'd been raised in a double-wide in the mountains of western North Carolina, but to get ahead in this life, she'd learned to keep the *South* outta her *mouth*. Yet no matter how many air miles she logged, how successful she became, she would never dig free of her Southern roots, nor did she want to.

"You are Eleanor Birdsong," he stated. "Is Birdsong a Native American name?"

How the hell did this man know her? The chill in her breastbone plunged to her gut, and suddenly she was terrified.

"You work for DynaCo, based in Atlantic City, and your boss is Dyna Collins. You deal in international real estate," he continued in a monotone.

"Have we met?" She inched away as far as possible, flattening her right side against the body of the airplane. She stole a peek at the stranger's dark, hawk-like eyes

He laughed, but the humor never reached those eyes. "No, we've never met, Ellie. Folks call you Ellie, right? I read the info on the cover of your proposal, before you locked it away. I recently met your boss, though. She's a mean poker player. I'll bet Dyna Collins is a bitch on steroids to work for. Am I right?"

She turned away, her heart racing. The jet bucked violently as they began their descent, and the baby in the forward seat squalled. Who the hell was this guy? He certainly didn't look like one of the mobster types who haunted the boardwalk in Atlantic City. Was he a real estate competitor, or just some horny loser looking for a date? Men hit on her more often than she cared to admit. They never tagged her as a lesbian, even though she firmly rejected their flirting.

"Who are you?" She was half afraid to look at him.

He reached across her and lowered the little plastic shade, blocking out the thunderstorm. In the process, his elbow bumped her breast.

"I'm your guardian angel." He smirked.

She hated it when guys copped a free feel, so her fear became fury. She delivered a sharp jab to his ribs with her left elbow. This joker was no angel.

At that moment their stewardess appeared in the aisle and tapped her companion's shoulder. "We're preparing to land. Sir, will you please return to your seat?"

Now this stewardess *was* an angel. She stood firm until Ellie's tormentor grunted and maneuvered his long limbs up and out of his seat.

"It's been a pleasure chatting with you, Ms. Birdsong. Perhaps we'll meet again someday."

God, she hoped not. She held her breath until the creep left and did not exhale until he was out of sight, leaving her more nervous than before about the ordeal awaiting her on terra firma.

CHAPTER TWO

The target...

The moment they deplaned, a heavenly stagehand turned on the floodlights, revealing the Puerto Rico promised in her brochures. Brilliant afternoon sun pierced through the clouds. It backlit the rows of majestic palm trees lining the boulevard beyond the terminal, etching their delicate green fronds in vivid relief against a blindingly blue sky.

This was how she had visualized this first act of her adventure, this ultimate challenge of her young career, so she refused to let the unsettling encounter with an unhinged, fallen angel throw her off course. Scuttling through the causeway ahead of the other passengers, she ducked into the women's restroom. After taking care of urgent business, she washed her hands and checked the mirror to be sure that the nervous tension of the past hours had not wrecked her outward persona.

She saw the unruly auburn hair inherited from her Irish mother. For this occasion, she had smoothed the long, curly mane back from her face and secured it in a loose ponytail. She saw bronzed skin, high cheekbones, and a determined jaw, gifts from her proud, misguided Cherokee father. Her smile was still too wide, lips too full, and her large dark eyes appeared slightly shell-shocked. But all in all, she looked okay.

Her inner tomboy, along with an insecure mountain girl masquerading in a voluptuous woman's body, was well disguised by the obscenely expensive wheat linen power suit Dyna had urged her to purchase specifically for today. Indeed, her boss had groomed her to look successful, and had taught her many things.

After snagging a scholarship and graduating from Temple University in Philadelphia, she'd felt isolated and alone in the big, impersonal city. In spite of a prestigious degree in marketing, she still had no idea what to do with her life. After two years of meaningless jobs—waitress to secretary in a large real estate firm—she'd made few friends, had little interest in dating, and lived alone in a ratty apartment above a kosher butcher shop. Yet she refused to run home with her tail between her legs, so she'd screwed up her courage, put on a basic black dress and attended a jobs fair, which was more like a fancy cocktail party. There she met the older, sophisticated Dyna, a "happily married" woman who seduced her and became her first lover. Dyna groomed her protégé, brought her into her real estate acquisitions firm, and then dropped their intimate relationship without ceremony. Heartbroken and emotionally distraught, Ellie had grieved for months until she realized that Dyna had given her a great gift: a validation of who she was and whom she wanted to love.

She had always been attracted to girls, but the thought of being gay in the conservative Southern town where she grew up was more than she could handle, until Dyna brought her "out."

Dyna had also given her the hunger to succeed. Entrusted with this unprecedented opportunity, Ellie would not let her down, although, like the obnoxious stranger said: Dyna Collins was a bitch.

Soon Ellie would meet her "mark" face-to-face, a total stranger who would become the focus of her life. Her target was wealthy landowner Carla Valdez. She was a world-traveler, highly educated, ten years Ellie's senior, and owner of the most desirable beach frontage on Puerto Rico's southern coast. Ellie's job was to convince her to sell her precious land to DynaCo.

Ellie's company would then develop it into a five-star gambling resort, a project Valdez would bitterly oppose on principle. Her mission was to seduce Valdez with the mighty all-American dollar and to disarm her with her womanly charms. This last tactic was never spoken, only implied, by Dyna, because after doing their research, they knew Carla Valdez was openly gay. Valdez's partner, Maria, had died four years ago, and as far as anyone knew, Valdez had never entered into another relationship.

Maria had also left Valdez in charge of her two young sons, products of an unhappy marriage. Bottom line? Dyna believed Valdez might be vulnerable to an attractive younger woman, so Ellie was given a major chance to prove herself.

Dyna thought she was ready. Ellie did not.

Nonetheless, she touched up her lipstick, adjusted the soft, patterned scarf around her throat, and then left the safety of the restroom. Running on nervous energy, she walked briskly through the terminal. As she worried about her imminent meeting with Valdez, the pretty scarf felt like a hangman's noose around her neck.

Once she descended from the causeway to the open-air baggage claim, the sudden heat and humidity spun her like meat in a microwave, melting her composure along with her makeup and the crisp linen suit. She was bombarded with the heady scents of sweet tropical flowers and jet fuel hanging in the still air, while her ears were accosted by the loud, musical chatter of people speaking Spanish and the unpleasant whine of planes taking off.

Luckily, she found herself at the opposite side of the baggage carousel from the man who had bothered her on the plane. He was shoving people out of his way to claim his stuff. He retrieved a small padded bag and frowned as he inspected the expensive camera inside, like he'd expected it to be damaged in transit. She figured he'd use it to take nude beach pictures. Or else he was an outright pornographer, the jerk!

She continued to lag behind, hoping the man would move on without spotting her. Closing her eyes tight, she put him out of her mind and instead visualized how she should react when Carla Valdez emerged from the crowd, looking for her. Dyna had promised that Valdez would be there to meet her on time.

She took a deep breath to compose herself. She had read Valdez's dossier a dozen times and felt she knew her inside out. Indeed, she believed she would actually admire Valdez if she were not *the enemy*, as Dyna put it. Because in the game of high-stakes real estate, the rules were less like business, more like war.

Normally she was not so uptight, but in her anxiety to pack, she had never made it to bed last night and suffered from sleep deprivation as well as a debilitating case of the jitters. As she bent over the carousel to grab her heaviest piece of luggage, a friendly flight attendant gave her a hand.

"Are you here on vacation?" he asked with a Puerto Rican accent.

"I'm here on business that will take me out on the island." She moved away the moment he gave her the suitcase.

"*Out on the island*? You talk like a native," he persisted.

Good. Fitting in was part of the master plan. She had studied the island's history, geography, culture, and even its political parties. She had spent endless hours attempting to learn Spanish on YouTube and various apps, but her lazy tongue couldn't quite roll the words properly, and her brain refused to become fluent.

Mostly, she had explored the personal history of Carla Valdez, become a voyeur in her unsuspecting victim's life. So when they finally met in a few minutes, she would be armed with secret knowledge one human rarely accumulated about another. She would have an unfair advantage, and she figured she would need it.

She thanked the flight attendant and left the baggage area, her adrenaline pumping overtime. She was so hyped she barely noticed the exotic sounds and sights all around her. She had dreamed of this encounter so often it was permanently engraved in her mind. So that when a soft male voice spoke at her elbow, she nearly jumped out of her skin.

"Señorita Birdsong? I am Juan Castillo. Doña Carla sent me to meet you, and to bring you home."

She stared into the kindly brown eyes of an elderly gentleman. His skin was dark and wrinkled from years in the tropical sun, and she recognized her two new suitcases gripped in his hands. "Where is Ms. Valdez?"

"She sends her apologies. She was too busy to come herself."

Ellie was speechless. Should she laugh, cry, or be annoyed? She frowned at the innocent messenger. So far, this day had been nothing like she had imagined. Carla Valdez not bothering to meet her was just a little more turbulence along the way.

CHAPTER THREE

American invasion…

"How did you recognize me?" Ellie asked the man named Juan.

"Doña Carla gave me your photograph, but you are much prettier in person. Come, the car is waiting."

"Did Ms. Valdez employ you to drive me to Ponce?"

"We are not going to Ponce, *señorita*. We are going to Casa Valdez. Doña Carla said I should bring you to her home."

"Look, I'm afraid you've made a mistake. I have reservations at a hotel in Ponce. I will not stay at Ms. Valdez's house."

The older man shrugged and smiled, an immoveable force of nature. "Come, we will be late." He balanced her suitcases in his two strong hands and trotted toward the parking lot.

She gripped her briefcase and laptop, then quickly followed him. He kept glancing back to be sure she was still coming, and each time she caught his gentle eyes, the more she felt inclined to trust him.

"Okay, I'll come with you, Mr. Castillo," she said once they stopped.

"Please call me *Juan*."

He helped her into the backseat of a new, grass-green Honda Accord Hybrid, and while the car was not as luxurious as the limo Ellie had ridden to the airport that morning, it was fuel efficient and jived with everything she'd read about its owner. She knew Carla Valdez was passionate about environmental issues, a true champion in the fight against global warming. She had also learned the island of Puerto Rico was only thirty-five miles wide by one hundred miles long, and that Valdez often drove the entire length in a typical business day. That made the hybrid a practical choice, as well as a *green* choice, and she couldn't help but admire the woman for her stance.

"Have you ever visited Puerto Rico?" Juan asked as he expertly bypassed San Juan, then picked up Highway 2 going west. "We are a land with many faces. We have beaches, mountains, and even the desert. Did you know this, Señorita Birdsong?"

"Please call me *Ellie*."

When he shook his head, she realized she'd asked him to cross a social barrier that could not be bridged. He squirmed in his suit coat, and she decided to try a different approach. "At least take off your coat, Juan. It's much too hot."

He hesitated, his eyes questioning from the rearview mirror, but soon he shed the uncomfortable jacket. "Doña Carla told me the coat was too warm for today, but I wanted to make a good impression."

With that remark, he captured her heart. He reminded her of her Grandpa Birdsong, a drunk who had adopted the Christian religion late in life. Every Sunday he would sit in the front pew of their rural country church in a suit, tie, and tight shoes—even on sweltering summer days when all the other parishioners wore short-sleeved shirts and shorts. Grandpa wanted to impress the preacher and the ladies in the congregation, make sure they understood that he was a reformed man. More times than not, he would faint dead away, so that Mama and she had to revive him and haul him home, their cheeks burning with shame.

She unwrapped the scarf from around her neck and smiled at her driver in the rearview mirror. Juan handed her a cold bottled water, which she gratefully accepted, and they lapsed into easy silence as their little car sped along the highway. She caught sight of the bright blue ocean. They circled fields of tall, sweet-smelling sugarcane and passed through colorful tunnels of flowering scarlet flamboyan trees that startled her with their dramatic beauty. She spotted occasional, ancient two-storied wooden country homes that reflected their grand Spanish heritage, but mostly she saw humble contemporary dwellings: concrete block ranch houses with very few rooms.

She saw strange trees bearing fruit much like large bananas. "What are those?"

"Platano trees. They feed poor families, keep us from starving."

In spite of the poverty, the setting was exotic and enchantingly beautiful. She wondered if Juan came from a poor family, if he had ever faced starvation. She wished he would tell her more about the people and how they lived, but he remained absolutely silent until they turned left onto Highway 10.

"Now we will cut through the mountains," he explained. "This road ends in Ponce, but we will drive on to Casa Valdez at Guanica."

The landscape changed abruptly as they dropped into valleys, then climbed up lush green hills. She saw weather-beaten, one-room shacks clinging on stilts to the sides of small mountains. Many were battered and broken beyond repair.

"Hurricane Maria," Juan intoned somberly. "We have not recovered."

Ellie remembered the devastating natural disaster that killed several thousand. The United States had done little to help.

Half-naked children, who should have been in school, played on the front porches. Suddenly, as they neared an entrance to the interstate, Juan pulled off the road, stopped, and climbed from the car.

"Where are you going?"

"I am very thirsty, *señorita*. Do you want a *cerveza*?"

She had noticed signs advertising *India* and *Corona*, which were local beers. "No thanks…" She glanced at her empty water bottle. "Can you find me a diet soda?"

When Juan approached a rickety roadside stand, a small boy about seven years old appeared from behind the counter and jumped into his arms. She watched in amazement as the child covered the old man's face with kisses.

Juan returned with a frosted beer. He handed her a warm Coke in a classic glass bottle. When she took a swig, she suspected the beverage was as ancient as its container. She didn't complain that the drink wasn't diet, she was simply grateful for a chance to wet her whistle. She did wonder briefly if Juan should be drinking and driving, but quickly dismissed the worry. Back home in the mountains, guys did it all the time without incident—mostly—and Juan inspired more confidence than those bozos.

"Who was that boy?" she asked.

"The boy is Luis, my son. I have three other grown sons and two daughters. They all work for Doña Carla."

"But where does Luis live? Where is his mama?" How could Juan be so casual about his little son wandering along a strange highway?

He pointed down Highway 111. "My home is out that way half a mile, in Lares. My wife lives there with Luis and our baby. Luis often works this roadside stand. For money, you understand?"

Sure, Ellie understood about money, but what about school? What about roving maniac child abductors, or didn't they have them in Puerto Rico? "Where do *you* live?" she asked Juan.

"I live with Doña Carla, of course. I drive for her and tend her garden. My two daughters work in the kitchen for Señorita Diaz."

"Who is Señorita Diaz?" Valdez's dossier had not included a description of this feudal system, complete with a chauffeur/gardener separated from his wife. And who was this mysterious Diaz woman?

"Why don't you take a nap?" Juan suggested. "We have many miles to go. I will wake you when we get there."

Great idea. Her eyes had seen more new sights than they could comfortably absorb, so she leaned into the headrest, and in spite of her nervous apprehension, she got drowsy as Juan hummed a slow Latin melody.

When she drifted into semiconsciousness, she revisited the black and white photo etched into her mind: a portrait of a ruggedly handsome, middle-aged woman with thick black hair, wing-tipped with white at the temples. Valdez's eyes were dark and deeply set above strong cheekbones, yet they were sad and haunted. Her full, sensuous lips curved in wry amusement, but her expression remained a mystery, although Ellie had studied the photo a hundred times. Was Valdez laughing at herself, or at the world?

As Ellie relaxed in the back seat of Valdez's car, she realized the portrait also implied a raw confidence, which was almost sexual in nature, as though the subject could defend herself from any or all attacks.

But Carla Valdez had never met Ellie. Could she withstand an American invasion?

CHAPTER FOUR

The porthole...

Carla Valdez gazed through the large round window set below the peaked roof of her study. It was the porthole where she commonly surveyed her land. From the exterior of the historic house, the window was the central architectural feature, a single eye, ever-watchful above the tin roof of the veranda, which stretched the full length of the hacienda. The window was wide open, so she felt the warm breeze drying her long hair, still moist from a shower. She smelled the floral fragrances from the gardens surrounding the driveway, and she heard her younger adopted son, Enrique, playing on the creaky old swing on the porch.

Her elbows were propped on the desk at the window, where she did most of her work, as she lifted her eyes to the horizon. The Cordillera Central Mountain Range protected the rear of the house to the north, while in the distance, across the fields, the Caribbean Sea glistened like an endless, aqua silk tapestry.

The farm had been in the Valdez family for generations, a lineage that would have ended with her, had Maria not left her two sons in Carla's care. Carla had adopted them, and the boys were now her rightful heirs. Her beloved Maria had been gone four long years, stolen by cancer, and every hour of every day Carla whispered Maria's name in her heart, which was broken. If not for Enrique and Antonio, her life would not be worth living.

But something had to change. The boys needed food, clothing, and someday in the not-too-distant future, quality college educations. Carla's sugarcane, rice, and coffee crops had been diminished by drought, hurricanes, and decreased demand. Puerto Rico now imported eighty-five percent of its food, so many of her eighty acres lay neglected and barren. She had been forced to fire much of her workforce and could barely pay the rest.

Something had to give. She figured she had to sell at least part of her land, and there were many interested buyers. She sighed, and again studied the screen on her laptop: DynaCo International, based in Atlantic City. The company was owned by Dyna Collins, who from her résumé, looked to be a very striking shark in designer clothing. Her representative, Eleanor Birdsong, who was currently on her way to Casa Valdez, was an entirely different kettle of fish. The name "Birdsong" was intriguing, almost certainly Native American, and Carla had a passionate interest in all indigenous cultures. The girl looked so young, but she knew Ms. Birdsong was twenty-eight, a woman, not a girl.

Eleanor's strong, angular features spoke of her native roots, but her unruly mass of dark, reddish hair defied understanding. Her expression was determined, yet somehow vulnerable—another dichotomy. From carefully reading her résumé, Carla deduced she was proud, ambitious, and likely a handful. Because the Internet info revealed nothing about her personal life, Carla was naturally curious, but firmly committed to keeping her emotional distance from this young woman who was undeniably attractive.

Undoubtedly DynaCo would offer a high-pressure pitch to buy Casa Valdez, but she was immune to all offers failing to meet her high standards. This decided, she closed her laptop, and saw a cloud of dust lifting off the ribbon of gravel leading to the house. The cloud appeared long before the Honda came into view.

Taking a deep breath, feeling a bit nervous, she watched Juan help Ms. Birdsong from the car. That breath caught in her throat. The woman was even more beautiful than her photo. Perhaps she had made a terrible mistake inviting her to stay at the house, especially in Maria's old bedroom. It was unlike Carla to second-guess herself, because she fully expected Eleanor to be an adversary, but her grandpa had taught her the old cliché: "Keep your friends close, and your enemies closer."

She figured Eleanor was ready to take her on, but was she ready for Eleanor?

CHAPTER FIVE

Sunset in paradise…

"Wake up, *señorita*, we are almost home."

Juan's voice, along with the bumpy road, jolted Ellie back to consciousness. She removed her sunglasses, because evening had fallen on the exotic landscape, and then she realized the rugged path they were traveling served as the approach to a plantation home in the distance. Yellow flamboyan trees arched along both sides of the roadway, and the odd, desert-like terrain was carpeted with flowering bushes and cacti tangling across the flat land. In the far distance, the Caribbean glistened like a wise green eye, lending a surreal beauty to the strange scene.

Juan parked beside a porch supported by tall square pillars. "Welcome to Casa Valdez."

The structure was not as large as the grand houses she had visited in the Antebellum American South, but its old wooden walls bore a fresh coat of white paint, so Casa Valdez boasted its own kind of grandeur.

"I love it, Juan, but why is the door wide open?"

A laugh rumbled up from deep in his chest. "We Puerto Ricans appreciate fresh air. Until recently, we followed the old ways—no glass or screens. The shutters are not decoration, they keep out hurricanes. We even welcome the little iguanas who come through the open door. No one cares when they come inside. Doña Carla's sons keep them as pets."

She laughed. "We had little critters like that where I grew up. Called them *skinks*, and I used to collect them." As a child, she had learned to enjoy all God's creatures. Now it was human encounters that made her nervous. "Where is Ms. Valdez?" she asked apprehensively.

"She is waiting for you inside."

As they climbed a flight of steps to the veranda, she was startled by two enormous black eyes peeking out from behind a wooden swing hung from the porch ceiling. The eyes were set in the dark face of a young boy, who bolted and ran away when she winked.

"Come back, Enrique!" Juan shouted. "This lady won't hurt you!" But the child had disappeared into a nearby field. "He is the shy one," Juan explained. "Antonio, his big brother, is not so shy."

As they passed through the front door into an open foyer with colorful tiles on the floor, she had the impression that the very outdoors—blossoms and salt-scented air—flowed through this house. Suddenly another boy, this one much taller, materialized from the shadows.

"Welcome, Ms. Birdsong. My mother is waiting in the library, but perhaps you will allow me to give you the grand tour before you meet her?" He hooked his fingers into the pockets of stylish jeans, squared his slim shoulders.

She stifled a giggle as the boy attempted to flirt. In spite of his cracking, adolescent voice, young Antonio seemed determined to be a ladies' man. Also, he spoke perfect, unaccented English.

"Save it for later, son." A deep, cultivated voice echoed from the dark beyond the archway. "Ms. Birdsong has traveled a long way." Antonio retreated as Ellie's hostess stepped forward, extending a strong, graceful hand. "I am Carla Valdez. Welcome to my home."

As she accepted Carla's firm handshake, she was rendered both shy and tongue-tied. After months of studying her, being suddenly face-to-face was overwhelming. The woman was much taller than she had imagined. Her frank, intense gaze totally disarmed her, and her photograph, attractive as it was, did not do her justice. Carla's long, shiny black hair was pulled back in a ponytail, emphasizing the woman's angular, aristocratic features.

"Well?" A faint smile curved upward at the corner of Carla's mouth. "Am I as you expected, or does the flesh and blood woman disappoint you?"

"I had no expectations," Ellie lied, as she breathed in the fresh scent of Carla's cologne, which reminded her of waves breaking on a windy beach.

"Very wise, indeed." Carla smiled. "I glanced at your DynaCo website, but that photo was inaccurate. You are younger and prettier than I imagined."

Carla was smooth as butter on a hot biscuit, Ellie would give her that. She'd heard Latino men were famous for delivering romantic lines, but she didn't expect something so direct from a woman. Thing was, her mama had always said Ellie possessed a built-in bullshit detector, and the good Lord knew she'd put it to good use over the years, but somehow she wanted to believe that Carla's compliment was sincere. Her alto voice and musical Spanish accent were honey from the hive. Her dark eyes were serious and attentive, but she was grinning like a fox in the henhouse, and Ellie did not intend to be her next meal.

"I planned to stay in a hotel in Ponce, Ms. Valdez. I appreciate your hospitality, but I can't stay here."

"Please call me *Carla*. When you call me *Ms. Valdez*, I feel old enough to be your mother. Am I old enough to be your mother, Ms. Birdsong?"

"Not unless you were a mother at ten, and call me *Ellie*, will you?"

"You have done your homework, because you know my exact age. Have you also memorized the details of my personal life?"

Ellie had spoken out of turn and revealed her hand, drawing a curtain of suspicion between them. "Yes, I've read your background. What did you expect? It's my job to know about people with whom we do business. No doubt you know something about me, too."

"Not much. I prefer to judge my associates face-to-face." Carla flashed her winning smile. "I admit I'm curious, though. One assumes a lovely American career woman has made a choice not to marry. Should you want a husband, I'm certain any number of suitable young men would line up to take you to the altar."

"What else do you assume about American women?" Ellie did not like the direction their conversation was taking, but she sensed Carla was feeling her way, trying to determine something about Ellie's sexual preferences. It was part of a delicate dance lesbians had perfected—a tango of hints and innuendo—and according to her dossier, Carla had never hidden her preference for women. It was another trait she admired about the woman, but for now, she preferred not to tip her hand.

"Excuse me, Doña Carla…" Juan chuckled. He had been standing just inside the door, pretending not to listen to their banter. "Where shall I put the *señorita's* bags?"

"Sorry to keep you waiting, Juan," Carla said. "Please take Ms. Birdsong's suitcases to the blue room, so she'll have a view of the sea."

"Perhaps you didn't hear me?" Ellie objected. "I don't intend to stay here. Will you drive me to Ponce, Juan?"

Carla and Juan glanced at one another, and then Carla cleared her throat. "Please be reasonable, Ellie. Juan has been working all day. He needs his supper and his rest. Can't you stay one night?"

So now she was the bad guy? "Okay, you win. But I will leave first thing in the morning."

"Agreed." Carla winked at Juan. "Thanks for everything, Juan. I'll try to convince Ms. Birdsong to accept our hospitality for several days, but should I fail, I'll call for the car at dawn."

"*Sí*, Doña Carla." The older man nodded, backed away.

Clearly Carla was mistress of the manor. Did she always expect her children, her servants, and possibly her guests to jump at her bidding? Once Juan departed with the luggage, Ellie picked up where she left off.

"So, what else have you heard about American women? I hope you realize that we are entrusted to negotiate business matters, and that you and I have a great deal to discuss." She gave her briefcase a meaningful pat.

Carla's infectious laugh echoed through the darkening foyer. "We Puerto Ricans don't live in the Dark Ages, Ellie."

She refused to be sidetracked from her purpose, yet did not protest when Carla's warm hand opened across the flat of her back, and with all the grace of a Southern gentleman, she guided Ellie into a large solarium. Her touch, the pressure of her strong fingers, felt surprisingly good, and suddenly she felt less like a stranger.

"Believe it or not," Carla spoke gently, "women are highly respected in all phases of professional life. After all, my country is your country, is it not? Puerto Rico is a US territory, and we share the same federal government. We have different customs, it's true, but we all live in the twenty-first century."

"I didn't mean to imply..." she began, but Carla lifted her hand off her back and gestured for her to be still. Ellie missed the warmth of the contact.

"I understand you want to discuss business, but first we must relax," Carla said. "We'll get to know one another, and then we'll talk. Can I offer you a drink?"

"You bet." Ellie was warming to this gracious stranger.

"Good." Carla smiled, gestured toward a couch in the middle of the room. "Please take a seat."

Ellie settled into the cushions of an elegant, wheat-colored linen sofa, and then gave the decor a once-over. Carla's furniture was simple, built of natural woods and upholstered in subtle fabrics. The aged brick floor was strewn with a few hand-woven rugs, some with an indigenous native design. Several pieces of seemingly ancient pottery, glazed in tones of rust and white, were prominently displayed on a modern glass cocktail table, while a dimly lit display case revealed an extensive collection of wooden figurines. The room would have seemed almost monastic without the art.

"Did you use an interior designer?"

"What?" Carla blinked in surprise.

"C'mon, did you hire a pro to decorate for you?"

The smile faded from Carla's face. She seemed uncommonly weary as she opened an antique carved wooden bar and stared at the bottles. "When my partner was alive, the house was quite charming. After her death, I gave everything away that reminded me of Maria. Later, I bought these things myself, so I'm to blame for how it looks now."

"But it's lovely! Tell me about the artifacts."

"Native Puerto Rican." A smile returned to her lips. "I'm a hopeless collector, you see…" She picked up a small statue, a brightly colored bird Ellie did not recognize. She held it lovingly in one hand, and then replaced it on a shelf. "But first, what do you drink, Ellie?"

"Bourbon 'n' branch?" She blurted it out as Carla lifted a chilled bottle of Chablis from an ice bucket. Guess she figured all American women drank wine. "It's an old Dixie custom," she hastily explained. "You know, whiskey and water?"

"You're a woman after my own heart." She poured them each a double.

Carla's manners were so practiced and polished, like a romance heroine from a classic movie, that Ellie almost forgot to be wary. Yet Carla was very much a woman of the present. Their fingers brushed as she handed her the drink, and Carla acknowledged the contact with the barest flicker of a smile.

Carla lifted her glass in a toast, then said, "All my art comes from the island. The pottery was created by the *Igneri*, a tribe of Indians who lived here long before the Spanish arrived, and the small wooden figures are called *Santos*. Even today, our artisans carve these little religious figures, and often a distinctive style is passed down from father to son."

"They are rare, aren't they?"

"I'm afraid the *Santos* have become a favorite with the wealthy tourists," Carla remarked bitterly. "And the pottery is extremely hard to find. Since you know so much about me, you must know I'm active in the Institute of Puerto Rican Culture. That's how I obtain the pottery."

In fact, Carla was one of the founders of the Institute. Ellie knew how generously she had contributed, down to the last dime. Carla was as passionate about preserving the Puerto Rican way of life as she was about preserving the environment, and the combination made her a tricky adversary. Somehow Ellie must convince her to welcome DynaCo into her own little piece of paradise, and the task would not be easy.

"I admire your support of Native Puerto Rican culture," she said with sincerity. "My father was Cherokee, so I've always been fascinated by such artifacts."

Carla pinned her with an odd, contemplative stare. "Yes, I suspected as much, Eleanor Birdsong. It was one of the reasons I was glad you were coming. Maybe you'll tell me something about your Native American background." She gently took Ellie's arm, helped her to her feet. "But now, I want to share something very special."

Seconds later they were standing at the large picture window, and the view beyond left Ellie breathless with wonder.

"So, Miss Lady Executive, what do you think of that display?"

Carla wasn't mocking her. Ellie heard the quiet, almost wistful quality in her voice and understood nature had conspired to produce the most magnificent sunset imaginable. Hues of fiery red, pink, and orange set the western sky ablaze above the placid Caribbean, which reflected the same colors, dipped in shadow. Between the house and the sea, the brush fields were glazed in dusty violet, while in the far distance, a row of palm trees rustled in black silhouette. Ellie wondered if Carla and her lost love, Maria, had watched the sunsets together from this spot.

"What can I say?" She was in awe.

"Say nothing. The heavens speak for themselves." Carla captured her hand.

Ellie knew it was a natural impulse, a basic human need to share such a moment of magic, but the gesture truly alarmed her. Again this woman's touch had triggered an unexpected response, a need as old as time itself. She slowly removed her hand and stepped a safe distance away.

She gazed out the window and wondered what would become of her in this strange, enchanted land. She wished the moment would never end, and struggled to regain her composure. But when she turned back to Carla, she realized that she too was lost in the fantasy world beyond the window.

"You said I would sleep in the blue room. May I go there, now? I'm really tired." Ellie's words shattered the ambiance. For a long moment, Carla stared in confusion, as though she had interrupted a holy interlude.

"Of course, where are my manners?" Carla's voice was thick with emotion. "The blue bedroom is upstairs, second on the left. Shall I call the maid to show you the way and help you unpack?"

"Hey, I found my way here from the States." She giggled nervously. "I suppose I can locate the bedroom." She turned her back and fled into the foyer, with Carla at her heels.

"But wait, Ellie…" Carla extended her hand. "Dinner is served at eight. Please join me."

She was already halfway up the stairs, but something in Carla's voice caused her to pivot and stare. Standing with the sunset behind her, the mistress of Casa Valdez was impressive indeed. She couldn't help but admire her proud, upright physique. Ellie knew she was thirty-eight, ten years her senior, yet Carla was built like a young, well-toned athlete. She wore a colorful, loose-fitting shirt tucked into stylish designer jeans, but beneath her clothing, Ellie detected small, perfect breasts and slim, well-muscled hips. As Carla awaited her answer, Ellie gave herself a lecture: *down, girl, let that dog lie.*

"Please, Ellie, don't you want to hear what else I've heard about American women?" she called up at her. "We can discuss it over dinner."

Ellie's face flushed hot with pleasure, but fortunately the lecture had done its work, so her mouth was able to speak contrary to the wishes of her heart. "Sorry, Carla, I'm afraid I wouldn't be good company tonight. May I eat in my room?"

"If that's what you want," she answered tonelessly. "I'll send the cook up for your special requests."

"Thanks," Ellie called over her shoulder, and ascended the steps as fast as her high heels would allow.

CHAPTER SIX

The blue room...

She easily located the blue room and opened the door to the afterglow of the spectacular sunset. Like in the solarium below, these windows looked out to the ever-present sea. Unlike the solarium, this space showed the distinct influence of a woman. Delicate lace curtains framed the shuttered doors leading to a balcony, while a floral canopy crowned an enormous four-poster bed. A fragile dressing table and mirror were positioned near the bed, with assorted perfumes assembled on a silver tray. Finally, the walls were papered in pale blue silk, the color of summer sky.

"*Buenas noches, señorita.* May I take your order, *por favor?*" The high, girlish voice nearly startled her out of her skin.

She spun around to discover a uniformed maid had followed her into the room. The girl's round face was pink with embarrassment and her pretty, somewhat blunt features, were vaguely familiar. "Oh, you must be Juan Castillo's daughter. Do you work in the kitchen?"

"I am Sylvie. My sister, Filo, works there, too."

Ellie smiled, hoping to put the girl at ease. "I met your father today. I see a family resemblance."

"You are Señorita Birdsong. Papa said you are beautiful, and it is true. You are hungry? Doña Carla said I should bring you some food."

"If it's not too much trouble, I'd love two eggs and some toast." As she pushed off her shoes and perched on the large bed, curiosity got the better of her. "Tell me, Sylvie, did Doña Carla choose the furniture for this room?"

"Oh, no," Sylvie gravely replied. "This room belonged to Doña Maria, her dead partner. Doña Carla never comes here. Never!"

The space was spotless, not one item out of place, not one dust mote floating. "But it's so clean. Does anyone use this room?"

"You are the first, except Señorita Diaz used to sleep here." The girl's eyes grew wide as she spoke.

"Where does she sleep now?" Juan had mentioned this woman, but never explained who she was. Perhaps she was the head housekeeper?

"Señorita Diaz stays downstairs in the front room. It's the biggest bedroom, right next to Doña Carla's," Sylvie confided, but not before looking over her shoulder, as though she was betraying some deep, dark secret.

"What is Señorita Diaz's job?" Ellie pressed, but Sylvie retreated into her shell, as though she had already said too much. Moments later, she scuttled from the room.

Ellie discovered her suite had an enormous bathroom, with a garden tub big enough to *wash two prize pigs*, as Mama would have said. She drew a warm, jasmine-scented bath and closed the door, so Sylvie could bring her dinner without being questioned by Ellie, the nosey *gringa*. After all, she didn't want everyone in the Valdez household to think she was snooping, though she was. For once in her life, she should mind her own business, which had never been her strong suit.

As she luxuriated in the soothing water, the mystery of Señorita Diaz still rankled. What employer gave her servant the biggest bedroom, the one adjacent to her own? Everyone knew the answer to that: an employer with a mistress.

Shoot, who cared? She sank into the fragrant bubbles, stretched each tired muscle as the hot bath worked its magic. She had read every scrap of material concerning Carla Valdez, so who was this Diaz woman, really?

She reminded herself that Carla had something Ellie wanted, or rather DynaCo International wanted. That made Carla Ellie's target, nothing more.

She had considered Carla a target, until she looked into her eyes and saw a human being inside. Now that she'd heard her voice, felt the touch of her hand, shared a sunset in paradise and prepared to sleep in her partner's bed, Ellie was back at square one.

Why would an attractive, exceptionally vital woman like Carla grieve so long for her lost partner? Had Maria been so special? She suffered an unexpected twinge of jealousy, and it annoyed her. She left the bath and toweled her skin raw. She gobbled the sumptuous omelet Sylvie had left. But before she could further explore her fickle psyche, she flopped down on the big bed and fell asleep, dead to the world.

Much later, she awoke with a start and found herself misplaced in a stranger's bedroom. As her reason slowly returned, she heard the plaintive cry of a tree frog. Its singing filled the night with melancholy, compelling her to rise and walk across the room to the balcony. She silently unlatched the shutters and stepped outside, where the scent of salt from the sea mingled with the sweet odor of frangipani from the garden below.

Just then, she sensed motion down on the patio and saw two candles flickering as they moved along the ground. She heard soft, furtive whispering: the voices of Carla and a woman speaking Spanish. As the candles burned brighter, she saw Carla's features were taut with some violent emotion. The woman with her was also agitated. She was a classic beauty with long, raven-black hair and eyes as intense as melting coal. The woman appeared to be Ellie's age, and she suspected she was spying upon the mysterious Señorita Diaz.

Though she knew it was wrong to eavesdrop, she stood transfixed while Carla wrapped one arm around the beautiful young woman and led her into the shadows. They were lovers! The truth swelled like a painful lump in her throat, and as she slipped back into her room unnoticed, she was unreasonably angry. Well, Carla had a perfect right to live her life. Carla was her target, her mark, just another statistic in a hopefully fruitful business negotiation, and she would do well to remember that in the future.

So she crawled back into the bed where once, years ago, Carla had lain with a former lover. She closed her eyes tight and took a deep breath, but even when sleep claimed her, it was a troubled sleep, and she dreamed of a stranger's arms, holding her and pulling her to her heart.

CHAPTER SEVEN

Fortuneteller…

"Doña Carla requests your company for breakfast on the patio," a soft voice informed Ellie as she walked downstairs. The surprisingly formal greeting came from a young woman who was obviously Juan's second daughter. She had the same blunt, but pretty features as Sylvie, but she was more mature and self-assured.

"You're Filo, right?"

The woman returned Ellie's smile and nodded. "My sister serves supper, while I am in charge of shopping and the daytime meals. I make sure all the men eat."

"What men?"

"They tend the sugar crop. We have only twenty now, but in the old days we had many more."

She followed Filo out onto a charming brick patio. A lush garden encroached from two sides, while the front opened to an astonishing view of the Caribbean. The wrought iron table was set for two.

"Please make yourself at home," Filo said. "Doña Carla will join you soon."

After Filo left, Ellie discovered the garden had a life of its own. She heard birds singing and smelled the salty ocean mingled with exotic floral scents she could not begin to identify. Once she took a seat, her mind drifted to the intimate scene she had witnessed during the night—Carla and her mysterious lady—until suddenly she sensed movement from the thick foliage. The broad leaves rustled, and an ornamental bronze sculpture at the patio's perimeter toppled over onto the brick.

"Who's there?" she cried out, jumping to her feet.

Gradually, a small, dark face emerged and stared from wide, frightened eyes. She recognized those eyes from last evening, when the same little boy had been hiding behind a wooden swing when she entered Carla's house.

"Don't be mad. I didn't break it," the child said.

"Enrique?" Clearly Carla's younger son was about to bolt. "Please don't run away again. My name is Ellie, and I'm a friend of Carla's. We met last night, remember?" The boy remained frozen, gazing at his bare feet. "What's wrong, cat got your tongue?"

At those words, Enrique's eyes expanded to platter size.

"Oh, I get it." She laughed. "That's an expression we use in America. It means *aren't you going to talk?*" She detected the trace of a smile, but the child shook his head. "What's that in your hand?" she persisted. "Are you hiding something?"

He offered a full-fledged, devilish grin and opened his small fist. A green and red lizard blinked up at her from buggy eyes, and she involuntarily jumped backward. Enrique giggled with delight, having solicited his desired response. "That's an iguana, right?" she asked.

He nodded.

"You found him in the garden?"

He nodded again, dangled the iguana from its tail, then held it close to her nose. This was her cue to run away, screaming in terror, but instead she opened her hand.

"Cool, you brought me a gift."

His smile drooped. "Aren't you scared, *señorita*?"

At least the kid could talk. "Heck, no, I kept these guys as pets when I was a little girl."

"This one is *mine!*" He shoved out his lower lip. "But you can hold him, if you want."

"Thanks." She took the little creature, stroked its smooth back as Enrique watched in surprise and grudging admiration. She held tight to the lizard's long tail to prevent its escape, then, as she returned the pet to its proper owner, a shadow fell across their hands.

"*Qué pasa?*" Carla chuckled over her shoulder. "Have you been bothering Señorita Birdsong, Enrique?"

Enrique smiled up at Ellie. They now shared a secret. "She likes my pet, Mama Carla. But I'd rather have a dog. Can I?"

"Not now, Enrique," Carla said, as she balanced a large silver tray on one hand. "You admire iguanas, Miss Birdsong?"

"Yes, ma'am." Ellie winked. "Add *that* to your list about American women." Her fast comeback startled Carla, but she was quick to recover.

"But you are not like most American women, are you? You are an exception to the rule." She carefully placed the tray, laden with breakfast goodies, on the wrought iron table. She set the silverware, poured two cups full of rich-smelling coffee.

"I expected Filo to serve us," Ellie said.

"Believe it or not, I can do a few things for myself." Carla winked.

Ellie felt a slow blush creeping up her neck as she focused on Enrique, who had retreated back into his shell. "Are you hungry?" she asked the boy.

"No, *señorita.*"

"Then what do you want, Enrique?" Carla demanded rather harshly.

The boy shrugged, then slowly crept away, vanishing into the shrubbery.

"Enrique rarely speaks to anyone." Carla sadly shook her head. "Did you enchant him, Ellie?"

"I certainly hope so. Why isn't he in school today?"

She threw back her head and laughed. "My dear Ellie, you suffer from jet lag. Today is Saturday. Even we ignorant islanders deserve a break from the books. Now, can we drop the chatter and eat?" Carla heaped her plate with chilled exotic fruits from a cut glass bowl.

Ellie's mouth watered when Carla passed the hot buttered rolls. While she sampled mangos, papayas, and figs, the fresh sea breeze heightened all her senses, so that each bite was a sensual experience. Eventually, she should introduce her real estate proposal, but surely that could wait until after breakfast.

"I have planned a grand adventure." Carla folded her napkin. "We didn't get to know each other last night, so I'll escort you to Ponce for a day on the town."

"Shouldn't we discuss business first?" Ellie licked her fingers, savoring the last drops of sweet chocolate syrup she'd used to dip her fresh pineapple. Finger licking was a habit she couldn't seem to break, but Carla seemed mesmerized by it.

Unexpectedly, Carla seized her fingers and gently spread her hand open, tracing the lifelines in her palm. "I am a fortune teller. We country folk have the gift, and I foresee a pleasant drive in your immediate future. I foresee a tour of the museum, a trip to the market, and finally, an intimate dinner in a quiet restaurant."

"You see all that?" The teasing path of Carla's fingers sent a powerful message to unexpected places.

Seeming to sense Ellie's response, Carla studied her hand. "Does my psychic gift impress you?"

She was certain Carla felt the electric current passing through their fingers. Their eyes met as Ellie gently pulled away. Ellie heard children laughing in the distance, and it gave her a prudent idea: Antonio and Enrique could be their chaperones. "Hey, since it is Saturday, let's take the boys along."

Carla frowned at the sudden break in their connection. "Why, for heaven's sake?"

"It'll be fun!"

"The boys are monsters, you know." Carla's frown deepened.

"But I love children!" she lied outright. In fact, she'd never had much time for children. At this stage in her career, kids, even if they came with a loving partner, would be major roadblocks to her success.

Carla took a long moment to stare at her own hands, but then conceded with a heavy sigh. "If that's want you want, Ellie, I will invite the boys, but you'll be sorry. No more intimate dinner in a quiet restaurant."

CHAPTER EIGHT

A family tradition…

Ellie dressed in a pale blue suit that defied wrinkles, added a wide belt and a tiny shell necklace, and hoped her outfit would suit the occasion. She brushed out her hair, allowing it to fall free, and cursed herself for a fool. Maybe that intimate dinner would have been fun? Too late now. By the time she arrived in the driveway, the Valdez family, mother and adopted sons, were leaning against the Honda, impatiently waiting for her.

Carla shouted so she could hear, "American or Puerto Rican, women always keep you waiting, boys."

Antonio laughed knowingly, while little Enrique threw Ellie a shy smile. Both boys were neatly clad in dark slacks and crisp shirts, and their mother wore soft tan slacks and European-style sandals. Carla also wore a woman's version of the traditional *guayabera*, a dress shirt fashioned of sand-colored cotton sewn together in squares. Her breast panels were embellished with embroidered pleats, also in sand-colored thread, so that the effect was both ornate, and understated. She was flattered that Carla had taken such care in dressing for their so-called grand adventure, but perhaps she always dressed with impeccable taste?

Her impression of Carla's gallant decorum faded the moment they piled into the Honda—boys in back, grown-ups up front—and then Carla peeled out of the driveway, leaving burning rubber on the concrete. She was speeding and grinning like a teenage hoodlum, apparently oblivious to Ellie's discomfort.

"Slow down!" Ellie shouted. "You're driving like a maniac!"

"Mama Carla *is* a maniac!" both boys said with prideful glee as they bounced on the back seat.

Out on the highway, Carla slowed to a reasonable, almost sedate pace, and the boys settled down with their handheld video games.

"Sorry if I scared you." Carla watched her from the corner of her dark eyes. "I always speed out the driveway. The boys would be disappointed otherwise. It's something of a family tradition."

If Carla expected her to be shocked, then she'd be sorely disappointed. After all, speeding had been something of a Birdsong family tradition, too. She and her badass brothers had burned plenty of rubber in their day, so it was everything she could do to keep from laughing. Maybe their cultures weren't so different, after all?

Ellie smiled and tried to ignore the magnetic female by her side. She gazed out the window and soon became genuinely interested in the passing scenery. "This land is absolutely beautiful. Where exactly are we?"

"My land ends over there at that row of palms." Carla pointed. "When you live here all the time, you sometimes take the beauty for granted."

Ellie's mind jumped to attention as she recognized the palms she had seen silhouetted in last night's sunset. She realized they were driving east along the curving edge of the Caribbean, alongside a beautiful stretch of sheltered water. She spotted a sign to El Tuque Public Beach and got her bearings.

"Now I know where we are." The image of a map appeared in her brain. "All this is your property, isn't it, Carla? This is the land my company plans to buy."

"*Hopes* to buy," Carla corrected her.

"Who wants our land?" Antonio piped up.

"Never mind, son. At this point, it's just an idea on paper."

Carla was right. At this point, Dyna's dream project was only in the planning stage, but Ellie saw every phase quite clearly: blueprints for the grand hotel and casino, golf and tennis courts, swimming pools and shopping centers, and of course, townhouse condominiums. The lush landscape outside was perfect for DynaCo's vision, unspoiled by human hands, except for the several acres of sugarcane planted on the inland side of the road. Those would have to go.

"Do you still work those fields?" she wondered aloud.

"They are an experiment." Carla glanced at her watch.

"What kind of experiment?"

"Are we almost there?" Enrique whined from the back.

"When we get to town, I'm going to the Plaza alone," teenaged Antonio announced.

"No, you must take Enrique with you," Carla answered sternly.

"Why should I?" Antonio growled. "*Él es un bebé.* The other kids won't hang with me when the baby's along."

"Enrique is not a baby, he's your brother. You want ice cream, don't you?"

"*Sí...*" Antonio lowered his eyes in defeat, and Ellie decided the teenage dilemma was the same everywhere. One moment Antonio had been all grown up, sassing his mother and likely dreaming about girls. The next moment he was lusting over ice cream.

CHAPTER NINE

The local problem...

When they arrived in Ponce, Ellie was captivated by the sleepy charm of the residential streets. The older, more traditional homes were cheerfully painted wooden structures with oversize covered porches. Since it was Saturday morning, the local families had already emerged to those porches or to their gardens, and occasionally she spotted chickens strutting in the fenced backyards, lending country comfort to the city.

"Señorita Birdsong?" Enrique leaned over her shoulder. "I bet you don't keep roosters in the yards of America."

"Oh, you'd be surprised," she answered. Carla gave her a puzzled look, but she wasn't about to explain how she'd earned her allowance by gathering eggs from the coop behind Mama's trailer. A girl was entitled to her secrets.

"Now we're entering the plaza," Carla said in her tour guide voice. "The church is the heart of every Puerto Rican town, and in Ponce, Our Lady of Guadeloupe graces this very unique double square..."

She tried to concentrate as Carla pointed out the many sights of interest in her melodic voice. She spoke with an endearing trace of accent, so Ellie found herself listening to her voice, rather than the words being spoken.

"Pay attention, Ellie," Carla scolded. "You haven't heard a word I've said."

She snapped to attention. "You were telling about the church."

Both boys howled with laughter. "That was two blocks ago!" Antonio giggled.

"You don't care about our past," Carla continued. "But our future turns you on, isn't that right? I bet you were picturing Ponce after your fancy resort envelopes our quiet little city."

What could she say? She certainly couldn't confess she'd been mesmerized by Carla's seductive voice. Clearly Carla was prickly proud of her heritage and easily offended, so Ellie vowed to be respectfully attentive from that moment on. "Tell me about that building over there...?" she prompted.

"That is the Parque de Bombas," Antonio answered. "It used to be a firehouse, but now it's a stupid tourist trap."

Carla laughed at her son's outburst, but approved his sentiment, while Ellie realized her hostess had a trigger-hot temper. Luckily, Carla didn't stay mad long, so Ellie figured her personality reflected the tropical climate, mild and gracious... but susceptible to sudden storms. Okay, she could live with that, but what if Ellie's presence in her home had put her on edge? They should wrap up their business negotiations as soon as possible, and then she would retreat from her life.

"Everybody out!" Carla shouted after she parked. "This little shop has the best ice cream on the island."

They all stared at a blackboard mounted on the shop's exterior, with the flavors of the day chalked across its face. "I've never heard of any of these," Ellie moaned. "What should I choose?"

Antonio picked *guanabana*, while Enrique selected *tamarindo*. Both types were made from tropical fruits.

"We have American flavors, too," Carla said.

"Okay, I'll try a *piña colada*." She ordered the one thing she could pronounce.

"*Dos piña coladas*," Carla told the man behind the counter.

"*Sí*, Doña Carla."

The vendor stared as he handed Ellie her ice cream. Because she was American, or because she was with Carla? How did Puerto Ricans feel about lesbians? Did they know Carla's history? As they strolled into the square, she felt other curious eyes upon her, and many people tipped their hats to Carla.

"Do you know everyone in this town?" she whispered.

"Most everyone. Quite a few of these older men once worked for my father in the cane fields. It was a big operation, and we supplied sugar to all the rum distilleries. When an American drank a rum 'n' tonic, likely the sugar came from the Valdez fields. Our hacienda was a little world unto itself, and we were all like family."

She could almost picture the old Valdez plantation, all those workers whose livelihood depended on one person, the landowner. That same landowner had looked after the workers' welfare, health, and even got involved in their family decisions. Had Carla taken on her father's paternal responsibilities to the workers when he died? Were people in this town beholden to her? If so, perhaps they looked the other way when it came to Carla's lifestyle. From everything she'd read, Carla had been quite open about her relationship to Maria, so perhaps the villagers were more tolerant than she expected.

"Of course, those days are gone for good," Carla reminisced as she and Ellie sat down on a park bench and the boys scampered off. "Farming is dead in Puerto Rico. Today young people prefer big cities. They want action, entertainment, and contact with the outside world. No one wants to work the land anymore, unless…"

"Unless what?"

She paused to search Ellie's face, almost like she was trying to decide if she could trust her. "Unless they are illegals. Farmers cannot pay a living wage anymore, so they hire illegal labor, mostly poor Dominicans who come ashore each day. Slave labor. I hate it."

As Carla's words sunk in, Ellie watched the busy square filled with children, many dressed in ragged clothes. She saw two painfully thin dogs nosing the vegetables vendors were offloading from their truck. Older men filled the public benches, smoking and passing the time of day, and the town priest shuffled from the church followed by a group of waddling ladies carrying baskets.

The plight of these Puerto Ricans was much like that of farmers in America, who had also lost their livelihood to big corporate food conglomerates using illegal labor. On the other hand, this local problem could provide her with an opportunity.

"So what's the answer, Carla? Maybe it's time to give your land over to the twenty-first century and put it to a more progressive use?"

Carla cocked her head, still deciding. "My father, my grandfather, and my Spanish ancestors before them owned this land. It's in my blood. I owe it the shirt on my back. Do I want to give my land over to progress...?" She offered an enigmatic smile. "I have a few ideas of my own, but mostly my answer depends on how do *you* define progress?"

CHAPTER TEN

Double Dutch...

Carla's dark eyes flashed, and Ellie wondered how she should define progress to achieve her objective. As she continued to watch the people—an old woman selling handmade dolls, a father tossing apples to his little daughter, who smiled and packed them into a burlap shopping bag—she asked herself, *do I really want all this to change?*

Clearly *Project Puerto Rico* was not a done deal, especially if Carla harbored some secret agenda for the cane fields. Carla claimed to be a fortune teller, so maybe she already knew how the deal would play out. Ellie shared no such insight. As she tried to formulate a neutral response, Carla's cell phone rang.

She fished it from her pocket, checked the caller ID, and then cursed under her breath. "Pardon, Ellie, I must take this call. Will you excuse me one moment?"

Okay, she could take a hint. She'd give Carla space, and use the time to buy a souvenir to support the local economy. She finished her ice cream and walked down the block, to where Enrique stood alone, watching some other kids having fun.

Ellie asked him, "Where is Antonio?"

He pointed to where his brother was playing catch. A group of teenage girls huddled nearby. They giggled and watched the boys with undisguised interest, while a gang of little girls Enrique's age jumped with two ropes.

"I can do that," Enrique shyly confided.

"You can jump Double Dutch?" He gave her a blank stare. She guessed *Double Dutch* was one of those expressions like *cat got your tongue*. It just didn't compute here. "Can you jump with a double rope?" He nodded. "Will you show me?"

Enrique grabbed her hand and held on tight as Carla approached like a brooding thundercloud.

"What's going on here?" she demanded.

"Enrique's going to jump rope."

He lowered his eyes. "I can't. It's for *girls*."

Ellie knew he wanted to play. "So what? Maybe you can show those girls how to do it right?" Before he could protest, she led him toward the flying ropes. The girls were waiting in line, so with a little push, Ellie coaxed Enrique to take his place.

"What do you think you're doing?" Carla hissed into her ear. "He should be playing with the boys."

"Please let him try. How can it hurt?"

"What if he fails? What if they laugh?"

"Look, he says he can do it. Give him a chance." She sounded brave, but if Enrique tripped, she'd blame herself.

Carla took a deep breath. "I can't believe Enrique actually talks to you. That is quite a compliment, Ellie."

Ellie wanted to say, *I can't believe that you, of all people, are gender stereotyping your own son.* Naturally, she kept that sentiment to herself.

Enrique was up for his turn. As he prepared to jump, Carla inched closer. Ellie felt the pressure of their arms touching, as though she sought reassurance. For a panicky moment, she feared Carla intended to hold her hand. Her first impulse was to pull away. She glanced over her shoulder to see if anyone had witnessed what felt like an intimate gesture, but of course, nobody cared. Then, when she saw Enrique's little features screw up with uncertainty, she was oddly grateful for the supportive contact.

"By God, he's really good!" Carla cried as he leapt into the swirling confusion. The boy was nimble and inventive as he landed on one foot, then the other. He created his own, daring dance, while all the girls on the sidelines clapped wildly for him.

"He's a rock star!" Ellie agreed. Now that the crisis was over, she was content just to enjoy the warmth of Carla's arm, onlookers be damned.

"Will you be all right if we leave you for a minute, son?" Carla called out.

"*Sí*, Mama Carla!" Enrique shouted triumphantly.

Carla self-consciously moved away and mumbled an apology as they left the plaza. Clearly embarrassed, she kept watching Enrique over her shoulder as three little girls gathered around and awarded him the honor of twirling the ropes. He was their undisputed hero. In the meantime, the older boys, including Antonio, paused from their game of catch to stare enviously at the little male who had penetrated that closed, female circle.

"Next the teenage boys will be jumping rope," Ellie said.

"I don't think so. You're lucky Enrique did well, otherwise you'd be guilty of setting him up for a fall."

"Say *what*?"

"I'm accustomed to directing my sons' activities without interference. You don't know them. Enrique is overly sensitive, so I don't approve of putting him into a situation where he risks failure."

"Well *excuse me*, I am so sorry."

Carla stopped walking. "You're not their mother, are you?"

"No, ma'am, I sure am not." One look at Carla's flushed face, and Ellie's temper flared. "So I'll back off, okay?"

Carla seemed momentarily stunned, but soon regained her composure. "Please, just leave my boys alone."

"Enrique's sensitive, all right," Ellie muttered through clenched teeth. "Because you've sheltered him all his life. If you give him more freedom, maybe he'll have more confidence."

Carla suddenly gripped Ellie's arm and spun her around to face her. A tiny pulse jiggled in her tightly clenched jaw, her breathing was harsh and uneven.

"Let go, you're hurting me!"

The fire died in Carla's eyes, and Ellie abruptly dropped her hand. Her shoulders drooped, and Ellie wondered if maybe she'd gone too far.

"I am so sorry," Carla spoke at last. "I received some bad news on the phone just now, but that's no excuse. I admit I go loco when it comes to Enrique."

Carla strode toward the sidewalk, while she followed several paces behind. They walked two blocks in total silence, and Ellie realized that thanks to her interference, the wonderful day Carla had predicted when she read her palm had proved to be a disaster. Carla's face was deathly pale beneath her tan, and she seemed to have something on her mind. Finally, just as Ellie's shoes began to pinch from their relentless trek, they halted before a magnificent building that looked like a miniature Parthenon.

Carla stood stock-still, stared at the sky. "Ellie, I need to explain about Enrique…"

"Hey, forget it. It's none of my business," she said, walking away.

CHAPTER ELEVEN

Sun and moon…

"No, please come back, Ellie!" Carla shouted. "The tour's not over yet."

Carla took a deep breath and prayed she had not alienated Ellie beyond redemption. Luckily, Ellie quit stomping away and turned back to face her, an inscrutable look in her eyes. She wanted to reach out and take her hand, but quickly thought better of it. Instead, she led her into The Ponce Museum of Art. In what she knew to be her tour guide's voice, she nervously explained the truly marvelous collection, including five centuries of master works. But Carla sensed Ellie's mind was wandering.

Why had she been so stupid?

She knew she was overly protective of Enrique, but with good reason. On the other hand, she had never seen her shy son respond to anyone as he had to Ellie. He was almost the happy, carefree child he had been before Maria died, and that was saying something.

They strolled into the museum's small gift shop, and Carla decided, against her better nature, to trust Ellie…at least a little. She captured her elbow and led her into a quiet corner.

"Please just hear me out. I really want to explain about Enrique." Ellie did not resist, so Carla began: "Enrique was born seven years ago, when my partner, Maria, was still trapped in a loveless marriage. It was dangerous for her to bear a second child, but her abusive husband wanted Antonio to have a sibling."

She faltered, but then gathered strength to proceed. "The doctors warned them, but Maria was willing to take the risk. The birth went wrong, and for several minutes after delivery, Enrique couldn't breathe."

Ellie reached out and took her hand. "But they saved him, of course. Now Enrique is just fine."

"I hope so. But the experts told Maria to watch him, that he might have suffered brain damage. When Maria got a divorce several months later and came to live with me, I took on that same responsibility. Poor Enrique was only three when his mama died."

Ellie squeezed her hand very tight. "Don't go borrowing trouble. Enrique seems normal, and very bright. I'm sure you've had him tested."

"Of course. He's been to the best doctors on the island. They say so far, so good, and he has above-average intelligence."

"There you go, so what's the problem?"

Carla groaned, pulled her hand free. "You've seen him. Something is holding him back. What's wrong with him?"

Ellie smiled reassuringly. "I know you love him, and that's what counts. I had a little brother a lot like Enrique. He had a hearing disability, so he never talked, and he was afraid to try anything new for fear of failing. But one fine day, he discovered he could skip stones clean across the river, better than any of the big kids. After that, he pulled out of his shell and started jabbering like a magpie. I'm sure it'll work out for Enrique."

Carla was overcome with gratitude. Few people had offered such encouragement, let alone a total stranger. She reached out to hug Ellie, but she moved quickly out of reach. She had again gone a step too far, and watched as the younger woman fled toward the other side of the gift shop.

"C'mon, Carla," she called. "I want to buy something."

She trailed in embarrassment as Ellie browsed through art books, T-shirts, and other trinkets. Soon she stopped at the jewelry counter and seemed to settle on something she liked. Carla came up behind her. "What did you find?"

"Look, isn't this beautiful?"

The handcrafted necklace was a silver charm depicting the sun and moon intertwined like lovers, and was hung on a loop of rough hemp. Ellie frowned at the price tag, and Carla figured it cost more than Ellie wanted to spend on a souvenir.

"Please allow me to buy this for you, Ellie. It would be my pleasure."

Before she could stop her, Carla purchased the lovely necklace. She fumbled to slip the tiny hemp fastener off its knot, and then circled it around Ellie's neck. Her fingers lingered on Ellie's cool skin as she closed it.

"Here, let me help you." Ellie reached back, brushing Carla's hand.

As they both worked with the clasp, Carla's fingertips felt the heat crawling up Ellie's neck and noticed she was blushing like a schoolgirl.

"Thank you so much, Carla. I don't know what to say…"

Carla smiled. "I say let's get out of here. The day is much too pretty to be cooped up inside."

CHAPTER TWELVE

The indoor market...

As Ellie tried to sort out her conflicted emotions, she was relieved to escape from the claustrophobic museum. Strolling with Carla through the streets was like walking through a dream. Dappled sunlight played on ancient stucco walls. White begonia flowers draped from pots on windowsills, and arched entryways hinted at secret gardens within. Eventually, Carla suggested they get something to drink.

They ducked into a dark indoor market. It was a bustling, noisy place compared to the drowsy day outside, and as Carla guided her through the bedlam, she saw people crowding the stalls to buy plantains, peppers, pineapple, and *bacalao*, which Carla explained was a kind of dried fish.

All the intermingling smells produced a heady sensation. Meats, oranges, and grapefruit, combined with the less pleasant odor of humanity, were soon overpowered by the aroma of coffee as they approached a group of men drinking espresso.

"Can I buy you a coffee, Carla?"

"Good idea, but I'm buying."

"No way, this one's on me." A cup of coffee was the least she could do to thank Carla for the generous gift. As Carla searched for two free seats at the bar, Ellie noticed an unusual sign on the rear wall: *Saints for Sale*. Lights twinkled above a row of carved wooden statues.

"What a bizarre concept!" she exclaimed.

But Carla paid no attention. Instead, she suddenly stiffened as a small man, meticulously dressed in a white Panama suit, approached them. He had dark olive skin, a carefully trimmed moustache, and although she judged him to be around Carla's age, the shadows of dissipation under his eyes, along with a beer belly, made him seem much older.

"*Buenos dias*, Doña Carla. *Qué pasa?*" He extended a plump hand with an obscenely large diamond ring on his pinkie.

The unpleasant little man stared at Ellie with a curiosity bordering on rudeness, while Carla declined to shake his hand or to introduce her.

"Hello, I'm Ellie Birdsong," she spoke up.

"Ah, *Americana*? Welcome to the city. Now, may I speak with Doña Carla in private?"

Without waiting for her permission, he rapidly led Carla away, leaving Ellie alone with the appraising eyes of the male coffee drinkers. Resisting an impulse to chase after Carla, she instead watched her every move as the two stood next to the bar, in a relatively deserted part of the market. The man took out his cell phone, held it up for Carla to view the screen. Even at a distance, she sensed Carla's distress. Their voices sounded angry, but since they were speaking Spanish, she had no clue what the dispute was about.

When Carla suddenly shoved the little man, it became clear their hostility was far more serious than a simple disagreement. From out of nowhere, a short guy wearing a Miami Dolphins T-shirt, stepped up behind Carla, as if to protect the guy in the Panama suit.

"Look out!" Ellie cried as the short thug drove his fist between Carla's shoulders, causing her to lurch forward against the bar. It was shocking to see a man attack a woman in public.

Carla spun around and actually slugged the short man, who wilted to the floor.

At the same time, an exceedingly tall man in an American-style business suit stepped in and bear-hugged Carla, pinning her arms to her ribs. With her pulled tight against his body, he whispered in her ear, as she struggled against the oddly intimate embrace.

"Somebody help her!" Ellie screamed.

A tiny old man in a straw hat attempted to come between them, but the tall goon merely laughed and batted him away. Next, Carla, to Ellie's undying admiration, employed the oldest self-defense maneuver in the book. She jerked her knee upward and nailed him in the balls. The tall guy howled, grabbed his crotch, and staggered backward.

Ellie couldn't take it anymore. By the time she reached the fight, the short guy on the ground was kicking at Carla's shins, while the tall one was preparing for a second assault. Ellie snatched a steaming cup of coffee off the bar and tossed it in the kicker's face. He screamed and rolled away under a vendor's table. Carla delivered a second blow, this one with her shoe, to the tall thug's family jewels and folded him like a squealing pig.

Belatedly, the cluster of surprised men in the room came to the women's rescue, grabbing and shouting at Carla's cowardly attackers.

"*Llama a la policía!*" the Good Samaritan in the straw hat shouted.

"No *policía, por favor!*" The dapper man in the white Panama suit, who had apparently started it all, but managed to stay out of the fight, vigorously shook his head. "Don't call the police," he repeated in English, with a finger in Ellie's face.

The short guy Ellie had scalded dabbed at his burned face with a coffee-soaked handkerchief. His Dolphins T-shirt was stained brown. His dead-fish eyes were filled with menace.

"Shame on you, Ellie Birdsong." The tall man, still doubled over by Carla's attacks, slowly stood to his impressive height and shook his finger at her. "Is that how you treat an old friend? Perhaps you should teach Ms. Valdez some manners."

Lord in heaven! As Ellie recognized the creep from the airplane, her heart thudded so hard she could hardly breathe. The short guy staggered up off the floor, joining the man in the Panama suit. The tall man from the plane winked at Ellie, then all three retreated, shoving their way through the gang of startled locals and going their separate ways.

Panama called back over his shoulder, "We'll talk again, Doña Carla. Perhaps next time you'll be more receptive to my offer."

Carla and she stood in shock as the bullies left the building. A vendor brought a roll of paper towels, and Carla clumsily attempted to clean the dirt from her hands and the abrasion on her knuckles. Ellie longed to find fresh water, antiseptic, and to do a proper job, but she knew better. After a morning of butting in where she didn't belong, she had learned a thing or two about Carla Valdez. Besides, it seemed everyone else in the market was now eager to help, but Carla stubbornly refused them all. Instead, she grabbed hold of Ellie's arm and rushed her outside. When they emerged into the sunlight, Carla picked up speed, dragging Ellie in her wake.

"Seriously?" Ellie panted. "Brawling in public? What was that all about?"

"He took pictures on his phone," Carla cried, "of Enrique jumping rope. He photographed Antonio, too."

So the man in the Panama suit had started it. "God, did he threaten you?"

"He threatened my boys, at least by implication."

"So who was the hell is he?"

"His name is Diego Martinez. You see, Ellie, your company is not the only party interested in my land."

As Ellie struggled to free herself, Carla abruptly slowed and stopped. They faced one another. Much to her surprise, Carla seemed to have let her guard down. It was shocking to see tears in the proud woman's eyes, and it broke Ellie's heart.

They had reached the plaza, where basically nothing had changed. Enrique and the three little girls had abandoned the jump rope and were now huddled on a wooden bench, giggling over something on one of the girl's phones. Antonio was still playing catch. Ellie noticed how his attention flickered between the ball and his younger brother. He was keeping a watchful eye.

Crisis averted—for now.

Carla exhaled and sank to a bench, where she too could keep a watchful eye. Ellie, still shaken, tentatively sat down beside her, taking care not to touch her tense companion. As she caught her breath, she tried to make sense of what had just happened.

Carla had said that DynaCo was not the only company interested in her land. Why hadn't this possibility occurred to Ellie before? If American developers wanted the Valdez property, why shouldn't locals like Martinez desire it too? She made a mental note to phone Dyna at the first convenient moment. Her boss would be upset to hear they had competition, especially contenders prone to violence.

She would also be angry because Ellie had spent the night at Carla's—not at all professional. On the other hand, she had advised Ellie to keep a close eye on "the enemy." Dyna always referred to their real estate marks as enemies, yet Ellie was finding it harder and harder to think of Carla that way.

As she was considering all this, Carla's expression turned stormy and she took hold of Ellie's arm. "We need to talk," she hissed. "How do you know the tall guy. The one I kicked. He sure as hell seemed to know you."

She panicked and kept it simple. "I don't know him, not really. Just some guy I met on the plane."

But having witnessed the tall, scar-faced fallen angel in action, she realized her first impressions of him had been dead-on. He was exactly like the lowlifes back on the boardwalk in Atlantic City, a Mafia wannabe, or else the real thing. She had no idea how to explain him to Carla, but she sensed she'd lost a measure of her trust.

"Okay, so you met him on the plane, and maybe that explains it." She released Ellie's arm, but couldn't disguise her skepticism. "I pray to God I never see that man again, you have no idea."

She studied Carla's flushed face and tried to piece it together. How had the tall man known Carla's name? Hadn't he asked

Ellie to "teach Ms. Valdez some manners"? Did they share some history? If so, it was unpleasant history indeed.

The tense moment seemed to pass. Carla stood up, and Ellie followed as they went to get the boys.

"Anyway, thanks for coming to my rescue, Ellie," Carla said as they walked. "Where did you learn to be a street fighter?"

"Hey, I grew up with three older brothers, need I say more?"

Although she was still upset by the exchange, Ellie decided she now had to focus on the fact that they'd soon be driving home through Ponce, the town where she'd originally made hotel reservations. The time had come to move to her proper lodgings.

"Listen, Carla, will you please drop me off at my hotel on your way home? Juan can bring the rest of my stuff in the morning."

"No, I will not do that," she said as they quickly walked toward the park to collect the kids.

Ellie stopped dead in her tracks. "Why not?"

"Because it's time to finalize our business deal. Isn't that what you want?"

The word "finalize" sent chills up her breastbone. Was it possible? Carla intended to sell without even hearing her sales pitch? She crossed her arms and stared in disbelief.

Carla smiled. "Don't look so surprised. You're already settled in at my place, so it makes practical sense for you to stay put. First thing in the morning, over breakfast on my patio, we'll go over the details and get it done."

This was too good to be true. "Promise?"

"Cross my heart." Carla gestured against her chest, but the movement looked more like a genuflection than a promise. "Besides, we have more pressing problems at the moment."

"Like what?"

Carla touched her raw knuckles. "I don't tolerate my boys fighting. How do I explain this?"

CHAPTER THIRTEEN

Stood up…

Moisture clung to the African tulips and orange oleanders in the garden. The sun had not risen high enough to burn off the pungent floral odors of the night, so the fragrance of the outdoors mingled with the scent of lavender soap on Ellie's skin, still moist from the shower. When she entered the Valdez kitchen, she smelled the rich aroma of rice and beans.

Filo and Sylvie looked up from the hot stove. Sylvie offered a shy smile, while Filo approached with a wooden spoon in her hand. "Good morning, Ms. Birdsong, did you sleep well?"

"Very well, thanks." In truth, she had tossed and turned through a series of disturbing dreams featuring the market brawl. Next she had nightmares about the contentious phone conversation she'd had with Dyna last night. But now it was time to get on with a magnificent, brand-new day.

"Are you hungry?" Filo asked. "We set your place on the patio."

Ellie looked through the double doors and noticed the wrought iron table had been laid with only one plate setting.

"Wait, you've made a mistake. I'm having breakfast with Carla this morning."

The sisters glanced at one another. "No, Señorita Birdsong." Sylvie shook her head. "Doña Carla left before dawn, with Señorita Diaz."

She gripped the handle of her briefcase and tried to swallow the lump of disappointment in her throat. "There must be some mistake. I have an appointment with Carla. Are you sure she left with Señorita Diaz?"

Again they peeked at one another, deciding how to respond. "We could be wrong," Filo said at last. "Maybe she'll be back soon."

But she knew Carla had stood her up. And what about this elusive Diaz woman? She smelled a conspiracy. If Diaz really was the head housekeeper, as she had first suspected, why did she never set foot in the kitchen or help with the chores? Maybe she really was Carla's mistress. Did she eat at the family table and talk to the children, or did she only inhabit the nocturnal regions of Carla's bedroom?

"Tell me about Señorita Diaz?" she asked the sisters.

"None of our business," Filo said with finality, refusing to meet Ellie's eyes. "Now, Ms. Birdsong, may we serve you?"

"Thanks anyway, ladies, but I can serve myself." She stomped to the griddle, slapped some rice and beans onto a plate, poured a steaming cup of coffee, and decided to eat standing at the sideboard. "And another thing, my name is Ellie. Can we drop the *señorita* nonsense?"

"Not a problem." Filo smiled and Sylvie giggled.

Ellie hated it when folks watched her chew and swallow, and both those activities were difficult to accomplish with a lump of disappointment in her throat. Finally she gave up, scraped the remains of her breakfast into the garbage. "The food was delicious," she assured them. "I'm just not hungry." She retrieved her briefcase and headed upstairs to change.

"What will you do today?" Filo called after her. "In case somebody asks?"

Ellie was stranded in paradise with no car. Things could be worse. "I reckon I'll explore," she answered.

Fifteen minutes later, she was headed down the rocky path leading toward the sea. Soon, just like yesterday, a tiny voice startled her.

"Where are you going, Señorita Birdsong?"

Seemed every time she encountered Enrique, he materialized from the very leaves on the trees.

"I'm going swimming, how 'bout you?"

"We can't go swimming in winter," he said, a look of surprise on his face.

Seriously? It was almost eighty degrees on that late November day.

"Only stupid tourists swim in winter. Besides, you're not wearing a swimsuit, *señorita*."

"Wanna bet?" She opened her yellow terrycloth robe so he could peek at her bikini.

He gaped in fascination. "But you better watch out for the bad current," he warned. "It sucks you underwater, and you die."

"Enrique, are you saying you have dangerous undertows on your beach?"

He nodded vigorously, while she searched her memory. DynaCo had done a thorough investigation of the tides and water patterns in the Valdez bay, and not one report mentioned an undertow.

"Don't worry, I'll be careful," she reassured the boy. "Sure you don't want to tag along?"

He shook his head, turned tail and ran toward the house. Carla was right about one thing: Enrique was a strange child and fearful of many things. Yet as Carla had so bluntly pointed out, Ellie was not his mother, so Enrique was not her concern. Fine. Carla Valdez was an arrogant, impossible woman—a promise breaker. Yesterday she'd said they would finalize their business this morning. That promise was the only reason she had agreed to sleep under her roof one more night. Yet here she was, might as well make the best of it.

As she kicked off her sandals and walked down the beach, she noticed the hot sand contained tiny pink shards that hurt her feet. The moment she entered the water, however, the sand was smooth and hard-packed, an ideal swimmer's beach. The water was cool and refreshing, transparent turquoise, so different from the salty brine off Atlantic City.

She waded out to her waist, then slid gracefully under the waves. She was determined to relax as she sidestroked, letting the gentle waters wash away Dyna's angry words. Last night she had told her boss about their competition from nasty little Diego Martinez. No need for a Google search, because it turned out Dyna knew all about Martinez, though she claimed to know nothing about the tall man from the plane.

Dyna said Diaz was a Dominican national who island-hopped across the Caribbean. He owned a company called Paradise Properties and had amassed a fortune by buying land with resort potential, then developing cheap, sub-standard condos that tended to self-destruct shortly after Martinez moved on. At least that's how Dyna characterized the violent little greaseball. Dyna also suspected the short man with the Dolphins T-shirt, who behaved like Martinez's bodyguard, was likely an unsavory associate from Miami, where Paradise Properties had a large branch office.

Dyna was definitely pissed because Martinez was in Puerto Rico and pissed because Ellie had not yet closed the deal, but she figured as long as Ellie was staying at Casa Valdez, she should turn up the heat on Carla. She had expected Ellie to have a signed contract in hand at breakfast, and no doubt she would be pissed when she learned she had failed. She'd be calling every hour, on the hour, for positive news, so Ellie had deliberately left her cell phone back at the house. Who needed the aggravation?

When she finished swimming, she judged by the angle of the sun that it was already early afternoon. Locating the blue towel she had borrowed from the bathroom, she wrapped it around her head like a turban, put on her robe and retrieved her sandals, then scanned the beach looking for shade. She soon spotted a rock jetty with an overhanging ledge that created a cave. She saw the rock was actually pink marble, which explained the rosy hue of the beach as well as the pink shards in the sand. In fact, the garden tub she had bathed in at Casa Valdez was fashioned of the same material. Carla's house was truly born of this land.

She located a gap in the rock and passed into a shadowy cave, where the receding tide had left behind a shallow pool. The aqua water shimmered like a large, sleepy eye in the smooth, sandy floor. Spreading her towel on the sand, she lay down, closed her eyes, and drifted asleep.

CHAPTER FOURTEEN

The cave...

"Pardon, *señorita*..." A deep, rich voice swam into her dreams. "You won't get a tan inside this cave."

She struggled to consciousness, sat bolt upright. A dark figure with a large hump on its back blocked the entry into her hideaway. With the glaring sun behind it, she saw only a slim silhouette wrapped in what appeared to be a towel. Realizing she was trapped, she tried not to panic, but then she remembered she had no cell phone, and her throat closed with fear.

"W-what do you want?" she stammered.

"You're trespassing," the oddly familiar voice said.

"No, I'm a guest of Carla Valdez." Her voice sounded tiny and frightened, like a little girl's. She watched in horror as the figure peeled the lump off its back and lowered it to the sand...a backpack.

"I *did* invite you, didn't I?" the person chuckled.

"Carla?" she squeaked, stunned by relief and embarrassment. "I couldn't see your face. You scared me half to death."

"I'm sorry, Ellie." Carla dropped her towel on the cave floor.

She found herself staring shamelessly at Carla's exquisitely feminine physique. Fully dressed, she was an elegant, urbane woman, but naked, except for the bikini accentuating her small, beautifully sculpted breasts, flat belly, and gently curving hips, she exuded an animal-like sensuality. She presented a soft, almost vulnerable contrast to the ruggedly beautiful landscape, and yet she remained somehow untamed. Her buttery bronze skin was smooth and soft in spite of years of exposure to sun and salt.

"What?" She seemed embarrassed by Ellie's scrutiny. "I'm dressed for a swim. So are you, I see."

Her expressive eyes traveled the length of Ellie's scantily clad body, causing Ellie to wish she had stayed in her robe, instead of tucking it under her head for a pillow. Her gaze lingered on Ellie's breasts, lifted slowly to her lips, and finally locked on her eyes in an age-old understanding. In this cave, far from the realities of life, they were simply two women fighting an attraction Ellie suspected they both felt.

Ellie realized she had an unfair advantage, knowing the intimate personal details of Carla's life and sexual orientation, while Carla had no way of knowing these things about her. Yet, they frankly appraised one another, and Carla seemed to like what she saw. It was too late to pretend the exchange had not happened, because it had. She watched Carla's dark brown eyes turn black with some unspoken emotion, while Ellie's heart beat faster, sending pulsing echoes throughout her body.

"You stood me up." Ellie accused her out of sheer nervousness.

"No, you took off before I got home. You should have waited. I found your footprints in the wet sand, so I followed you here."

"Filo said you left with the Diaz woman."

"That is not your concern." Her eyes flashed a warning as she knelt beside Ellie's makeshift bed.

Clearly Señorita Diaz remained a forbidden subject, yet just now, Ellie was more than willing to let it drop. Could Carla hear the pounding of her heart? Maybe it was her imagination, but she swore Carla's heartbeats matched her own. She explored the classic contours of Carla's face with her eyes and discovered a tiny network of smile lines etched around her mouth. They betrayed her maturity and attested to the joys and sorrows she had known in her life. To Ellie, her face was heartbreakingly beautiful, so she impulsively touched her cheek.

Then Carla's gentle hand found Ellie's shoulder, one finger tracing the line of her swimsuit strap. It left a fiery path wherever it traveled.

"Sunburn..." Carla explained as a strange, hoarse quality entered her voice. "You should be more careful."

Carla stretched out on the sand beside her, propped up on her left elbow, while her right finger followed the ridge of Ellie's collarbone, pausing at the base of her neck, where a tiny pulse raced madly in her throat. Carla's touch was featherlight, sending a hot charge to unexpected places.

"I came in here to avoid the sun, and I always use sunscreen," Ellie stupidly responded. She couldn't seem to move her eyes from Carla's face, so she impulsively began her own exploration. She traced the edges of Carla's generous mouth, then the line of her jaw down to the graceful curve of her neck.

"What are you doing, Ellie?" Carla whispered.

She spoke Ellie's name just before her mouth closed over her anxious lips. The kiss was hungry and insistent, surprising Ellie with the intensity of her need. In return, she locked both arms around Carla's neck, while her lips parted to receive Carla's probing tongue. Carla tasted the soft lining of her upper lip, sending shock-like vibrations through her entire body. And Ellie thanked God she was anchored on solid sand, for had she been standing, the power of that kiss would have collapsed the legs out from under her.

When Ellie probed with her tongue, Carla's response was electric. A shudder passed through her lithe frame, as she gently positioned herself above Ellie. The soft mounds of her breasts pressed against Ellie's tender skin, and Ellie felt the rapid beating of her heart.

"Carla, what are we doing?" she gasped when Carla released her mouth. She knew she should end this right now. It was completely unprofessional and more than a little dangerous.

Had she really invited this advance? She knew she had, and God help her, she was not sorry.

When Carla's teasing lips nibbled the sensitive flesh beneath her chin, Ellie couldn't bear to interrupt the frenzied dance they had begun. When she felt the pressure of Carla's smooth, warm thighs against her cool legs, her resistance fell completely away. She longed to feel the full weight of her, yet how could that be justified? She had been down this road before, but never this fast and never with such emotional intensity. With all the will she could muster, she finally pushed against her with both fists.

"Please stop!" she pleaded. "We shouldn't do this."

Carla's sigh came from some deep, untraveled place, but she relaxed her hold on Ellie and slowly rolled away. Her dark eyes were clouded and confused by the sudden interruption of passion, and they seemed to ask an unspoken question.

"Carla, I'm sorry…" was all Ellie could manage as she listened to the fast, rhythmic pounding of the waves, which precisely matched the beating of their hearts.

A strange, wounded expression flashed briefly across Carla's face, but just as quickly, the moment passed. As her eyes faded from black to their natural brown, she sadly shook her head. "I'm sorry, too. I don't know what came over me, Ellie. I completely misread you, and I hope you can forgive me." She dragged a trembling hand across her forehead. "Perhaps I was the one who was out in the sun too long." Climbing unsteadily to her feet, she stood on shaky legs as her ragged breathing returned to normal.

Ellie lay still, with her arms by her side, praying the blood racing through her veins would slow to an acceptable pace. She felt lost and alone, like she had relinquished something vital to her very being. She also felt like a terrible tease, an imposter, and had no idea where to go from there. At last, when she was certain her voice wouldn't betray her, she rose up on one elbow.

"No, Carla, it was my fault. I wanted it, too."

Carla extended a helping hand, lifting Ellie to her feet. She did not ask why Ellie had stopped her. Carla had put herself in an extremely awkward position by initiating the advance, so

Ellie should confess then and there that she was a lesbian, but instead she said, "Who told you I was at the beach?"

Ellie quickly put on her robe and sandals.

Carla continued to watch, a curious expression on her face. Finally, she cleared her throat. "Enrique said you were likely to drown."

"Are there really dangerous undertows?"

Carla searched her eyes before walking out of the cave and onto a natural stone jetty stretching into the sea. Ellie followed. "No, Ellie, the waters could be dangerous for a young boy like Enrique until he becomes a strong swimmer, but I promise you, it was far more dangerous for his mother to enter that cave with you inside."

CHAPTER FIFTEEN

Dignidad…

Carla retrieved her backpack, wrapped the long towel around her shoulders, and then led Ellie away from their grotto. She guided her up a steep pink dune to a flat stretch of cactus-covered landscape, where a dusty road penetrated the horizon, and wondered if she could somehow forget the entire embarrassing episode. She was so shaken, she almost tripped on the rocks.

"Don't give up," she said when Ellie stumbled. "Your reward is just over the rise."

As they rounded a bend, Carla recognized the strong, pungent odor contrasting with the familiar aromas of blossoms and salty sea. It was a smoky smell, like fat dripping into an open flame. At the same moment, she spotted the ancient pickup truck parked along the side of the road, where the driver had set up a primitive grill.

"What is he doing?" Ellie asked.

"Pedro sets up every day around lunchtime. The highway is just over the hill, you see. All the locals know where to grab a quick bite at a fair price. Pedro is our very own fast food franchise."

"Sounds good to me!" Ellie started to charge up the hill.

"Wait, Ellie!" Carla grabbed her arm. "Please sash up your robe first. Pedro is a good Catholic. He's married, you understand, and the sight of a beautiful, nearly naked *Americana* might upset his equilibrium."

Ellie punched her playfully, but obediently closed her robe. "Satisfied?"

"*Sí*, you are gorgeous...*preciosa*."

Ellie glanced pointedly at Carla's own bikini, peeking out from under her towel. "Don't you have some clothes in that backpack of yours? Maybe you should cover up, too."

"Pedro knows me well. He won't notice."

"He may pretend not to notice, but I know he'll look. If you have something, please cover up, for my sake."

Carla lifted her eyebrows at the remark, but then pulled a pair of wrinkled khakis and a rumpled jacket from her pack. Moments later, she was decent. "Satisfied, *señorita*?"

"Shut up and feed me." Ellie laughed as they approached the old truck.

Carla smiled, feeling that somehow the day was back on track and that they had both regained their balance.

"*Buenos días*, Doña Carla." The roadside chef bowed deeply.

"*Buenos días*, Pedro," Carla answered, and then introduced Ellie.

"Yum, everything smells delicious," Ellie said as Carla led her to a large metal drum cut lengthwise and laid on its side to serve as a grill. The drum was filled with flaming coal. "What's this?"

"*Pollo*...roast chicken."

At the other end of the grill, a tub of boiling fat was being used to cook the finger foods to crispy perfection. "What about those?" Ellie asked.

"Those are *empanadas*, little fried meat pies, and the others are *chicharrón*, fried pork rind."

"What should we choose?" Ellie asked.

"Let's sample one of everything." Carla smiled, then ordered in rapid Spanish.

As Pedro wrapped their hot food in brown paper, he seemed agitated, asking the same difficult question again and again. Carla knew she couldn't give him a satisfactory answer, so she shrugged and begged him for patience.

"What was that all about?" Ellie asked as they walked away.

"Follow me," she said, and led her quickly toward the beach.

"Slow down, will you?" Ellie begged as she scrambled up a steep bluff.

They came to rest under the branches of an ancient ceiba tree, and from that vantage point, they could see for miles out to the dazzling Caribbean. In the far distance, sailboats floated like doves of peace on the shimmering water.

"Are we still on Valdez land?" Ellie asked.

She nodded slowly. "This is my favorite spot." She took a colorful blanket from her backpack and spread it in the shade. "Please have a seat, Ellie."

Ellie dropped onto the blanket. The swim, fresh air, long hike, and the emotional energy expended in the cave seemed to have exhausted her. She claimed to be hungry beyond belief.

Carla produced a chilled bottle of Spanish wine from her magic pack. "This is *Torres Viña Sol*, perfect for a warm day and spicy food." She brought out paper plates, napkins, and two glasses. "Like your American Girl Scouts say, *be prepared*. Here's to you, Ellie."

Ellie smiled over the rim of her glass, acknowledging her toast.

The wine was light and refreshing. It helped Carla relax, filling her with a sense of well-being as she greedily devoured the delicious lunch. The combination of spicy flavors teased her tongue and filled her belly, and once that was accomplished, she felt less unnerved by the young woman lounging beside her.

"How would *you* know about the Girl Scouts?" Ellie surprised her with the question.

"You'd be surprised how deeply your culture has penetrated ours. When I was a schoolgirl, I studied your holidays. We even cut out paper turkeys at Thanksgiving. I never minded being force-fed American customs, but many people do resent it. My parents, for instance, were divided on the issue of United States interference."

Ellie paused a moment, seemingly letting Carla's words sink in. In the distance, a car pulled off the highway, and Pedro laughed as he greeted another customer.

Ellie said, "Tell me about your parents."

"My father, Don Carlos, was a self-made man. He was born on a poor mountain farm and was one of the original *Jíbaros*—that means he was a peasant with simple, patriotic virtues. We call that quality *dignidad*, or pride in oneself. It's at the heart of every Puerto Rican."

"I've read about that. Your Independence Party is founded on that idea, right?"

"That's right, but some of my countrymen, *Los Macheteros*, carry that concept too far. Have you heard about them, Ellie?"

"They are revolutionaries?"

"They call themselves *Boricua Popular*, the People's Army, but in fact, they are a gang of thugs who want to free Puerto Rico from what they call the United States' colonial rule."

"Haven't those guys done bombings and robberies? They've even attacked the US military. If I'm not mistaken, the FBI has classified them as a terrorist organization."

"Unfortunately, those facts are true. But as you know, we Puerto Ricans have voted multiple times in favor of becoming the fifty-first state in the United States. Our proposal is still sitting in your Congress, waiting to be approved."

"Yeah, I know. Our new administration would love to get it passed, so we would gain two more Senators—likely Democrats."

Carla chuckled. "It really could happen this time, but do you understand what that would mean, Ellie? It would change everything for the better, in my opinion. Our island would finally have representation and the benefits of full-fledged citizenship."

"It would also make your land more valuable, when more Americans flooded in."

"Which means your company, DynaCo, should pay much more for it, yes?" she teased.

Carla could see the idea upset Ellie, so she steered the topic back on course. "You asked about my parents. Well, Father made his fortune with sugarcane. He used his money to buy more and more land, spending very little for frivolous things. When sugar was king, he employed many workers, but in this new economy, our property no longer provides jobs. That's why Pedro is angry."

Ellie glanced back at the man who had grilled their lunch. Pedro was kicking the dust with his shoe as he stared down the road, hoping for more customers. "But surely Pedro doesn't blame you?"

Carla sighed, poured them each more wine. "I think he does. I had to lay him off, but I fear I also gave him and the others false hope."

"I don't understand...?" Ellie took a deep swallow. "What kind of plan do you have up your sleeve?"

CHAPTER SIXTEEN

The dream…

Carla laughed and finished her drink in one long gulp. She put down her glass, hesitated a moment, then took Ellie's hand. "It's just a wild dream, Miss Lady Executive, and I'm not sure it will help our negotiations if I confide in you."

Ellie squeezed Carla's fingers and tapped her bare foot with her toes. "Spit it out, will you?"

Carla squinted at a gull circling in the bright blue sky, picked up a shell and drew a little design in the sand. Finally, she looked squarely into Ellie's face and decided to trust her. "Well, they have implemented the plan in Brazil, and very successfully. You know about bioethanol? It's an alternative fuel source distilled from corn or sugarcane. It's the brainchild of conservationists, like me, who hope to wean our world off petroleum dependency."

"Don't tell me you intend to convert your sugarcane to bioethanol? Hey, are you serious about this?"

Carla flopped down on her back, stared at the sky. "Actually, it's the waste products from the sugarcane we convert, but the dream requires a bigger investment than I can afford. Bioethanol is expensive to produce, more costly for the consumer at the pump, and it may not be as clean as we hoped. Until science proves it won't hurt our air quality, I will not proceed."

"I like your idea, Carla. Maybe we can compromise? Maybe if you sell part of your estate to DynaCo, you'll earn enough money to achieve the bioethanol dream?"

Carla looked up. Ellie's liquid brown eyes were shifting in thought, waiting for her response. The distant buzz of traffic competed with the natural roar of the waves. The two sounds perfectly orchestrated the dichotomy they were discussing: the clash of civilization with nature, each competing for the upper hand.

Eventually, she cleared her throat. "Well, I've told you about my father. Now I'll tell you about my mother, who traveled here from Spain. She came to this country as an arranged bride for my father."

"Are you serious? I thought arranged marriages went out with the Dark Ages?"

"Not at all. Once my father earned his fortune, he did as his father told him. Marriage to a pure-blooded Spaniard was considered a social coup back then."

"That doesn't sound like your father, the proud *Jíbaro*. What happened to *dignidad*?"

"You're right. Father didn't like the idea, and neither did I when he tried to marry me off to a man imported from Spain."

"No way! Are you saying your father tried to market you as a mail-order bride? God, I can't imagine such a thing!" Ellie giggled.

"I wouldn't put it quite that way, but yes, Father wanted desperately for me to be straight and behave like a traditional, dutiful daughter. When I told my parents I was gay, my mother was heartbroken, and my father nearly disowned me. Only on his deathbed did he grudgingly admit that I handled the farm well, and that he wanted me to inherit the estate."

Their conversation cast unhappy shadows on the otherwise perfect afternoon. Only one hour ago, she had been swept away by Ellie's kiss, and now they were discussing the sometimes tragic consequences of being gay.

"I'm so sorry," Ellie said. "Please go on with your story."

"I admit my parents' marriage wasn't without conflicts. My father was Puerto Rican through and through. He bitterly resented the United States and tried to keep me from attending their schools. Mother was worldly and understood the advantages of an American-style education. Since in Spanish families, the mother is in charge of small children, her will prevailed."

"What about you, Carla? How do you feel about an American occupation?"

She sat upright, wrapped her arms around her knees, and stared at a lone sailboat drifting on the horizon. "I am the daughter of both my parents."

CHAPTER SEVENTEEN

Glass-bottomed boat...

Ellie packed her suitcase and weighed her options. She was feeling as blue as her bedroom when a determined knock sounded on her locked door.

"Open up, Ellie!" Carla's voice startled her.

Clad only in a bathrobe, her hair still wet, she opened the door a tiny crack and saw Carla's face alive with excitement. Apparently the emotional aftershocks of their tumultuous afternoon had been completely forgotten.

"Tonight there will be no moon," Carla said. "I'll expect you downstairs in thirty minutes for our date. Please don't be late."

"I wouldn't dream of it."

She dressed in record time, in a pale green cotton sundress. When she fastened the necklace Carla had given her, she noticed a pink blush to her skin and remembered the tantalizing sensation of Carla's fingers exploring her sunburn. Damn, double damn. Seemed like when Carla said *jump*, she said *how high?* Mama would say Ellie was *runnin' blind as a possum at noon*, and maybe Mama was right.

"Bravo, this time you did not keep me waiting," Carla said as they walked to the Honda.

She likes what she sees, Ellie noted with satisfaction as Carla appraised her. "Where are we going?"

"Not far, you'll see."

Carla looked sexy in a loose, multicolored open-weave sweater and tight designer jeans. The subtle scent of her musky cologne made Ellie want to slither across the seat and nibble her neck. Instead, she sat stiffly upright and stared straight ahead.

"Maybe we should discuss business?" Ellie sounded as cold and mechanical as a robot, and hated herself for it.

"All in good time, but tonight I want you to observe our people and absorb the flavor of the land you hope to make over."

"Make over? You make it sound like DynaCo wants to drastically change your little community, when in fact we intend to improve it—just tweak it here and there."

"Tweak?" Carla laughed. "What kind of word is that? Listen, Ellie, after I show you around, if you still believe your project will benefit the area, then we'll talk."

So be it.

They passed a sign announcing the Parguera city limits. As they neared the bay, Ellie realized the town was a little fishing village, much smaller than Ponce, which they had visited two days ago. They parked outside a quaint old hotel, but why were they here? The silent streets indicated that everyone had already gone to bed, yet Carla led her down a narrow path behind the hotel and into a dense garden.

"Where are we going? I can't see my own feet."

"Yes, that's the point." Carla took her hand to guide her down the path. "As I said, tonight there will be no moon."

Ellie was baffled. Was Carla a Hispanic werewolf? What was she up to? She pulled Ellie close as they walked, supposedly to help her keep her balance. She felt Carla's warm breath on the back of her neck. What did all this touching mean? That afternoon she had discouraged Carla's advances. *My loss*, she thought.

"There, you see? I wasn't leading you astray." Carla pointed at a string of lights up ahead. They had arrived at the water's edge, where swinging lanterns illuminated a wide wooden dock. A large crowd had assembled, and the parking lot was filled with cars.

"Where are we?"

"Look again," Carla urged.

A large launch was moored at the dock, and folks were beginning to board the craft. As they came closer, she heard American-style English being spoken. "These people are tourists, aren't they? Are we going on this boat?"

"Yes to both questions." Carla steered them into the queue and took out her wallet. "You've heard about Phosphorescent Bay? Well, this is it."

Ellie recalled her research. "Yes, the bay of sparkling water."

"Close enough. On moonless nights, you can see the luminescence caused by all the tiny marine creatures. Their movements give off sparks of chemical light, making the whole bay shimmer. This place is unique in all the world. In fact, our government has purchased the surrounding land in order to protect it."

"From developers like me," she teased.

"Exactly. It's a popular tourist spot, but you mustn't feel like a tourist, because tonight you're with me. When I was a child, my family would dine at this hotel, and then my parents would bring me down to the dock through that garden. It was all part of the adventure."

"You're right, Carla, this is a marvelous adventure."

Suddenly she felt like a little girl again, but as they climbed the gangplank, Carla let go of her hand. At that moment, an overdressed woman with a New York accent stared curiously in their direction, then fixed on Carla with obvious admiration. The woman's hungry look set off Ellie's gaydar. It made her feel proud and possessive of her attractive native escort, even if the illusion lasted for only one romantic evening.

Carla and she seemed to generate interest everywhere, as several men on the shore tipped their hats to Carla and whispered amongst themselves.

A young police officer, who had been directing traffic, noticed Carla for the first time. "*Buenas noches*, Doña Carla!" he called. "When you return from the boat ride, we must talk!"

Carla shouted a reply in Spanish, and the policeman seemed highly annoyed by her answer.

"What did he want?"

"It's not important. Come, I'll take you to the best seat in the house."

Carla guided her to the stern, where they found seats far away from the crowd. As she settled onto a bench, she noticed the floor of the boat was made of glass. "My God! I feel like we're going to fall into the bay. It makes me dizzy, Carla."

"Relax. It's not as scary as it seems. The boat was designed so we could view the phenomenon below us in the water."

Sure enough, as the captain motored away from the pier, the boat's wake was suddenly stitched with white light. She trailed her hand in the water, and like magic, her fingers were bathed in silvery silk. In the distance, a leaping fish created a dazzling shower of natural fireworks. "It's awesome!"

"Like your Fourth of July?"

"No, Carla, it's much more peaceful, like looking down into the stars."

Carla smiled dreamily. She started to wrap her arm around Ellie's shoulder, but then changed her mind. Ellie understood the need for discretion, yet she was disappointed, and in spite of the balmy night, a chill passed through her. She wanted to snuggle close to Carla's warmth.

"Ellie?" Carla murmured against her hair. "I'm sorry about what happened at the beach."

"In the cave?" Ellie shivered harder as she remembered her kiss.

"No, I don't regret that part." Carla's dark eyes sparked like the phosphorescent waters surrounding them. "I'm sorry about dredging up my past. You didn't need to hear all that, and people tell me I need to start living in the present."

"People are right," she gently responded, drowning in Carla's eyes.

Ellie imagined their lips brushing, barely touching, as light and teasing as the electricity sparkling on the waves. She imagined exploring the outer contours of Carla's mouth with her tongue, far more arousing than a direct kiss. Were the other passengers watching? Did they know Carla? If so, what would they think if Ellie initiated such a kiss? In a last grab at sanity, she peered at the other passengers, who were moving like gray shadows in some other world.

"Forget them," Carla whispered. "They don't care. Go back to what you were thinking, because I was thinking it, too. Pretend you and I are alone with the sea and the sky."

She lowered her cheek onto Carla's shoulder, then tilting her chin upward, she saw the heaven above was a dark blanket, sequined with tiny white stars. The captain's narration faded to mute, while the very floor beneath their feet shattered with faceted light.

She snuggled closer and rested her cheek on Carla's arm, so she could watch both the light churning in the wake of their propeller and the swirling kaleidoscope colors of phosphorescence under their feet. Carla gently stroked her hair, hummed a slow, haunting lullaby. Her rhythmic touch and the low melody made Ellie's eyelids heavy, and soon she was adrift in a peaceful place at the edge of consciousness.

The engine's vibration massaged her body, and she breathed in harmony with the cadence of the rolling waves. She remained mesmerized in that warm, safe dream until suddenly the vibrations stopped and they bumped against something hard and final.

CHAPTER EIGHTEEN

Under arrest...

Ellie sat up with a jolt, completely disoriented. "Did I miss anything?"

"Just more sparkles and light. You are beautiful when you sleep, so I didn't have the heart to wake you." Carla's words ushered her back to reality. "The cruise is over, and we're back at the dock."

"Oh no, I *did* miss it! I'm so sorry."

Carla laughed. "We'll do it again, dear Ellie, and next time I promise not to put you to sleep."

Next time? She glanced at Carla to weigh the truth of her offer, but realized her eyes and mind were elsewhere, positively riveted to a commotion taking place on the dock. She recognized the uniformed policeman who had been directing traffic. A second cop had joined him, and the pair stood on either side of the gangplank, inspecting all the passengers as they left the boat.

"Do we have a terrorist aboard?" Ellie joked.

Carla was not amused. Next Ellie spotted a patrol car, its cherry light spinning, and when it was their turn to debark, both officers closed in. The one who had spoken to Carla before the cruise put his hand on her arm and took her aside.

"What do you want?" Angrily shoving the officer's hand away, Carla spoke in English, for Ellie's benefit.

"We need to talk, Doña Carla. Lieutenant Colon agrees. He's waiting for you now." The young man nodded toward the parking lot. "You understand I had to call him, yes?"

"No," Carla snapped, then gave Ellie a dark look. "Wait for me in the car."

Clearly this was the wrong moment to argue. The tiny pulse in Carla's clenched jaw started to jiggle, just as it had when Ellie interfered with Enrique. But Ellie was desperate to understand what was going on, so without directly contradicting her, she followed several paces behind as the officers led Carla away.

For a moment she lost them in the crowd, but then spotted an unmarked police car inching to the curb. It was a beige Ford Crown Victoria, just like cops used in the States. She knew this because her youngest brother, who had collected speeding tickets like baseball cards, taught her to recognize these vehicles.

Sure enough, an officious young guy stepped from the Crown Vic's passenger seat, just as Carla and her escorts reached the car. He wore a stylish blue blazer with a crisply ironed shirt and tan slacks. He discreetly flashed a wallet badge, which apparently infuriated Carla.

"For Christ sake, Colon, I know who you are," she hissed. "I've known you since you were a baby." Using both hands, Carla pushed the two uniformed officers aside, and with a nod from their young boss, those officers retreated to do crowd control.

Soon the altercation between Carla and Lieutenant Colon attracted curious bystanders, and Ellie felt embarrassed for Carla. Most of these folks were tourists who didn't know her, but those who did averted their eyes, not wanting to acknowledge that their powerful neighbor was in trouble. Ellie figured this press of humanity worked in her favor. Maybe she could blend in unnoticed.

Problem was, the confrontation had escalated in Spanish, so she couldn't make much sense of anything, except the name

Carmen Diaz came up again and again, as Carla vigorously shook her head in denial.

Interesting. Much as she hated to see Carla being grilled by the police, she was morbidly curious to know what Carla's mystery woman had done. She was compiling an imaginary list of criminal offenses committed by Ms. Diaz, when Lieutenant Colon spotted her.

Obviously he had seen Carla and her leaving the boat together, so he assumed they were in cahoots—whatever that meant. He raised his arm and crooked his finger in her direction, commanding her to approach.

Carla sighed heavily. "Damn it, why didn't you go to the car like I told you?" Carla then reluctantly introduced her in English. "I'm sorry about the confusion, Ellie, but Lieutenant Colon is making a big mistake."

Up close, the lieutenant was far from formidable. He had a button nose and a thin moustache, the kind Ellie and her girlfriends used to draw on their upper lips with an eyebrow pencil.

"It's a pleasure to meet you, Señorita Birdsong. I hope you are enjoying your stay on our island."

"Not at the moment." She scowled at Colon, who seemed torn between playing the proper host and harassing Carla. She knew better than to sass a cop, especially in a land where she didn't speak the language, but his interference was infuriating and she'd never been one to buckle to bullies. Yet she didn't want to make Carla's situation worse, so she moderated her tone. "Sorry, it's just that we were on our way to a late dinner." She smiled.

Carla blinked in surprise, but her remark got Colon chewing his gum double-time. He smelled of Juicy Fruit as his blue eyes narrowed under a straw-colored buzz cut. He was a blue-eyed, blond Puerto Rican, who seemed somehow more sinister for this aberration.

"Sorry to spoil your evening," he continued coldly. "But perhaps you can help me, Señorita Birdsong. You have been staying at Casa Valdez, so you must tell me, where is Carmen Diaz?"

"Who?" Although unreasonably jealous of Diaz, her sympathies lay firmly with Carla. She reached out, touched Carla's arm. She searched her eyes and offered an encouraging smile.

"Señorita Carmen Diaz," Colon repeated, losing his patience.

"Never heard of her," she lied with wide-eyed innocence. "Can we go now?"

Carla's mouth tugged up at the corners as she gave Ellie an almost imperceptible nod of approval. "Leave Ms. Birdsong out of it. She knows nothing."

Well, that was God's own truth. She knew less than nothing, but from the way Colon was fuming and masticating his gum, she guessed Señorita Diaz, Carla's lady of the night, must be Public Enemy Number One.

"I'm taking you to the police station, Doña Carla," Colon insisted. "Where we can discuss this privately."

Carla moved closer to Ellie, but the two uniforms intervened. One cop gently seized her right arm, the other her left.

"Be reasonable, Doña Carla," Colon pleaded like a little boy. "Remember when you coached our Little League football team? You told us to follow the path of least resistance. Perhaps you should take that advice right now." He folded back his jacket, exposing a set of handcuffs looped to his belt.

Carla glanced at Ellie, her face scarlet with fury, but did not raise her voice or lose her temper. "Can you find your way home?" She reached into her pocket, fished out her car keys.

Ellie nodded, and their fingers brushed as Carla handed her the keys. "God, are you under arrest?" she asked incredulously.

"I'm sure it's nothing serious, but please go home and tell Juan what has happened," Carla called over her shoulder as Colon ushered her to the unmarked car. "And if I am not home for breakfast, tell him to send out the troops."

Ellie nodded, waved, and remained speechless while one cop tucked Carla into the back of the cruiser. She watched in stunned silence until the Crown Vic's taillights disappeared, like two bloodshot eyes into the night.

CHAPTER NINETEEN

Creatures of the night...

Ellie stood absolutely still, breathing in, then out, until all the curious bystanders left the crowded parking lot. Only then, as she started up the dark garden path toward the hotel, did she realize the enormity of her predicament. Carla arrested? How could that be? Was it about Carmen Diaz, or something else? Carla had fought with that greasy little gangster, Diego Martinez, in the Ponce market. Was her association with that unsavory man less than innocent? She believed in Carla, but she'd learned early on that big bad wolves often inhabited the most genteel of clothing.

As she stumbled up the garden pathway, coiling vines grabbed at her ankles. She imagined the vines were venomous snakes, and the droplets of moisture attracting the dim, available light were actually menacing animal eyes following her through the jungle. The silence was absolute, but for the scurrying of small night creatures and the staccato beating of her heart.

Twice she stumbled on uneven pavers, lightly skinning her hands and knees, yet she tried to focus on the flickering hotel lights glowing in the distance. Funny, this route hadn't seemed nearly so long or treacherous when Carla was holding her hand, but now Carla was gone. Ellie had been abandoned, and the thought made her unreasonably angry as she picked her way through a particularly dense stand of foliage.

As her panic escalated, she heard the heavy thudding of some large beast right behind her, and before she could process the meaning of the snapping branches, something punched her in the back.

The pain was intense, knocking the wind from her chest. The vicious blow sent her flying. She held out her hands to break the fall, but her ribs crashed against an unyielding stone bench, and as shock waves radiated through her entire body, she swore she heard her ribs cracking.

"Go home, bitch!" The gravelly voice was muffled against her hair, and when she opened her mouth to scream, a large hand covered it. His fingers stank of cigarettes as his powerful grip crushed her jaw. "Shut up, or I'll break your neck!"

Dear God, please don't let him kill me! The mantra repeated itself in her short-circuiting brain as the impulse to fight kicked in. The monster grabbed her shoulder with his free hand, breaking one strap of her sundress. The precious necklace Carla had given her fell off into the weeds. *Dear God, don't let him rape me!* As adrenaline pumped through her veins, she realized he was stealing her shoulder bag. And when he released her mouth, raking the bag's strap down across her sunburned arm, her fury knew no bounds.

She fought the pain and slithered through his grasp to the ground. When she squirmed around to face him, she noticed two bizarre things at once: the asshole was wearing a black ski mask with three holes, and he was laughing. His breath smelled like stale coffee, and his dead fish eyes belonged to a stone-cold killer.

She opened her mouth to scream, but the thug lifted his hand and slapped her hard across the face, toppling her onto her back. When she tasted blood, something broke loose inside. Copying a page from Carla's fight book, she cocked her knee.

When she kicked upward with all the force she could muster, the sharp heel of her sandal connected with the sweet spot between his legs.

Her attacker howled in agony and cradled his crotch. His scream vibrated through the dark garden, shocking the creatures of the night to silence, but waking the sleeping hotel, and Ellie knew she had won.

The whites of his eyes expanded inside the two black holes. "Go home, bitch," he squawked in a tortured falsetto. And then, still holding his balls in one hand and her purse in the other, he hobbled away as fast as his injuries allowed, whimpering like a whipped hound.

Only then did her tears flow. She would have laughed, but it hurt too much. Eventually she extended both legs and felt for damage, but found only a network of sticky abrasions. So she was okay from the hips down, but when she leaned her aching head back against the bench, her ribs contracted in protest and her jaw felt like a day at the dentist's—without Novocaine.

Shit, shit, shit! She inched upright, and soon she saw two sets of flashlights bobbing through the blur across her eyes. And while she was grateful to be rescued, she didn't want to be found like someone's broken Raggedy Ann doll. *Damn, damn, damn!* She pulled up the right side of her sundress, now strapless, to ensure she was decent, and then struggled to her feet.

One man and one woman approached, speaking excitedly in Spanish, and when their beams trained on Ellie's face, their expressions said it all. She was a battered, blubbering wreck, terrifying to behold. Clearly her rescuers were also frightened, but they cautiously approached, took hold of her arms. Maybe they assumed she was about to faint on the spot, and they could well be right.

Although her ears were ringing and she couldn't understand a single word they said, the language of comfort was the same all over the world. She kept nodding in the affirmative, indicating she was able to walk, so gradually they all made their way out of the garden.

Her rescuers had come from the hotel kitchen, and when they entered the rear of the building, the welcoming lights and the aroma of foods cooking induced a fresh flood of tears.

"Please sit, *señorita*." By then the man, a portly fellow in his early sixties, understood she was American and had switched to broken English.

He helped her onto a straight-backed chair at a white enameled metal table. The table's surface felt cold to her skinned elbows. This man was obviously the hotel chef. His white coat was smeared with traces of red, which she assumed was her blood, and as he watched her cry, he seemed at a loss.

Her female savior, who spoke no English, was a practical young thing in her late teens who immediately filled a stainless steel bowl with lukewarm water, brought clean washcloths and towels. She placed them on the metal table and searched Ellie's eyes with a shared female concern. Using both hands, she touched the private place between her legs and lifted her eyebrows in a question.

"Oh, no, he didn't rape me," Ellie said at once. "He took my purse."

The chef seemed embarrassed by her straight talk and his round cheeks turned ruddy, yet he translated what needed no translation, and the teenaged cook nodded in sympathy. She dipped a cloth into the bowl and held it toward her, asking permission to bathe her face.

"No, *gracias, señorita*, I can do it." She accepted the cloth. It hurt when she smiled, so after pressing the warm liquid to her eyes, hoping to stop her cowardly tears, she got to work on her lips and mouth, dipping and washing until the water in the bowl was stained pink.

"I will call the hospital," the man said.

"No, I'll be okay. Just call the police, will you?"

The two consulted with one another. They thought she was crazy to refuse medical help, but Ellie had survived enough football skirmishes with her three brothers to know that a couple of sore ribs and a bunged-up jaw were not life-threatening injuries.

"Water and aspirin?" she asked them.

That request was also universally understood, so like magic, the girl rushed to the sink as the man dialed 911. She brought the water and a bottle of pills, while her boss gave animated instructions to the authorities. Ellie swallowed three tablets, dropped three more into the glass. She swirled them until they dissolved, then swished the painkilling potion around in her mouth. Each time she spat, she added more pink liquid to the bowl.

"Brush and mirror?" She mimed her request to the girl, who understood instantly.

When the girl fetched those items from her own purse, Ellie flipped open the compact mirror and inspected her mouth. *Shit.* Her lips were swollen like two links of breakfast sausage, but the bleeding had stopped. She had bitten her tongue, but all her teeth were still firmly rooted in her gums. So far, so good. She closed the compact and brushed a small collection of dried vegetation from her hair, but the action of lifting her arm tortured her ribs, so she gave up.

She suppressed a groan, smiled at her two new friends, but before she could adequately thank these angels from the kitchen, a squad car arrived with its siren blaring. Two uniformed officers rushed inside and surrounded Ellie like she was the criminal, not the victim, and only after a long-winded explanation from the chef, did the cops give her a break.

"Do you want to see a doctor?" the first cop said.

She recognized the young traffic policeman who had spoken to Carla when they first arrived at Phosphorescent Bay. These two were the same policemen who had taken Carla away. Small world.

She explained once again that she didn't need medical attention, and after the cops had weighed their liability, they agreed she could skip the emergency room.

"As you wish then, *señorita*. We'll take your statement at the station, and then file a report."

CHAPTER TWENTY

The Keystone Cops...

Ellie thought of them as Cop One and Cop Two, since she couldn't seem to remember their names. As they drove through town, the men tried to engage her through the wire mesh, but she closed her eyes and rested her battered head against the back seat. Could she trust them? She had learned that Puerto Rican cops could be corrupt, but what were her options? She hurt like hell, was fighting a massive headache, and was in no mood for chitchat. It could wait until they got to the station, where she prayed to find Carla, hopefully not behind bars.

The thought of being reunited with Carla made her ordeal more bearable, although her ribs ached with every bump in the road. Those aspirins weren't working, not by a long shot, and her pain rekindled the rage she had felt in the garden. Who needed the aggravation? She'd been in Puerto Rico a few short days, and so far she had interfered with Carla's child-rearing technique, been seduced in a cave, broken up a brawl in the market, been roughed up by a thug in a ski mask, and had her emotions spun up and down like a yo-yo.

Her boss, Dyna, would be royally pissed. She had lost her purse—including her cell phone, driver's license, two credit cards, and more cash than she usually toted around. Worst of all, she had lost the precious necklace Carla had given her, and had she enough energy, she'd go back to the garden to search for it. Finally, but way less important, she had surely botched *Project Puerto Rico*, so perhaps her attacker was right: she should just give up and go home.

"Are you all right?" Cop One asked as they led her up a short flight of stairs to the Ponce Police Department.

"Do I look all right?"

"Sorry," Cop Two muttered as he seated her at a hard table under bright lights.

She knew her attitude was uncalled for. These were the good guys, they hadn't hurt her, but she'd reached the end of her emotional rope. "Do you have anything stronger than aspirin here?" she asked nicely, hoping lawmen kept some heavy-duty meds handy.

"Sorry, it's against regulations to medicate visitors," Cop Two said.

She rolled her eyes at the stained ceiling. "Okay, can you find me a safety pin?"

They gaped at one another, but Cop One rummaged through his desk and came up with one. They both stared as she pinned her torn strap to the bodice of her sundress.

"Okay, where is Carla?" she demanded through her pain. Each time she lifted her arms, her ribs rebelled. "You're questioning her here, right?"

"Carla?" Cop Two drew a blank.

She glanced at the big round clock on the wall, saw it was well after midnight. "Carla Valdez. Lieutenant Colon brought her here about an hour ago."

Cop One threw back his head and laughed. "Oh no, the lieutenant works in the city. He took Doña Carla to San Juan."

"All the way to San Juan? Why, for God's sake?"

"That is not your concern." Cop One pushed a lined pad and pencil across the table. "This is about your case, not hers.

Will you write down everything that happened, or shall we do an oral debriefing?"

Her spirits plunged when she learned Carla was not there to save her, to hold her, to tell her everything was going to be all right. She was utterly and depressingly alone, and while she knew Carla was not to blame, her absence felt like a betrayal.

To make matters worse, Cop One's officious manner and self-important tone was infuriating. She laughed out loud, not a smart move. But she wasn't about to sit on a hard chair and write out a stupid report. "Let's just *talk*. Is that okay with you, sugar?" she drawled sarcastically.

Her humor was not appreciated. But, hey, it was late, and they were all tired.

Without cracking a smile, Cop Two turned on a tape recorder, introduced everyone present, and they began the session. As she spoke, her throat felt numb and she stifled several yawns. When she got to the part about the ski mask, Cop Two giggled.

"That is nonsense, *señorita*. What thief wears a ski mask in the tropics?"

"He probably brought it from the States," she snapped. "I think he's from Miami, but he works for a disgusting little man named Diego Martinez." She had put it together back in the garden—the short bodyguard who had worn a Dolphins T-shirt, the thug Carla had punched in the face. She'd recognized his smell and stature.

"Really? Did your attacker confess all this?" Cop One laughed.

"Look, I recognized the guy. He has eyes like a dead fish."

The cops smirked at one another. "Let me get this straight…" Cop Two chuckled. "The thief is an American because he wears a ski mask, and you recognized him because he has fish eyes?"

So her testimony was a big fat joke. "Look, if you Keystone Cops could catch him, I could identify him."

"No doubt, but unfortunately we have many American assholes on our island, so how do we catch *your* thieving *gringo*?" Cop One sneered. "And who the hell is Diego Martinez?"

She clamped her mouth shut. Let them do their own research on Mr. Martinez.

"Did your assailant drive a black Range Rover?" Cop One continued.

"What are you talking about?"

He yawned, looked at the clock. It was now after one in the morning. He punched off the tape recorder. "Never mind. It's just that a Range Rover was the only vehicle we passed on the road when we responded to your emergency. It was coming from the direction of the hotel and speeding fast, until it spotted our squad car. Normally we would have pursued, but we were coming to your rescue."

"On the other hand," Cop Two added. "It might not have been the thief at all. He could have escaped in the opposite direction."

"Don't you get it?" she interrupted. "This isn't about robbery. The jerk wanted to scare me off. He wanted me to go back to the States."

"So why don't you?" the cops said in unison.

CHAPTER TWENTY-ONE

Hispanic Florence Nightingale…

The cops didn't believe her. Or else they didn't care. They drove her back to Parguera, where she had left Carla's Honda, and she could tell by their attitude that her case would be shifted to their back burner. They saw her as just another unlucky tourist who waved American dollars in the face of local poverty and got what she deserved.

Maybe that was too harsh. Maybe they felt a teensy bit sorry for her, but in the greater scheme of things, a common *snatch-and-run* was not top priority. As she drove unfamiliar roads, twice taking wrong turns, yawning and straining to keep her eyes open, she counted herself lucky. After all, she had stashed Carla's car keys in her pocket rather than in her ill-fated purse. Nagging pain kept her awake long enough to reach Casa Valdez and prevented her from having an accident without a driver's license, which had also been stolen.

Thank heavens for small blessings she told herself as she walked through the moonless night to an all-dark house. On the far horizon, the first pink rays of dawn above the placid Caribbean confirmed that she had lost any chance for a full night's sleep. She hesitated before ringing the doorbell, hating to awaken the household, but she needed help.

So she pressed the button, listened to chimes echoing inside, and was about to fall asleep on her feet when Filo finally opened the door. The maid was barefoot, clad in a purple, knee-length shift, and her rumpled mass of black hair framed her startled eyes.

"Where is Doña Carla?" she demanded before letting her enter the dim foyer.

Ellie pushed past, hobbling into the light from a hurricane lantern mounted on the wall. "Near as I can tell, Carla is cooling her heels in a San Juan jail," she answered, thankful her vocal cords still worked. "Where is your father? Carla really wanted Juan to know what has happened."

Filo rubbed her eyes. She was still half asleep, trying to process the insane information. "My father went home to Lares for the weekend, and my sister Sylvie went with him, so I am alone here with the boys."

Ellie wilted onto a wooden bench under the lantern, leaned into the stucco wall. "Do you have aspirin and orange juice?" She squinted up at Filo, who then got her first clear look at Ellie.

"*Madre Maria*, what happened to you?"

"It feels like I got plowed under by a tractor, but in fact, I got mugged in the garden at Phosphorescent Bay."

Filo began to hyperventilate. "That is terrible, but where is Doña Carla?"

She had already explained that Carla was in jail, but obviously Filo could not imagine such a thing. "Please, Filo, will you help me upstairs?"

In the end, Filo proved to be the Hispanic Florence Nightingale. She gave her juice, and pills that packed a wallop far more potent than aspirin. It seemed Casa Valdez was equipped like a mini emergency room to deal with field hand accidents, and Filo was an expert nurse. They decided any further first aid could wait until morning, so the moment her head hit the pillow in the blue room, Ellie fell into a deep, drug-induced sleep.

All too soon, she heard roosters crowing at dawn and the patter of tiny footsteps outside her door. Boyish voices whispered as the faces of Antonio and Enrique peeked in without entering. They were curious about the injured *Americana*. Soon she heard the school bus collect the boys from the dusty road outside her window and the clatter of trucks hauling field hands to the cane fields. By the time breakfast smells reached her, Casa Valdez had undertaken a new day, and so must she.

"Are you awake, Ellie?" Filo shyly poked her head into the room.

She helped Ellie sit up on the edge of the bed, administered more orange juice, assisted her into the bathroom, and then left.

After a warm, restorative soak in the garden tub, Ellie clumsily washed her hair and blew it dry. Returning to her bedroom, she was surprised to find Filo waiting to treat her abrasions with antiseptics. Upon closer inspection, they agreed her ribs were neither broken nor cracked, which was a minor miracle. Filo helped her into a loose, comfortable outfit much like a karate suit, with baggy shirt and string-tied trousers. Finally, the young woman left her alone, with makeup and a mirror.

Heaven help us. Ellie groaned at her reflection.

Yet aside from glassy brown eyes, a greenish-yellow bruise on her jaw, and lips pumped up like an inner tube, perhaps no one would notice she was the walking wounded. She applied Erase under her eyes and foundation to her face, almost concealing the bruising. Adding blush to her cheeks, she figured she was good to go.

She hobbled downstairs, limping like a sidelined quarterback and praying that her screaming muscles would loosen up sooner than later. She was especially thankful when Filo allowed her to eat without asking questions, and after greedily swallowing rice and beans, scrambled eggs, and more juice, she smiled gratefully.

"Are you feeling better now, Ellie?"

"Right as rain. Thanks so much."

"Good, I am glad." But then Filo's spine stiffened and she crossed her arms. Her dark eyebrows knit together in a frown above her small, flaring nose. "Now cut the bullshit. What the hell happened last night?"

She was so startled by Filo's outburst that she told her everything, start to finish. She had a captive, if incredulous, audience. Filo did not interrupt or ask questions until her recitation was done.

Then she shook her head disapprovingly and frowned. "This may have nothing to do with it, but a nasty woman keeps phoning you. She called last evening, every hour on the hour, and she was very rude."

Ellie considered only a moment, for the answer was a no-brainer. The impatient caller was Dyna Collins. "Don't worry, Filo, I'm sure it was only my boss. Did she say what she wanted?"

"No, but she was calling from Atlantic City, and she was very angry. She kept waking the boys up, until I turned the phone off and stopped answering. Do you want to call her now?"

She glanced at the landline telephone mounted on the wall and digested this new complication. Last night she had turned off her cell phone during the cruise, since the captain required it. Then, of course, she had lost it in the garden. The last thing she wanted now, though, was an unpleasant confrontation with Dyna. She would face that when she felt stronger.

"Thanks, but I'll talk to my boss later. Right now, I'm worried about Carla. Last night she said we should 'call out the troops' if she wasn't home for breakfast."

Filo shrugged. "*Sí*, that sounds just like her, but Doña Carla told me not to worry when she phoned this morning."

"Carla called *this morning*?"

Filo smiled mischievously. "*Sí*, the police held her only one hour, but since it was late and she had no car, she decided to spend the night in a hotel."

Ellie's temper flared. "You knew this all along, but you didn't tell me? You made me go through the whole story, when you already knew the ending?"

"Oh, but it was so interesting to hear it from both points of view."

Filo carried the dirty dishes to the sink, while Ellie wondered if strangling the girl with her bare hands would be considered justifiable homicide. "Did you tell Carla I got mugged?"

She laughed. "No, I thought you should tell her yourself. She will be very upset, you know. Also, Doña Carla expects you to pick her up at noon."

"Damn it, Filo!" She pounded her fist on the table, making the silverware jump. "Are you saying Carla expects me to drive to San Juan? Hell, I don't know how to get there. I don't even have a license. Can't you call someone in from the fields to pick her up?"

"Oh, no, Ellie. All the men are busy doing their work." Filo handed her a sheet of paper from the counter. "But Antonio Googled your directions before he left for school. They will lead you directly to the Banco de San Juan, where Carla will be picking up the deed and other papers about her land. She said you would understand…" Filo paused to give her a look of disapproval. "She said you must bring an overnight bag, in case you are delayed and have to stay over in the city."

"What else did Her Highness say?"

"She said she will treat you to lunch." Filo winked. "But do not be late."

CHAPTER TWENTY-TWO

An intimate table…

So history repeated itself. Carla said *jump*, Ellie said *how high?* Equipped with her overnight bag and the bottle of Demerol Filo had given her, she followed Antonio's directions to San Juan. She had packed cosmetics, a nightgown, and a change of clothes because she needed options. Whether their negotiations went well, or poorly, she could no longer depend on Carla for the roof above her head and intended to book lodgings in town. Then she would fetch the rest of her belongings from Casa Valdez before heading back to the States.

But what if Carla was planning to share a hotel room? To celebrate a successful merger? She had to admit, the fantasy of a sleepover with Carla made her emotions soar and fall like a roller coaster. Clearly a romantic entanglement was a figment of her imagination, so she calmed her racing mind by focusing on the job at hand. She found a CD in her bag, *The Tourist's Guide to San Juan*, and slid it into the player.

Ellie followed along with the audio tour, so that by the time she turned into the narrow, tree-lined streets of the old city, she felt like she'd been there before. She actually arrived early, and when she parked in front of Banco de San Juan, she spotted Carla pacing on the sidewalk under a shade tree, watching for her. She locked the hybrid and concentrated on walking normally, in spite of her angry rib muscles. Although she felt much better, she didn't want to burden Carla with her ordeal prematurely, not until the time was right.

"Thank God, Ellie!" Carla hurried to meet her. "I'm so relieved to see you. I was so worried after leaving you to fend for yourself last night. I am so sorry."

As Carla approached, Ellie noticed she no longer wore the multicolored sweater and jeans from last night. Instead, she wore an exquisitely tailored American-style power suit—wheat-colored linen jacket and slacks, softened by a peach silk blouse and stylish boots. Either Carla had a hideaway apartment in the city, or she had done some early morning shopping. Certainly her short stint at the police station had left her none the worse for wear. As she drew Ellie into her arms for a tentative hug, Ellie tried not to wince from the pain.

"Did you find your way home all right?" Carla's eyes were disturbingly concealed behind a pair of dark sunglasses.

She desperately wanted to ask Carla what had gone on at the police station last night. She was dying to know more about Carla's relationship with Carmen. She needed to tell the truth about being attacked in the garden, but Carla's anxious concern made her hesitate. Yes, she would ask her questions and tell the truth later. Luckily, it seemed Carla's sunglasses kept her from noticing her bruises.

"Have you finished your business at the bank?" she asked, evading Carla's question.

"Yes, I have everything we need, so let's discuss it over lunch." She smiled disarmingly. "Afterward, we'll do some sightseeing, agreed?"

What could she say? Carla was a take-charge kind of gal, so Ellie didn't protest when she casually slipped her hand under her elbow and steered her down the street. Ellie's mission was to complete their business, so she was doing her job. Besides, considering how unstable she still felt from the attack, she welcomed the support of such an attractive crutch.

Once they closed the deal, she'd tell Carla about the goon in the garden and ask her advice about getting some money and a new driver's license, but for now she was content to watch people smile as they passed. Likely they thought Carla and she were best friends as Carla guided her through an ornate iron gate leading to a hidden garden restaurant.

"You'll appreciate the privacy here, Ellie. The owner doesn't advertise, so tourists never find this place, and we regulars keep coming back for the gourmet menu."

Carla chose an intimate table in the shade of a banana tree. Nearby, a softly bubbling fountain flowed into a pool of small goldfish, and although two other couples were also eating in the garden, they seemed far away, partially concealed by the lush foliage. Alone at their little table, Ellie felt like they'd been stranded in paradise.

"Carla, would you mind taking off your sunglasses?" she gently requested. "I can't see your eyes."

She nodded and tucked the dark lenses into her purse. Her eyes were soft with affection, and Ellie was so embarrassed by the raw emotion in her gaze, that she quickly looked away. At the same time, Carla reached across the table and captured her hand.

"What's wrong, Ellie? You asked me to remove my glasses, but now you refuse to look at me?"

She was right. Carla's intensity had triggered a response Ellie didn't want her to see, but then Carla tilted her chin upward and forced her to meet her gaze. Thank heavens they were seated in dark shadow, otherwise Carla would surely notice her bruises.

"Much better," Carla whispered. "You have exceptional eyes, Ellie, and they change with every moment. Yesterday at the Caribbean they were amber, but today they are as dark and deep as the ocean on a moonless night."

"Your eyes change, too, Carla."

"Oh really, when do they change?" she teased.

She vividly recalled how Carla's eyes had turned black with passion as they lay together in the beach cave. The very memory caused some delightful discomfort that had nothing to do with her injuries.

"When do my eyes change, Ellie?"

Judging from Carla's knowing grin, she felt sure that other women had already told Carla about her eyes. "Never mind, can we order now?"

A waiter had arrived unnoticed to their table. He handed Carla a menu and wine list, and as Carla leaned close to consult with Ellie, warmth emanated from her body. "Lord, I don't know what to pick. Will you choose for me, Carla?"

They began with an enticing array of cold-spiced meats and a delicate herb soup. Next, they enjoyed lightly steamed vegetables in cream sauce served with warm sesame rolls. A potent white wine enhanced all the flavors.

"This meal isn't authentic Puerto Rican, is it?" she asked between mouthfuls.

"No, it is not, but I'll treat you to local cuisine at a late dinner."

Dinner? Surely their business wouldn't take all day, but she was not inclined to argue. When the first bottle was empty, Carla called for a second. The flavor was as mellow as the golden afternoon, so she relaxed, enjoying the sunlight filtering through banana leaves. The fabric of Carla's slacks brushed Ellie's knee, only to be expected in such close quarters, so she allowed her leg to relax against Carla's. The contact felt natural and right. She listened to her melodic voice and was more content than she'd been in a very long time. By the time the waiter appeared and offered dessert, they hadn't even glanced at the papers in Carla's briefcase. Needing to sober up, Ellie said no to dessert, and they both ordered coffee.

"Now, are you ready to tell me what *really* happened?" Carla regarded her from above the rim of her cup.

Her scrutiny anchored Ellie with a sudden jolt. "What are you talking about?"

"Your face, I can see the bruises. Please don't tell me you walked into a door." Carla frowned. "And I could tell by the way you were walking, that you were hurting."

Ellie twisted her napkin. "Do we have to talk about this now?"

Carla sighed, signaled for the bill. "I understand, and I hate to break this magic spell, but I'm worried about you, *comprende*? I'm upset. Whoever did this to you, will answer to me."

As she watched Carla's right fist clench, then unclench, she glimpsed a darker side to her gentle companion. It seemed her rage lived right below the surface, and Ellie didn't want to go there. This wasn't a case of Carla playing *butch* to Ellie's *femme*, because like Ellie, she sensed Carla never thought of herself in those terms. In the straight world, they would both pass as attractive heterosexual women with strong opinions, a tad too much ambition, perhaps, and decided stubborn streaks. Be that as it may, she was still not ready to burden Carla with the full story of the assault.

"Please, Carla, I promise I'll explain it all later. Right now, let's just complete our business."

Carla's expressive eyebrows, usually arched like graceful raven's wings, suddenly dipped in a frown. "If your explanation must wait, then so must our transaction. We still have some trust issues, don't you agree?" Carla stood up, left a generous tip, and then tucked the briefcase snugly under her arm, out of Ellie's reach. Ellie was sure it contained the deeds to her land. She helped Ellie to her feet. "Maybe if we drive down to the ocean, the breeze will help blow the mistrust away?"

The strong coffee had helped diminish the effects of the wine, but when they stepped out to the sidewalk, where the bright light hurt her eyes, she once again hoped for Carla's support. The old-fashioned custom of an escort guiding his lady on his arm would ordinarily make her bristle with feminist resentment, but from Carla, the attention had seemed right, and nice. Unfortunately this time, after their spat, she did not offer a hand under Ellie's elbow, but rather she walked on ahead. Slightly miffed, Ellie told herself that Carla was from a different culture, practically from a different generation, so no wonder they had trust issues.

CHAPTER TWENTY-THREE

El Morro...

Carla took the driver's seat and treated her to a beautiful smile, as though nothing had ever happened. "I am taking you to El Morro," she announced. "This is the great fort that protected Puerto Rico from many conquerors."

Ellie decided to forget their disagreement. Instead, she tried to recall what she had learned of the island's history. "El Morro is located at the tip of the city, right?"

"Of course, so our soldiers could see the enemy approaching from the sea."

She relaxed against the headrest and studied the woman beside her. She had never seen Carla coming—from the sea or otherwise. And she was grateful she had removed her sunglasses, because like Mama always said: *you must look your enemy in the eye, before you can read his heart.* But was Carla her enemy?

Carla pointed out landmarks of interest along their route: the San Juan Museum of Art and History, the Plaza de San José, the Pablo Casals Museum, the Dominican Convent, and Carla's favorite, the Institute of Puerto Rican Culture.

Eventually, they drove into a green parkway and parked as close as they could to the great fort of El Morro, and when they followed a winding path up into the mighty battlements, Ellie experienced an eerie sensation of slipping backward into history. Carla paid their admission, and they began circling up the walled six levels of fortress, rising one hundred and forty feet above the sea. The exercise actually made her battered ribs feel better.

"You should rest," Carla said as she guided her slowly through a cold stone tunnel. "Let's find a bench."

"No, I'm fine," Ellie insisted.

They emerged into a sun-drenched courtyard, where ancient black cannons pointed out to sea. The fresh wind whipped through Ellie's hair, pulling strands from her loosely gathered ponytail and flailing them against her face. Carla led her to the edge of the wall. Far below, people bustled like ants in the parking lot, while out at sea, enormous cruise ships floated like toy boats on the horizon.

"Well, Ellie, what do you think? Are we at the edge of the world?"

She leaned against Carla as they gazed at the endless panorama. Carla's soft breath tickled her neck while they stood high above the dizzying drop. "We're at the edge of *something*," Ellie agreed, moving closer into the magnetic sphere of Carla's body. Suddenly she was tired of the deceit, sick of playing games, and totally exhausted from fighting the attraction she felt for this amazing woman. She encircled Carla with both her arms, then gently turned her until they were face-to-face.

"Kiss me, Carla," she pleaded in a voice she hardly recognized as her own.

Carla's eyes searched her face. "I don't understand…?"

"I've been lying. At least, I haven't told you the whole truth." Ellie took a deep breath. "I want the same thing you want. At least I hope you want it…"

Carla's heartbeat seemed to escalate along with her confusion. "But you know I'm a lesbian, Ellie. This is not a game to me."

"It's not a game to me either, damn it. Don't you get it, Carla? I'm a lesbian, too."

For one suspended moment they stared at one another, somehow stunned by the truth suddenly thrust between them. Carla began to tremble in Ellie's arms, so she pulled her closer and held on tight. "For God's sake, Carla, must I beg? Will you please kiss me?"

No need to ask twice. Carla's lips sought hers with searing hot intensity, and when her tongue explored, urging Ellie to open, the last remnants of her control fell away. She melted against the pillowed warmth of Carla's breasts and leaned into the tense muscles of her thighs. "Please hold me tighter. I think I'm falling…"

Carla moaned when Ellie slipped her hands under her jacket, exploring the curved planes of her back, and then cupping her soft breasts.

"Please, Ellie. If you keep that up, it won't matter if every tourist in the city is watching, I won't be able to stop."

But Ellie didn't want to stop. She buried her face between Carla's breasts, listened to the rapid pounding of her heart, and didn't give a flying fig what any curious bystanders might think. Her exquisite pain demanded a release only Carla could provide, and the feeling was a revelation. No woman had ever caused her to react that way before, and she longed to surrender completely to that new, achingly powerful force. She struggled to hold back her tears of relief, and joy.

"Not now, my sweet Ellie," Carla murmured.

"When then?" She was shockingly aware that her question seemed like an invitation to her bed, a blatant plea to a woman she'd known for only a few short days. Nothing in her past had prepared her for this role, but her heart insisted her instincts were right.

"Consider this…" Carla gently pulled away. "We had too much wine at lunch, and you may regret what you say. Look at me. I'm not a young American college girl. I've never made love in the back seat of a car, then gone on with my life like nothing happened."

Her protest tickled Ellie's funny bone. "No kidding? In case you haven't noticed, I'm no college girl, either. Believe it or not, I've never made love in the back seat of a car, nor do I intend to.

And I've never been a hit and run driver, if that's what's worrying you."

Carla's laugh started deep in her chest, then exploded from her mouth. "I'm often dense, but I'm not blind, Ellie. I see you are very much a woman, and while most of my countrymen think the Americans conquered us back in 1898, it seems I'm being conquered all over again."

Ellie was still giggling, responding to the corny, yet effective line, when she felt Carla stiffen in her arms and heard the laughter die in her throat. Her eyes hardened as she frowned at the parking lot far below.

Following her gaze, Ellie saw a white luxury sedan double-parked near the entrance gate. The tall man standing beside it had a pair of high-powered binoculars trained directly at them.

"You recognize him, don't you?" Carla's voice was suddenly wary. "He assaulted me at the market, and I kicked him in the balls."

"What does he want?"

"I thought *you* might answer that question." A tone of sad resignation entered Carla's voice.

"Like I told you before, he approached me on the plane from Atlantic City, but I don't know why."

"Okay, what about this, then. Your boss, Dyna Collins, has been leaving threatening messages in my voice mail, and from her tone, I wonder if she and the other man from the market, Diego Martinez, might not be joining forces to get my land?"

"No, that's impossible. Martinez is Dyna's competitor, nothing more."

Carla gave her a long, searching look. "Business is one thing, Ellie, but that man down in the parking lot is something else again. Your association with him would be intolerable."

Ellie exhaled slowly, all her emotions spent as she sank onto the nearest bench. Only moments before they had been lost in one another's arms, and now they had suffered another utter breakdown of trust.

"Look, Carla, I'm sure it was Diego's goon who attacked me in the garden last night. Why would he do that if we were working together?"

Carla also wilted onto the bench, taking care not to touch her. "Your boss called this morning and mentioned Diego by name, so I assumed she knew the man. Dyna knew details about the fight in the market and implied that if you and I did not complete our business in a timely fashion, I should expect more trouble."

"Carla, I told Dyna about our encounter with Diego in the market. That's how she knew those details."

"You also told her you'd been assaulted by Diego's bodyguard in the garden?"

"No, I never had a chance. That asshole stole my purse, including my cell phone, and I've been incommunicado ever since." She stopped talking, touched the little hollow at the base of her throat. She couldn't bring herself to confess that the necklace Carla had given her had also been lost in the scuffle.

Yet it hurt that Carla doubted her, had actually imagined she was involved with scumbags like Diego and his bodyguard. "You owe me an apology," she said quietly.

Carla glanced at her from the corners of her eyes. "Do I? What about that tall man down there?"

Ellie was confused. The guy was still watching. "Don't tell me he's after Casa Valdez, too?"

It seemed Carla was close to tears when she answered. "I fear it's much worse than that, Ellie. His name is Joey Arroyo, and he's after Antonio and Enrique. He was married to my Maria. He is their father."

CHAPTER TWENTY-FOUR

El Rincón...

White stucco walls and dark wooden beams gave the restaurant a distinctly Spanish flair. The floor was fashioned of colorful quarry tile, and their table was covered with spotless white linen. A single red rose on each table softened the otherwise austere atmosphere as flickering candlelight revealed other diners seated in the soft shadows. The separate conversations and the clinking of silverware were hushed and unobtrusive, while the clear, resonant notes from a classical guitar floated from beneath the fingers of a skilled musician featured in a single, pale spotlight.

They had managed to sneak away from El Morro without being spotted by Joey Arroyo. Once Carla had been sure he wasn't tailing them, she'd promised Ellie that she would explain all about him—later. She hadn't wanted to spoil their lovely day together, and she hoped Ellie felt the same.

Carla sighed with contentment as they finished the exquisite meal, which had begun with *asopao*, a thick, chicken-based soup. Next they enjoyed *paella*, rice prepared with chicken and seafood, and finally, she had introduced Ellie to *tostones*, a banana-like fruit pounded into inch-long pieces, then fried in olive oil.

"Wow, talk about calories!" Ellie patted her full tummy.

"You must have *guavas* for dessert."

"Bring it on, it's worth it."

"That's the spirit." Carla was happy as she watched Ellie eating the sweet fruit paste and goat's cheese. The emotion was new to her. She had deliberately buried her lingering suspicion that Ellie had some connection to Diego Martinez, or any other dark ulterior motive. If Carla was being willfully naïve, then so be it, because she hadn't felt so relaxed and at ease with a woman since Maria.

She delighted in Ellie's reaction to the native food, and couldn't believe they were spending the night together at El Rincón, her favorite hotel at the ocean's edge. "All very proper," Carla had assured her. "I've taken the liberty of booking two rooms, so we can put off the long drive home until tomorrow."

She had proposed the idea in an offhand way, taking Ellie by surprise. Carla had been startled when Ellie eagerly agreed. She supposed Ellie's quick acceptance was entirely innocent, but after the kiss she'd delivered that afternoon at El Morro, she wondered if Ellie's quick acquiescence was a not-so-subtle invitation to share her bed. If so, was Carla up for it? It had been a very long time.

But as they left the restaurant, Ellie seemed nervous.

"Carla, is putting off our drive home like putting off signing contracts?"

The evening air was surprisingly chilly as they climbed into the Honda. "I have the documents with me, and we'll both have clearer heads in the morning, after breakfast. Then we'll sign on the dotted lines, get you some cash, and apply for your temporary driver's license on the way out of town."

She watched Ellie relax into the seat and stare out the window at the city of San Juan, which was coasting by like a glittering fairyland. Carla found some soft music on the radio, as Ellie leaned against her shoulder.

She had decided back at El Morro to put aside the distrust between them and to ignore the elephant in the room: Maria's ex-husband, Joey Arroyo. No doubt he was in Puerto Rico to make another play for partial custody. Ellie had urged her to talk about it, but she had put the topic off-limits.

As they neared the hotel, she told herself, *whatever happens, happens.* Yet she could not ignore the churning that started somewhere behind her heart, then traveled much lower. She understood, once and for all, that she desperately wanted to make love to Ellie, and if Ellie wanted it too, then Carla would be hers—at least for one night.

She had conveniently left her right hand lying vulnerable on the seat between them as she drove with her left. Ellie captured it and placed it on her lap, smiled up into her eyes. Fifteen minutes later, they turned down a quiet street and stopped at the edge of the ocean. In the glow from a streetlight, she could just make out the dark form of the old-fashioned wooden structure…El Rincón.

"God, this place feels like déjà vu," Ellie said. "That hotel looks just like the seaside tourist resorts back in Atlantic City, those old Victorian homes where families came to stay year after year, long before gambling changed everything."

Carla's spirits fell. "Sorry, I was hoping this place would seem special to you. If you prefer a more modern hotel, we can go to the Condado. But I prefer El Rincón, which means *cozy hideaway.*"

"Oh, I prefer it, too!" Ellie exclaimed as she lifted her overnight case from the car, then climbed up the wide steps to the front porch. "I love old hotels, Carla."

"Forgive me. I seem to be overly protective of my favorite habitats. I was afraid a young American might not understand my obsession with the antique."

Ellie stopped in her tracks, crossed her arms, and glared at her. "Carla. I'm sick and tired of hearing how old you are, and how young I am. Please, do me a favor and forget it. Let's just be ourselves, all right? The rest is unimportant."

Carla cleared her throat and shifted from foot to foot. Fact was, she was nervous. She had never spent a night with a near-stranger, and in spite of her earlier suspicions, she was beginning to think romantic encounters were not an everyday occurrence for Ellie, either.

"You are right, Ellie. No more age comparisons. Shall we go in now?"

They stepped into an ornate foyer.

"*Buenas noches*, Doña Carla!" A dapper man in a dark suit and tie approached, beaming and bowing from the waist. Ellie seemed startled by the formal greeting from Carla's old acquaintance, the owner of El Rincón.

"*Buenas noches*, Don Miguel." She nodded. "Meet Ms. Eleanor Birdsong, the American I told you about."

"Welcome, Ms. Birdsong. Doña Carla said she was bringing a business associate, but she did not say her associate was a beautiful lady."

Carla was annoyed when Miguel stared at Ellie's breasts, but proud when Ellie did not extend her hand for him to shake. Clearly she knew an old goat when she saw one.

He turned back to Carla, a look of disapproval in his beady eyes. "And how is your lovely partner? Could Maria not make it to town this time?"

His words stung like a slap to her face. Obviously, Miguel had not heard that Maria died four years ago. But how could he know? She had only come here with Maria. It had been their special place, so she had not visited since Maria's death. Carla composed herself, and then explained in Spanish.

Their host apologized profusely, but the damage had already been done. Ellie was looking at her with pity in her eyes.

Miguel gave them their keys, bid them good night, then began walking away with a knowing smirk on his face. The hotel owner seemed to assume Ellie was Maria's replacement. His attitude infuriated Carla, and apparently, it infuriated Ellie, too.

"Excuse me, Ellie…" Carla turned and followed Miguel. She hooked the little man by the arm and led him aside for a spirited dressing down in Spanish. When it was over, Miguel glanced up at Ellie, a sheepish grin on his face, and bowed respectfully from the waist before scuttling down the hall.

"What did you say to him?" Ellie asked.

"Let's just say that Miguel is unlikely to look at you that way again."

"What way?" Ellie teased.

Carla refused to elaborate, but so what if Ellie really had been her mistress? Was that such a sin? She had rented two separate rooms, putting extra money into the unpleasant owner's pocket, so why had he automatically assumed they were lovers? Hopefully it had nothing to do with the look on Carla's face.

Besides, likely nothing would come of their night together. She should expect nothing more than an innocent sleep, apart from one another. One thing was certain, if she didn't get hold of her runaway emotions, she was lost.

"Our rooms are side by side," Carla explained as they waited for the elevator. "Would you like a drink at the bar before we go up?"

"No thanks," Ellie said.

"How do you feel? Do you still hurt from last night's attack?"

"Nope, I'm feeling much better. Thanks for asking."

Why did Ellie suddenly sound so weird and formal? And why had Carla asked about her physical condition? Was she as nervous as Ellie was?

"This hotel hasn't changed much through the years," Carla babbled on. "The furniture has been reupholstered..." She paused as they climbed aboard the elevator, then continued when they stepped out into a wide hallway. "The rooms I reserved are quite grand. They overlook the ocean, and in the morning, we will have an amazing view."

Ellie followed wordlessly until Carla inserted a key into one of two doors at the end of the hall.

She looked up at Carla, a question in her eyes.

CHAPTER TWENTY-FIVE

Ellie's room…

"No, our rooms are not adjoining, Ellie, but we do share a common balcony. This room is yours."

Ellie caught her breath when Carla turned on the light. The space had been created for a princess. It included an enormous brass bed covered with a floral-patterned spread sewn of coral and green silk. Matching solid fabrics graced the seats of two Queen Anne chairs, while a pale oriental rug adorned the hardwood floor. Finally, just as Carla had promised, painted shutters opened to the balcony and the sound of pounding surf.

"Oh, Carla, did you know my room would be so pretty?"

"I know it used to be. I'm glad it hasn't changed."

"Is your room this nice?"

"It's less pastel." She blushed. "At least it used to be."

"Which do you prefer?" Her voice sounded low and husky as she lifted her hand to Carla's face. Then Carla slowly guided her into her arms. She gently stroked Ellie's hair, while Ellie threw both arms around her neck and held her tight. Just as suddenly, Carla released her.

"My sweet Ellie, everything has happened so fast. I'm going to my room now, but I'll wait on the balcony, and you can join me. If you don't come, I will understand."

She left before Ellie could compose herself, and then she heard Carla's door slam. *Dear God, what does she want from me?*

Feeling like an emotional yo-yo, she locked herself in the elegant bathroom, peeled off her clothes, and tested her injured ribs. Sure enough, aside from some minor bruising, she felt good to go. A long, hot, tub bath eased her lingering aches, but did nothing to soothe her jangled nerves. When she leaned her head against the tiled wall, she heard her reluctant date showering next door. She toweled herself until her skin was red, then splashed on her favorite cologne. She put on her white cotton nightgown, unfortunately designed for "the girl next door," and vigorously brushed her hair.

Grandpa used to say *oxen are slow, but the earth is patient*, but Ellie knew her time in Puerto Rico was limited. She was hundreds of miles from home, with only a thin wall separating her from the most desirable woman she had ever known. So as her brother the marine might have said in a similar situation: *Carpe Diem*—seize the day.

Before courage deserted her, she opened the shutters to the balcony and stepped out.

Carla was waiting as promised, smelling of fresh soap. She had shed her jacket. Her silk blouse was seductively unbuttoned to just shy of indecent, while her glossy black hair had been freed from its ponytail. Still damp and wild from the shower, it framed her elegant features. And she was barefoot, making her seem endearingly vulnerable as Ellie faced her in the cool night air. The hair at Carla's temples was silver in the moonlight, and her eyes were unfathomable pools above her sensuous mouth.

Carla held out a bottle of champagne. "I ordered this from room service. You didn't want a drink downstairs, but I thought you might enjoy one on our private balcony."

"You knew I would come?"

"If you had not, I would've drunk the whole bottle by myself, to ease the disappointment."

Carla laughed, but Ellie could tell she was shy, and possibly as nervous as she was. Her hands trembled when she popped the cork, which fell into the lush garden below, and then she handed her a glass of the bubbling liquid. "To our partnership!"

"To us…" As the words left Ellie's mouth, Carla pulled her forward and rested her smooth cheek on her forehead. Ellie recognized the familiar rush of heat as their bodies met, and believed she had been waiting all her life for this moment.

Carla reached under her gown and gently ran warm fingers along her bruised ribs. "I don't want to hurt you. Please, if your injuries are a problem, you must stop me now."

Ellie trusted with all her heart that Carla would not hurt her. "I'm fine, so don't you dare stop!"

CHAPTER TWENTY-SIX

Carla's room…

Soon they left the night behind, abandoning their bottle of champagne on the patio table, deserting their glasses on the wide rail of the balcony. Carla led her through French doors with lace draperies swaying in the gentle breeze, and into the sanctuary of her room, where the flickering of a single thick candle illuminated the sumptuous space.

Wobbling shadows revealed dark, heavily carved Spanish furniture, a patterned tile floor strewn with exotic rugs, an enormous four-poster bed with the covers turned down.

Carla guided her closer, tilting her chin upward to better search her eyes. "My dear Ellie, are you sure?"

Ellie silenced her doubts with a kiss. Stretching on tiptoes, she pulled Carla's head forward and leaned into that kiss, locking their mouths in a rough embrace penetrated with the darting tip of her tongue.

Carla's reaction was stunning. Electric shock waves rippled through her body. She gripped Ellie's upper arms and held her against her breast, where her thudding heart beat a counterpoint to Ellie's irregular, frenetic rhythm. Ellie's tongue explored the sensitive lining of her upper lip, while Carla's tongue pushed past to discover Ellie's secrets. Again and again, Carla plunged, conquering her mouth with a relentless expertise that ignited all her senses with an all-consuming fever. Just when Ellie thought she could endure no more, Carla gently eased them apart, leaving her gasping with need.

"Please, Ellie, let's go slow…"

Good idea, otherwise they'd never make it to the bed. Carla gently opened Ellie's robe, helped her remove it, and tossed it at a chair in the corner, leaving her standing in her white cotton nightgown. Ellie wished to God she had packed something sexier for the occasion.

Reaching out to keep her knees from buckling, she latched onto the waistband of Carla's slacks. Once she steadied herself, she decided turnabout was fair play and slowly unbuttoned Carla's blouse, helped her remove it, and then freed her lovely breasts from their soft bra. She then tossed everything onto that same chair.

This was the Carla she remembered from the beach cave: athletic, tan, not one ounce of fat on her womanly frame. She exuded an animal magnetism, both sensual and untamed, but tonight, unlike that day at the ocean, Ellie would not stop what they had begun.

She ran her hand up under Carla's breasts, and with one finger, traced a path between them. Carla gasped with pleasure. Ellie drew light, feathery circles around each nipple, and with her other hand, again grabbed Carla's waistband.

"How slow do you want to go?" Ellie barely recognized her own throaty voice, let alone the aggressive woman behind that voice.

Carla untangled Ellie's fingers from her waist, then quickly slid Ellie's white gown up and over her head. "*Dios mío, eres preciosa.* I love you in the candlelight."

Her skin burned where Carla's eyes traveled along her body.

"Now it is my turn…" Carla caressed Ellie's breasts in the cradle of her hands. She tantalized each nipple with the balls of her thumbs until they peaked with delight, until her back arched in intense pleasure.

Her hands traveled down to Ellie's panties, and she slid one hand gently inside, between her legs. The exquisite sensation of her fingers intimately touching was unbearably good. With several deft maneuvers, Ellie eased her panties down below her knees and pushed them off with her feet, taking special care not to interrupt Carla's momentum.

Before Carla's talented fingers continued what they had so effectively begun, Ellie pressed the palm of her hand against Carla's chest, stopping her long enough to unzip her pants. In the end, Carla had to help with the unzipping and stripping, because Ellie's trembling fingers were impeding their progress. After more fumbling and joyous laughter, Carla stood naked before her, the pale moonlight pouring through the window, and Ellie returned the same compliment Carla had given her moments before, this time in English. "You are beautiful. You are a goddess."

She meant it with every fiber of her being. Carla's body would send any Renaissance sculptor worth his salt scurrying for marble, mallet, and chisel. Her elegantly squared shoulders, small perfect breasts, slim hips, and understated muscularity exuded both strength and femininity, an enticing combination.

Even in the dim light, she saw Carla blushing under her scrutiny. Normally so self-possessed and in control, the formidable Carla Valdez seemed undone by the compliment and decided they had waited long enough. She literally dragged Ellie to the bed, and for the first time in her life, Ellie was weightless with happiness.

Carla was the sun, and she was the moon, like the silver design on her lost necklace. And she was ready when Carla lowered her, taking great care not to put too much weight on her ribs. Carla positioned herself above her, and they locked eyes in an eternal understanding. She trembled, eager to capture Carla's light, to guide it into her darkness and hold it there forever.

CHAPTER TWENTY-SEVEN

Lose your heart...

Carla came to consciousness slowly. Even before she opened her eyes, she was aware of stiff muscles and a foreign scent on her skin. In the distance, traffic sounds mingled with the dull roar of surf on sand, and as reality intruded, she felt content and almost lethargic. She stretched her long legs and turned to embrace the woman who had brought her to this state of euphoria, but she was gone. Ellie's pillow was sunken, her side of the bed still warm, and she realized she was already up and showering.

Feeling somehow cheated, she struggled upright and opened her eyes to the familiar room glowing with early morning light. Sunbeams danced on the dark wood furniture and Persian rug. The shuttered doors to the balcony were wide open to the Atlantic, which dazzled her with its brilliance.

She swung her legs off the side of the bed, grateful they still worked, and decided she was still the same Carla Valdez she'd been yesterday morning. Love had not altered her beyond all recognition, as some folks claimed it did, yet she did sense a vital part of her had now merged with Ellie. Was that what it meant to *lose your heart?*

She touched her chest, her heart was still there. It was the same heart she once gave to Maria, many years ago, in this same room. How many times had they secretly met here, shamelessly, even while Maria was still trapped in her unhappy marriage? The memory should hurt more than it did, because she had promised her heart to Maria. But Maria was gone.

Ellie was here. And somehow it seemed her old heart could share, after all.

Last night, she had tried her best to shield Ellie's sore ribs from her full weight, but in the end, Ellie hadn't let her. And she hadn't been able to stop herself. But bruising Ellie's body was quite different from abusing her love, and Carla vowed she would never ever do that.

She smiled, remembering her total abandonment, in spite of their mutual desire to go slow. She had never felt more passionate, or aggressive. And Ellie had returned the favor in spades, surprising her. She glanced wistfully at the closed bathroom door. What would Ellie do if she burst in to join her? She pictured the driving water streaming down her breasts, her womanly hips, and smooth thighs. The vivid image sent her blood rushing to all the likely places.

Shaken, she stood upright on the solid floor and found her clothes neatly folded on the chair. Did she have the nerve to invade Ellie's shower? Less than one week ago, Carla suspected she'd been little more than a name in Ellie's DynaCo report—Ellie's *target*. Well, Ellie had hit a bullseye, and Carla would be eternally grateful.

CHAPTER TWENTY-EIGHT

Encore performance…

Ellie emerged from the shower and saw Carla sitting on the side of the bed, an unfathomable expression on her face. Stunned by the depth of feeling in her eyes, she was stricken by shyness and a need to escape. So, wrapped in her robe, clutching her white nightgown, she fled.

Shivering, she tiptoed onto the balcony and hurried into her own room, where everything remained pristine and untouched, just as she left it. Soon Carla would emerge fully dressed and ready for a new day, and so should she.

While she was in Carla's shower, with water rinsing away all traces of their intimacy, she had felt uncommonly sad. True, she would carry Carla's scent in her mind, if not on her body, and she would never forget one moment of their first lovemaking.

But would there be a second and third time? Or would their relationship slide away like water down the drain? Was their intimacy only a one-night stand? Such liaisons were not unusual, not sinful, and not necessarily love. She must not assume that Carla cared for her as totally and desperately as Ellie cared for her. In fact, in a few short days, they had exhibited strong differences of opinion, and they were both stubborn by nature. How could they last?

Oh, for Pete's sake, she scolded herself. *You sound like a lovesick fifth-grader.*

Her reflection in the mirror looked surprisingly vibrant, considering her injuries and some serious sleep deprivation, but her eyes betrayed her fear. If this was a game, could she survive losing? Everything she had learned about Carla led her to believe she was honorable and not inclined to take advantage, but how could she be sure?

"Are you in there, Ellie?" Carla's voice, deep and anxious, scared her so badly she dropped the gown.

Carla was pounding on the patio door. "Why did you leave?"

She sashed her robe tighter, opened the door, and suddenly they were face-to-face. Carla was clad only in a long T-shirt that barely cleared her waist. Her bare feet were planted firmly on the floor, her arms were folded across her chest, and her forehead was knit in a worried frown.

"Why did you leave?" she repeated.

"I panicked," Ellie answered truthfully. Seeing Carla filled her with joy. "You look beautiful," she added.

Carla opened her arms, inviting an encore performance.

Ellie needed no coaxing. She rushed into her embrace. She trembled, but not from the cold, as Carla removed the fabric impediments between them, leaving them skin to skin.

"You are even lovelier in the morning light," Carla murmured against her ear. "You are like an island flower, your petals softly opening."

Carla's fingers strayed between her thighs, proving the point. Ellie was exactly like the flower as she welcomed Carla, and closed her eyes. "Carla, what will your friend the hotel owner think when he sees I haven't even used my bed?"

"We will correct that problem right now."

Next thing she knew, someone was rapping on the hotel room door. The loud voice awakened them from a deep, satisfied sleep.

"Señorita Birdsong?" the man called. "Do you wish to check out, or reserve for another day?"

She sat bolt upright and gaped at the door with alarm. She gently shook Carla, who when asleep, looked as defenseless as a child. Gradually, her sleepy brown eyes opened and crinkled in a smile.

"Thank you again, my sweet Ellie," she said drowsily.

Yet Ellie was terrified by the thought of a stranger barging in on them. "What the hell should we do? That sounds like Miguel, and I'm sure he has a key."

Carla sat upright on their punished mattress and blinked at the light. "Miguel would not dare disturb us. Tell him we will be checking out, but ask him to bring his famous El Rincón brunch to us on the balcony."

"Why can't *you* tell him?" she whined.

"Won't you be embarrassed if he knows we are together?" Carla teased.

"Like he doesn't already know?" She gave her a silly, cross-eyed look.

Carla laughed, then left the bed. She pulled on her T-shirt, and after a swift kiss, cracked the door to give Miguel her instructions before returning to her own room.

CHAPTER TWENTY-NINE

Room service...

Two showers in one morning—either Ellie was very clean, or very dirty. Considering her recent wanton behavior, most folks would assume she was the latter. Entertained by naughty thoughts, she dressed in the only change of clothes available. She felt like a sloppy, yawning, frightened mess, but that wasn't Carla's fault. She had been a charming hostess and a more-than-tender lover, who had made no promises, so Ellie should expect nothing more.

Expect nothing, she kept telling herself as she listened to room service preparing their table outside. She heard the soft clinking of silverware as delicious odors of hot food wafted into her room. Suddenly she was light-headed, not caused by hunger alone. She was dizzy with longing, pure and simple, and couldn't wait to see Carla again.

If she was setting herself up for a fall, so be it. If they were destined to enjoy only a few more days together, let them be good ones. She brushed back her hair, applied a touch of lipstick, and soon greeted Carla with a smile.

She took Ellie into her arms, kissed her long and earnestly, and then pulled out her chair, helped her sit. "I missed you."

"Missed you, too." She swallowed the lump in her throat. "But I'm starving."

Her mama always said it was a woman's role to get folks talking about themselves, but as the brisk wind from the Atlantic gusted across their table, causing the linen tablecloth to flap against their knees, Carla's skillful interrogation style got Ellie talking about herself. As she gobbled to fill the hole in her belly, almost oblivious to the gourmet food being served, she gabbed on and on about her past.

She described her childhood in the mountains of Cherokee, North Carolina, as the daughter of a hard-drinking Native American casino worker. She told her about her three delinquent brothers, her hot-tempered Irish mama, and how she had dropped out of the local community college to nurse her mother through an illness her mother would not survive. She even admitted to her inglorious rearing in a double-wide trailer. While she listened, Carla's expressive features first registered surprise, and then an intense empathy.

"My poor Ellie, did you ever go back to college?" she asked as they finished chilled bowls of tropical fruit.

"Yeah, eventually I got a scholarship to Temple in Philadelphia. One of my girlfriends back home went into real estate. She made lots of money, so I figured a marketing degree from a good school could help me follow in her footsteps."

"So you wanted to be rich, too?" Carla watched her intently.

"I sure as heck didn't intend to live like my parents."

"So, is money still so important?"

As the waiter cleared away the last of their dishes, money was the least important thing on her mind. Most important was the woman sitting directly across from her, yet she couldn't say that. Not yet. "Well…" she began as she self-consciously folded her napkin. "In the real world, money still counts."

"You could always hook up with someone who has money. A wealthy partner could provide those luxuries you never had as a child." Carla laughed.

When Ellie looked her straight in the eye, she couldn't tell if Carla's remark was a joke, or some sort of test. "Listen, Carla, I have no interest in having a relationship for money. I am able to provide nicely for myself without anyone's help, and to afford a lifestyle that suits me quite well."

With that, Ellie climbed to her feet and crossed to the edge of the balcony. She squinted out to sea, where a tropical storm was brewing on the horizon. She knew she sounded defensive, but her emotions were raw. Her bullshit detector was on the blink, and frankly, she was scared to death of losing Carla.

Maybe it was time to sign those papers.

CHAPTER THIRTY

A meeting of the minds...

Carla refused to sign the papers. She said she needed more time to think it over, promised to complete the transaction by the end of the day, and made Ellie mad enough to either spit nails, or else hammer them into the first innocent victim who crossed her.

In the end, they left El Rincón without incident and got on the road.

As they left San Juan and headed for Casa Valdez, Carla's stubborn jaw was set and humorless, but eventually the beautiful scenery gliding along the roadway helped restore their easy companionship. Ellie realized she was too vulnerable to hold a grudge, and after sharing one night of indescribable passion, she convinced herself that Carla could not be blind to her true nature. She could not honestly believe that she was after her money.

A few short days ago, she might have slept with Carla to win a contract, but she seriously doubted it. In spite of her driving ambition, her need to prove herself in this man's world, at core she was still a fairly traditional girl who had been raised with good values. Often her hometown upbringing seemed at war with her new, career woman persona, but she'd been dealing with that dichotomy just fine until she met Carla.

"I'm taking you home on a different route," Carla informed her. "We'll travel through Toro Negro State Forest."

"That means *black bull*, doesn't it?"

"Yes, it's a pretty road. We'll stop at the recreation area, and I'll show you the countryside."

Ellie leaned back, pretending to be fascinated by the lush foliage, but secretly she watched Carla habitually checking the rearview mirror. She seemed edgy, perhaps fearful that they were being followed—by Lieutenant Colon's beige Crown Victoria, or the black Range Rover likely driven by Diego Martinez's bodyguard, or Joey Arroyo's expensive white sedan. Had she selected this alternate route to throw all those hounds off her scent? Her preoccupation saddened Ellie, because after spending the night in one another's arms, Carla should trust her enough to confide.

"We'll park and walk." Carla suddenly pulled off the road. "There's an observation tower hidden up that hill, through those trees. Let's stretch our legs and have a look, all right?"

She nodded, knowing she was up against an immoveable force. Her body ached from the attack in the garden and their marathon lovemaking, but if Carla wanted to hike, they'd hike. She grabbed Ellie's hand and led her along a flowering woodland path. A lively brook bubbled along beside them until they reached a little park with several picnic tables and a barbeque pit. Her legs protested as she kept pace with Carla's long strides, so she gratefully accepted her support as they began the steep climb up to the soaring observation tower.

"Well, what do you think?" From their platform high above the forest, Carla encircled Ellie's waist and guided her through a slow rotation, so she could view the verdant panorama unfolding on all sides.

"Another unforgettable sight, another haunting memory," she confessed wistfully.

"*Memory?* But surely you'll come here again. You like my country, don't you, Ellie?"

"Like it? I'm falling in love with it."

Carla watched for one long moment, brushed a strand of hair from Ellie's forehead. Ellie sensed she was about to kiss her, but the moment passed.

Carla cleared her throat and walked to the walled edge of the precipice. "If you love Puerto Rico, then you will agree that any contract I sign with DynaCo must benefit the land and the people. The money you offer is secondary."

Ellie stepped close and touched her sleeve. "Of course, I agree. My boss, Dyna Collins, agrees, too. We want a good settlement all around."

"Do you?" Carla moved away from her touch. "How many Puerto Ricans will be able to afford your condominiums? How many will be hired by your restaurants and clubs? And how many families will lose their grocery money if you build casinos?"

The showdown was at hand. Ellie had dreaded this moment for days, yet she had willed it to come. They were no longer lovers or friends. They were cold-blooded negotiators, each wanting something from the other. Was she up to the challenge? Certainly she had trained many months for this critical confrontation, but her heart was no longer in it. A sudden chill invaded her body as she turned away and took a deep breath.

"DynaCo wants only the best for Puerto Rico," she began, hoping to God it was true. For ten full minutes she outlined the proposal, and Carla listened attentively, without interrupting. "So, we both want the same things for your country."

Carla glanced at her, a look of respect in her eyes, but then she looked out over the land. "Your presentation was excellent, Ellie. You are very persuasive, very professional, and no doubt you deserve all the money you make in your field, but I'm afraid you're wrong. We don't want the same things."

"Of course, we do."

"No, your ideas would include my countrymen only as busboys, cooks, and janitors, don't you see? If we are to do business, we must establish controls and restrictions."

"Controls and restrictions?"

"Well, a set percentage of the management team must be Puerto Rican. The real estate must be made available to my people, as well as to yours, so that the ownership will be balanced. Native architects and laborers must be hired, when qualified, and local officials must have some voice in the decisions made in the DynaCo community. Most of all, I want to retain enough land for my bioethanol project and to keep Casa Valdez."

She found no fault with Carla's suggestions. After all, natives had more at stake than outsiders and would likely be more concerned with the long-term good, rather than short-term profit.

"That sounds reasonable. Anything else?"

"Yes, all buildings must be constructed of materials found on the island: wood, clay tile, and marble—to harmonize with the land. Structures must be painted in earth tones that blend, rather than contrast, with the environment. An environmental group will be appointed to make sure no waste pollutes the water or the air, and…"

"Stop right there…" Ellie interrupted. "I get the message—no pink flamingos, everything green and Earth friendly, right? If it were up to me, I'd insist that you personally select each paint chip, and I can't see why Dyna would object. Is that all?"

"Not quite…" Unexpectedly, Carla found her hand and pulled her close. "I will allow no gambling, no casinos."

Ellie struggled to free herself. "But casinos are the heart of our plan, and gambling is its lifeblood. Casinos draw the clientele and bring in the profit."

"Who profits?" Carla held tight to her wrist, refusing to release her.

Ellie time-warped back to her childhood in Cherokee. Although known for its natural mountain beauty, her hometown was most famous for its huge casinos, which were originally intended to compensate the Native Americans for the unspeakable wrongs committed against them by white pioneers.

Her daddy had worked in the gambling resorts, got drunk in the casinos, and ultimately lost what little income he had to his addictions. But that was then, this was now, and she couldn't afford to remember that aspect of her unhappy past.

"Americans and Puerto Ricans both love to roll the dice," she reminded Carla. Your people practically worship *San Cayetano*, the patron saint of gambling."

"You've done your homework, but you haven't answered my question: who wins, Ellie?"

"Some players win," she argued weakly, knowing it was a lie.

"Very few. You and I both know the odds make losers of us all."

She searched her bag of tricks, but couldn't find a single comeback. Carla was right. "If you're so opposed to gambling, why did you allow me to travel all the way down here?"

Carla ran a gentle hand through Ellie's hair, tucked a few more wild strands back behind her ears. "I didn't intend to waste your time, believe me. I hoped once you saw the land and our way of life, your company might think of the venture in a new light. A profit can be made here without gambling. Will you help me, Ellie? Can you convince DynaCo to do this project right?"

She impulsively touched the little worry lines at the corner of Carla's eyes. "Believe me, I'm on your side, and I'll do what I can."

"Does Dyna listen to you?"

"Yes, she listens."

Carla paused only a moment before her mouth sought Ellie's for a long, grateful kiss. As they clung together, high above the fertile jungle, their embrace was less a sexual expression, more a meeting of the minds. The kiss was very different from a business handshake, the kind normally used to cement deals. Instead it was a loving affirmation that they agreed on what was right, what was wrong. And as she held Carla close, she hoped with all her heart that Dyna would also agree.

CHAPTER THIRTY-ONE

A dear friend of the family…

They rode home in silence. Ellie tried to sort out her thoughts as she snuggled against Carla's warmth. The contact served as a buffer against the doubts that had haunted her throughout their tortured affair, but as they neared Casa Valdez, she instinctively pulled away to her side of the seat. After all, she couldn't assume the intimacy they shared in San Juan would continue under Carla's roof.

Sure enough, as soon as Carla cut the engine, Antonio and Enrique bombarded their mother with questions.

"Where have you been?" Antonio jutted out his lower lip. "I wanted to spend the night at José's, but Filo wouldn't let me without your permission."

"Why didn't you come home?" Enrique whined.

"Calm down, boys. I am here now, so what's the problem?"

"But where were you *last night*?" Antonio persisted. "Were you with *her*?" He glared at Ellie.

"Is she your new girlfriend?" Enrique giggled.

Antonio examined her with his inquisitive, adolescent eyes. When it came to sexual relationships, no one was more curious than a teenage boy.

"Ms. Birdsong and I were together in San Juan," Carla answered sternly. "If all goes well, her company will be buying our land."

"But how can you sell our land?" Antonio cried and kicked angrily at the dirt.

"Where will we live?" Enrique wailed.

"We will continue to live right here." Carla gave Antonio a warning look, then faced Ellie. "Ms. Birdsong agrees. We will keep this house and the land between here and the sea. This is our home, and no matter how much everything changes around us, our house will remain as it is now, as it has always been. Eventually, it will pass on to you boys as your heritage."

Both children stared wide-eyed as their future was discussed, a topic usually reserved for adult ears only. At the same time, Ellie couldn't help but smile at the smooth way Carla had slipped her personal fine print into the deal. She nodded, an unspoken affirmation that she would do everything she could to make it happen. She now truly understood how devastating it would be if the family lost their home. She couldn't imagine them living anywhere else. Yet she knew DynaCo's current plan for the resort community did not include an old-fashioned house like Casa Valdez.

"Let's go inside," Carla suggested. "I want lemonade."

"Me too!" the boys chimed in unison.

As they crossed the wide veranda and entered the cool foyer, Ellie was stricken by a powerful sense of *coming home*, an emotion she had no right to claim.

"*Buenos días*, Carla," a low, feminine voice echoed from the stairs. "*Cómo estás?*"

"I'm fine, Carmen. Speak English, please." Carla nodded in Ellie's direction.

Carmen glanced dismissively at Ellie, then turned to Carla. "Okay, where the hell have you been?

Carla sighed. "Sorry. Yes, I'm late, but I didn't mean to worry you."

Ellie searched Señorita Diaz's smoky black eyes, but the woman ignored her completely. Carmen was elegantly dressed in a deep purple sheath with a silver belt and killer high heels, making Ellie feel suddenly rumpled and inadequate as Carla formally introduced them.

Carmen said, "Forgive me, Ms. Birdsong, I knew you were staying here, so it was rude of me not to greet you sooner."

"Pleased to meet you." She extended her hand to the beautiful creature, whom Carla had just described as *a dear friend of the family*. Carmen's touch was cool, her bearing aristocratic, but in spite of the handshake and cordial words, Ellie felt a hostile vibe. Carmen's eyes burned with an emotion akin to hatred, causing her to shrink away and wonder what she'd done to inspire such animosity.

Carmen took possession of Carla's arm. "We missed Mama Carla, didn't we, boys?"

Both boys agreed, then promptly disappeared in the direction of the kitchen for lemonade.

Was Carmen jealous? The idea sent a chill through Ellie, but of course, that was absurd. She was the Jane-Come-Lately, so surely Carmen saw she posed no real threat. Carla had called Carmen a *dear friend*. What exactly did that mean?

"Will you excuse us, Ms. Birdsong?" Carmen's voice was pure ice. "Carla and I must talk privately."

"Go ahead, I'm fine."

With that, Carmen led Carla away like a docile pet on a leash. They stepped out onto the porch, leaving her alone wondering what to do with herself until dinner. Deciding a nap would at least ease her physical disabilities, she was on her way upstairs when she heard Carmen's voice raised in anger. Ellie sneaked toward the front door, where she accidentally on purpose overheard their heated exchange.

"Did you sleep with that woman?" Carmen shrieked. "Don't you know what she's up to?"

"What is she up to?" Carla's voice betrayed her exhaustion.

"She's after the land, you idiot! That's all she wants. If she showed you affection, she did it to get her way. She's a professional, can't you see that? You are her *job*, nothing more. Honestly, I can't believe you fell for it."

Ellie's ears rang and her cheeks burned with shame. She almost wished Carmen's tirade had been in Spanish, so she'd have been spared the humiliation. In fact, Carmen's English was so damned perfect, she decided Carmen must have grown up in the States.

"You know nothing about Ellie's motives," Carla objected.

"Don't I? God, I hope you didn't sign any papers. Did you make a deal?"

"I think we reached a mutual understanding."

Carmen's laugh was harsh and abrupt. "Oh well, it doesn't matter anyway. We both know you can't make a legal commitment on your own."

Ellie waited for Carla's adamant denial, which never came. She wondered what Carmen meant. Wasn't Carla the sole owner of her estate?

Carmen said, "Carla, I know you think you have our best interests at heart, but we need to sit down and talk about it, darling."

"Not here," Carla answered crossly. "Let's go to the country place and keep this argument in the family, where it belongs."

Ellie was terrified to be caught eavesdropping, so she froze in place until the two drove away in Carla's Honda. She was about to run upstairs to sort it all out, when Filo emerged from the kitchen and latched onto her arm.

"Ellie, you look exhausted. How can I help?"

"Please, I just need some sleep." Had Filo heard the sorrow in her voice, or read the pain in her eyes? All she wanted was to be left alone, but Filo wouldn't let go. "What do you want?"

"That woman has been calling again, Ellie. The same rude woman who called two nights ago, but now she's really mad."

"I'm sorry she's been bothering you. I'll take care of it."

But Filo kept fussing, offering her food, until Ellie finally managed to escape upstairs. If Dyna was angry, that was too damned bad. Ellie had done her best. Had the world gone mad? If so, it would still be crazy when she faced it in the morning. As she crawled into bed, she prayed some rest would restore her strength and focus her perspective, but as she sank into troubled dreams, she doubted it.

CHAPTER THIRTY-TWO

Antonio/Tony...

Sure enough, morning brought a new day, but when she looked down into the driveway and discovered Carla's car was still gone, she realized Carla and Carmen had not returned to Casa Valdez. They had spent the night together elsewhere. She felt as stiff as yesterday's mashed potatoes as she dragged herself out of bed. She knew Filo would be waiting downstairs to nurture and feed her, but she wasn't up for all that attention. In fact, she had a visceral need to escape the house. She required fresh wind to clear her mind and vigorous exercise to limber her body, so gritting her teeth, she struggled into her bikini and yellow terrycloth robe.

She laughed bitterly and splashed her face with cold water. Déjà vu. On Sunday, wearing this same bikini and robe, she went swimming in the Caribbean for the very first time, and Carla had surprised her. She had appeared in her cave like a bronze goddess, and they had shared their first kiss.

She tiptoed downstairs wondering, had she loved Carla even then? Did she love her now? Was it possible her life had changed irrevocably in a few short days? And where was this *country place* where Carla had taken Carmen for their *private discussions*? Did Carla honestly have the energy, let alone the inclination, to make love to both of them in the same twenty-four-hour period?

Try as she might, she could not drive Carla from her heart. Three days ago she found peace on Carla's beach, so perhaps it would work again. At the very least, she would expel her demons with a good, hard swim.

She waited until she heard Filo moving around in the living room, and then she crept into the kitchen, drank a glass of water, and devoured a banana. She sneaked out the back door and beat a path through the cacti to her favorite stretch of pink sand.

The sea was rough, with churning emerald green surf, foamy white waves and a brisk breeze bending palm trees along the bay. The active surf was appealing as she kicked off her sandals, dropped her terry robe on the shore, and dove headlong into the water.

She cut through the billowing waves with sure, clean strokes, and as each pull carried her farther out to sea, she reveled in the stretching of her arms and legs. Her first swim in the Caribbean had been a leisurely, sensual experience, but today she intended to punish herself in the water and drown her newly awakened passions in the silent deep. She longed to exhaust her traitorous body so it would no longer want, need, or dream of the pleasures Carla had given.

"Señorita Birdsong!" a shrill voice interrupted her exorcism. It screamed across the waves, restoring her to her senses. "Please, *señorita*, you are too far out!"

She slowed down and dog-paddled, peering in toward the shore. Sun shone through her wet lashes, casting rainbow prisms on her eyes, while far away the beach was a narrow pink ribbon, with a small black head bobbing in the waves halfway out.

"Come back!" the tiny voice cried.

Slowly comprehending the situation, she called out in alarm, "I'm all right, Antonio! You swim back, and I'll follow."

Much to her relief, the boy executed a graceful turnabout and swam effortlessly toward the shore. Apparently Carla's eldest son was not afraid of the sea, and she felt a misplaced surge of pride as she followed in his wake. Truth was, she was grateful he had called her, because she was wearier than she'd realized and had strayed out farther than she should. When her feet finally touched bottom and she staggered to the beach, she plopped down onto the sand, thankful for dry land.

"My mother will scold you," Antonio said as he sat down beside her. "Once she spanked me for swimming out that far."

She smiled at the adolescent shivering inside his fluffy red towel. "Well, your mother won't spank *me*."

Antonio grinned from ear to ear. "She would if she dared. My mother likes pretty *señoritas*."

She frowned at the cheeky teenager. Was he making this up for her benefit? Obviously the idea of his mother having gay sex didn't seem to upset the boy in any way. Seemingly Carla's openness with her sons had produced two emotionally healthy, inclusive kids.

"What about you, Antonio, do you have a girlfriend?"

The boy blushed as red as his towel and pretended to be fascinated by the sand beneath his feet, but she refused to let him off the hook. "C'mon, tell me about your girlfriend."

Gradually, he lifted his dark eyes, but instead of meeting her gaze, he stared at her bosom. "Yes, I like many girls, but I'm too young to settle for only one. And my name is *Tony*, not *Antonio*, so please don't call me that."

She chuckled. The child's expressive brown eyes, determined jaw, and full, sensuous mouth were small replicas of Carla's, even though they weren't related by blood. She lifted his chin and forced him to meet her eyes. "You are a handsome young man. Take your time and choose the right girl, it's an important decision. And how come you want to be called Tony?"

"My father is American. He calls me Tony."

Interesting. She did some math and calculated that "Tony" would have been six or seven when Carla's Maria and the tall man named Joey were divorced. "Do you remember your father?"

"Of course, I remember him. He's a basketball superhero. He played for the 76ers, but he's a coach in Philly now."

Also interesting. She could believe the tall jerk she knew from the plane and the market was a basketball player, but a superhero? "Do you see him often?"

The boy shrugged. "Not really. Mama Carla won't allow it. He visits the island a couple of times each year, to work with the Puerto Rican Basketball Federation, but he's not allowed at the house."

"How do you feel about that?"

Antonio shrugged again. "I'd like to see him. I want to go to college in the States, so it'd be cool to have a place to crash when I'm there, but my little brother never wants to talk about him."

"Enrique probably doesn't even remember him." She knew from Carla that the younger son had been only an infant when she and Maria got together.

"Our father calls him Ricky, not Enrique."

That figured. Clearly Antonio/Tony aspired to be American, from the swagger to the slang, an attitude that likely aggravated Carla every day. She doubted he knew anything about Joey's designs to gain some sort of custody of the children, so she didn't pump him. Besides, the subject seemed to make him uncomfortable. Already she had learned more from him than she had from Carla.

The boy's color had deepened, but he continued to face her with a frank, almost defiant attitude. "I don't want to talk about him, I want to talk about Carmen. She said you'd do anything to steal our land. Are you fucking Mama Carla?" he bluntly demanded.

His crude question and the hostility behind it fired her temper, and suddenly, as though it had a mind of its own, her hand flew out and slapped his cheek. The resounding crack echoed across the deserted beach. For long seconds they glared at one another, and although his eyes brimmed with tears, he did not cry.

Immediately she was mortally ashamed. She would never, ever, choose to hit a child. "I am so, so sorry, but you have no right to speak to me that way. Who do you think you are?"

"I am Mama Carla's son." He jumped to his feet and crossed his skinny arms. He took a wide, aggressive stance, daring her to cross him. He threw his red towel on the ground.

What the hell was that remark supposed to mean? Carla had used similar words that day on the beach, the day she taught Ellie about *dignidad*. But while Carla might consider herself a proud Puerto Rican nationalist, her kid had a mouth like an American street punk. The silence dragged on dangerously long between them, and she was sure they both wished they could erase their bad behavior.

"I'm sorry." Antonio gave in first. "But I don't want you to hurt my mother. You're only nice to her because you want our land."

She exhaled in relief. The standoff was over. She reached out and touched his bare arm. Clearly the boy had overheard Carmen's angry accusations last night, and her words had planted the seed of mistrust in his mind. "Do you believe everything you hear, Tony?"

She decided to call him by his preferred name, hopefully to ease the tension between them.

"You're an American, right?" He sneered. "Most Americans think we are stupid and try to steal from us."

She suppressed an urge to shake his hunched little shoulders. "Who told you that? Not your mother, she knows better."

"Roberto told me." Antonio jutted out his jaw.

"Is Roberto one of your friends?"

"No, Roberto is my…" Antonio abruptly cut off, clearly afraid to finish his sentence. "Roberto knows the truth, and he tells it like it is."

She sighed in frustration, unwilling to deal with this child's unshakable prejudice. She climbed to her feet, brushed off the sand, pulled on her robe, and then left him to rant as she walked briskly up the path toward the house. The last thing she needed was a militant youngster's lecture on the *Ugly American*.

But he retrieved his towel, and followed on her heels. "Roberto says all Americans should be driven out of our country at gunpoint," he shouted.

When she stopped dead in her tracks, he plowed clumsily into her. She grabbed his thin wrists. "Don't you have a mind of your own, Tony? You sound like a silly parrot repeating everything it hears. What's wrong with you? You don't know anything about me, let alone *all Americans*, so how can you judge me, or anyone else?"

She detected a flicker of remorse, but he stood his ground and refused to answer. She said, "If you hate me, why are you following me? Don't you have better things to do?"

With that, she released his wrists, lightly shoved him away, and headed back toward the house.

CHAPTER THIRTY-THREE

Brush with death…

Antonio blinked a few times, but then focused. "I came looking for Enrique. He followed you down to the beach, *señorita*. Have you seen him?"

"But Enrique's afraid of the water, isn't he?"

Antonio kicked at the sand with his bare toes. "Yeah, but the stupid kid has a crush on you. He'd follow you anywhere."

One minute Antonio was ready to drive her out of the country at gunpoint, the next he was reporting that his little brother was enamored of her. "I haven't seen Enrique, but maybe he passed by when I was swimming. He wouldn't go near the rocks with the undertow, would he?"

His eyes stretched wide with fear. "He's been warned a million times, but like I said, he would follow you anywhere."

She didn't wait to hear more. She ran headlong toward the beach, casting off her sandals and robe as she went, ignoring the shards of sharp marble lacerating her feet. Her breath came in short, constricted gasps as her sore ribs expanded, then rebelled, and naked fear knocked at her heart.

"Enrique!" she shouted into the wind. "Where are you?" As she neared the ominous rock ledge, her fear became reality when she spotted Enrique's tiny form near the very edge of the jetty. Heavy winds whipped his shock of black hair and puffed the cloth of his bright blue jacket. "Enrique!" she screamed, but the child couldn't hear.

She knew the boy was terrified of the water, yet he leaned out too far and peered into the choppy abyss, searching for something...for her? She tried to run faster, her chest bursting with love and concern, but her muscles wouldn't cooperate. And as she gasped for oxygen, events unfolded as in a dream—or nightmare.

An evil wind slapped hair into her eyes and lifted the sand like dust. As a cloud passed over the sun, the wind teased the water into foamy green peaks. It filled the back of Enrique's little jacket, and in slow motion, as he lost his balance, the wind seemed to lift the child and drop him into the sea. His arm broke through the surface once, only to vanish again into nothingness.

God! Her outcry was a prayer, not a curse, yet it took a lifetime to cover the distance between them. As she dove under, she saw a surreal green light when she opened her eyes in the briny undersea world. She searched the bottom twice before coming up for air. She shook her head, clearing it to concentrate, then dove again, noting how the current pulled sideways, rather than out to sea. Swimming as hard as she could, she allowed the undertow to capture her body, carrying her closer to the bright blue bundle skidding along the seabed.

She hooked Enrique by the collar and swam for the sun. Her lungs begged for oxygen and her eyes stung from the salt, but when she finally pushed through to blessed air and blue sky, it felt like salvation.

She dragged her sodden burden onto the sand, knelt over him, and found no signs of life. When she rapidly turned Enrique onto his back and began resuscitation, Antonio inched closer, with tears in his eyes.

"What are you doing?" he asked in a small, frightened voice. "Will he be all right?"

"Enrique will be fine," she gulped, trying to convince herself. She cleared his mouth, puffed breath between his cold lips, and silently counted the strokes. *Dear God, please let him live!* As soon as the desperate prayer filled her heart, Enrique choked, then coughed up water. His strangled breathing was the most beautiful sound she had ever heard. She laughed hysterically through her tears and gathered him upright into her arms. As she stroked his hair and rubbed his back, he expelled more seawater and began to cry.

"You're safe now, honey," she whispered, kissing his wet hair.

"Yeah, don't cry," Antonio added, his voice surly with anguish. "You're fine, so don't act like a baby."

She shot a warning look at Antonio, but understood his harsh words were the result of a bad scare. "Come here and help me, Tony. Enrique needs your towel."

Grateful to have a job, Antonio quickly removed the red towel from his quivering shoulders and fell to his knees. With the gentle hands of a father, he started drying his brother. "She saved your life, dummy."

Enrique's blurred eyes sought hers. "Did you really save my life?"

"She kissed you on the lips!" Antonio smirked.

"You kissed me?" Enrique blinked. "Do you love me?"

"Yes, I love you," she answered truthfully.

"But that's not why she kissed you," Antonio pointed out. "She did that to save you, like Mama Carla taught us. Where'd you learn that, *señorita*?"

"That's so cool!" Enrique grinned and hugged her.

As both children gaped in awe, she was relieved Enrique had so quickly forgotten his close brush with death, and Antonio, at least for the moment, no longer considered her a foreign devil. Yet no amount of hero worship could erase the shock of this near-tragedy. She sat down hard in the sand, ran fingers through her sodden hair, and squeezed back her tears.

"I learned when I was your age, Tony," she said. "I took a lifesaving class at a small lake near my town."

Antonio looked away, suddenly embarrassed. "Mama Carla taught me CPR, but I didn't help you, I was frozen…"

"Mama Carla never taught me. Will *you* teach me, *señorita*?" Enrique asked.

"I'd love to, but I might not be here much longer."

"Sure you will." Antonio said. "If you expect to buy our land, you'll be here a very long time."

She hoped the boy was right, but likely she'd never set foot on this beautiful beach again, a place where she'd first tasted love, and had her first confrontation with death. The near tragedy had even made her imagine the joy and pain of motherhood, so that she, who didn't have a maternal bone in her body, longed to hold these precious children and protect them forever.

The thought forced her to remember that another woman had actually given birth to these children, and although she'd never seen a picture of Maria, she was overwhelmed with sympathy for her. In a moment of heartrending clarity, she experienced Carla's loss and Maria's sacrifice. The jealousy she once felt gave way to pity and compassion.

"Why are you crying?" Antonio gently took her hand.

Yes, Antonio was, in every significant way, Carla's son, while Enrique must take after Maria, the mother he never knew. "I am not crying," she told them emphatically. "I just have salt in my eyes, and I'm really, really hungry."

"Then we must feed you." Antonio beamed with grown-up assurance. "Come to the house, and Filo will make us lunch."

Enrique captured her other hand, and they both helped her stand up. Her legs wobbled as the brothers marched her toward Casa Valdez. Her heart tripped inside her aching ribs. She couldn't have loved them more had they been her own flesh and blood. While she squeezed each small hand, she wondered how it would feel to mother Carla's children. The thought uncovered emotions that were best left buried, but at that moment, she was happy. Should God choose to leave her stranded in this special time and magical place, her every prayer would be answered.

CHAPTER THIRTY-FOUR

Unwelcome visitor...

Oddly, the door to Casa Valdez was locked when they arrived. As they rang the bell, she smiled at her young companions dripping on the porch floor. They had called her a hero all the way home, but to her way of thinking, they were all heroes, and she was proud of them all. She was also shaken. Someone in the household needed to know what had happened to Enrique, but she figured the boys would broadcast the details faster than she could.

"Oh, Ellie, *gracias Dios* you are back!" Filo hustled them into the foyer. Her sister, Sylvie, was close behind, fluttering like an anxious hen. Both women were flushed with excitement.

"What's happening?" Ellie asked.

"There is a *woman* in our kitchen," Filo panted. "She is looking for you, and she would not believe me when I said you were out."

"What woman?" Antonio and Enrique chimed in unison.

"The woman of your dreams, who else?" The suave voice, smooth as warm butter, oozed from the figure stepping boldly from the kitchen. She was tall, exquisitely handsome, her silver hair was cut in a severely short style, and she was fashionably clad in crisp gray slacks and a navy blazer.

"My God, Dyna, what are you doing here?" Ellie's mouth dropped open as she beheld her boss, so far from home. "Why didn't you tell me you were coming?"

Filo, Sylvie, and the boys were transfixed. They couldn't take their eyes off the forceful stranger.

Dyna strode over and ruffled both boys' hair. "These are the Valdez kids, right? I didn't know you enjoyed babysitting, Ellie."

Antonio stiffened with indignation and pulled away. Even Enrique seemed hurt by the insult.

Ellie wrapped a protective arm around the younger child and guided him away from her boss. "These are young men, Dyna. Neither requires a babysitter."

"My mistake." Dyna rolled her eyes. "Will you *young men* please leave me alone with Ms. Birdsong? We have grownup business to discuss."

"It's okay," Ellie reassured the boys. "Mrs. Collins is my boss from America." She gently pushed them toward Filo and Sylvie. "Go to the kitchen, and Tony, please make sure Enrique eats some hot soup and takes a nap, okay? Tell Filo what happened at the beach."

"But aren't you hungry, Señorita Birdsong?" Enrique balked.

"Yeah, you said you were starving," Antonio said.

"Go on, I'll eat later."

The two trooped off like brave little soldiers, while Filo, sensing they needed further attention, followed close behind. Sylvie hung back, a look of rapt interest on her young face. Ellie had had much the same reaction when she first laid eyes on Dyna, who always looked like she stepped straight off the cover of Vogue Magazine. To a mountain girl like Ellie, Dyna had seemed the ultimate sophisticate, an intoxicatingly powerful woman to emulate. That was before they became lovers, and then Ellie was more like a pawn than a pupil.

Dyna cleared her throat and frowned at Sylvie. "Tell me, miss, where can I take this lady for a private talk?"

"The den is this way, *señora...*" Sylvie led Dyna toward Carla's private study.

"Not so fast..." Ellie pulled away from the authoritative hand Dyna had placed on her elbow. "Can't you see I'm soaking wet? I won't enter that room in a dripping swimsuit."

"I agree, you look like a drowned rat, a pretty one, of course." She playfully fondled Ellie's wet curls. "Go change your clothes. I'll wait for you in the lioness's den."

Ellie swatted her perfectly manicured hand away, but lost no time doing her bidding. She charged into the blue room, took a fast shower, and dried her hair. As she hurriedly dressed in a soft cocoa blouse and skirt ensemble, an outfit Dyna had always admired, she wondered why the hell Dyna had come. Ellie had the negotiations under control, so her sudden arrival did not feel like a vote of confidence.

She approached the ornate dressing table that had once belonged to Maria and was pleasantly surprised to find she looked respectable, in spite of her recent physical challenges: a vicious attack, energetic lovemaking, and so-called heroics. Was she really a heroine? Would the boys tell Carla what happened at the beach? She didn't feel especially valiant as she hurriedly applied makeup to her bruised face and color to her still-puffy lips.

When she rushed downstairs and found Dyna making herself at home in Carla's study, where Ellie and Carla had shared that magnificent sunset her first night on the island, her boss's presence seemed all wrong.

"Ah, now you look like the woman I know and adore." Dyna stood behind Carla's desk, gave a soft whistle of approval, and then rapidly closed the distance between them. She snatched Ellie's hand, taking her by surprise.

"Why did you come?" Ellie demanded. Dyna's grip was hot and unwelcome.

"Aren't you glad to see me, doll? After everything that's happened, I'd think my arrival would be a great comfort."

She tried to pull away, but Dyna tightened her grasp on her fingers.

Dyna didn't know the half of it. She didn't know she'd been attacked in the garden. "Sure I'm glad to see you," she answered carefully. "But I have things under control. You could have saved the airfare."

"Under control? You sure?" She lifted Ellie's hand and kissed her knuckles, leaving a bright red lipstick smudge.

Her touch made Ellie's skin crawl. She jerked loose and backed a safe distance away. Over the years, she'd come to recognize Dyna's moods, especially her romantic overtures, which were completely unwelcome.

"I've been trying to call you," Dyna whined. "You were supposed to check in at the Ponce Hotel, but you never showed. Next I called here, but that obnoxious maid said you and Valdez were both missing in action. What the hell's going on, Ellie?"

She took a deep breath and moved to the window, where treacherous waves churned up whitecaps on the distant Caribbean. "Calm down, Dyna. I stayed at Casa Valdez to make our negotiations more convenient."

"Was it *convenient* to spend a night with Valdez in San Juan?"

She had never seen her boss so distraught. Her fair skin was blotchy with rage. "Lower your voice! We went to San Juan to fetch the paperwork and close the deal."

"Did you sleep with her?"

Heat scorched Ellie's face, and she gripped the windowsill for support. "How dare you?"

Dyna squared her broad shoulders and raked her with angry eyes. "Was it worth it? Did you close the fucking deal?"

She considered punching Dyna's pugnacious jaw. Instead, she waited until her pulse slowed, until her voice no longer threatened to betray her, then glared into Dyna's furious eyes. "I believe Carla and I have come to terms."

"What the hell does that mean? I trusted you with this project, so you better not screw it up." She got in Ellie's face, folded her arms across her chest.

Ellie smelled a trace of liquor on her breath. "Believe me, Dyna, we're good to go."

Ellie desperately wanted that to be true. She hoped Dyna would accept Carla's conditions and restrictions, but feared Carla's refusal to allow gambling was a deal-breaker. She waited until Dyna's color and breathing returned to normal, then prayed for the strength to convince her.

"And what about Diego Martinez?" Dyna asked. "He's dangerous, out for a quick buck. After doing more research, I'm convinced he's connected to the Mob: Organized Crime. He'll stop at nothing to get his way, so we better close this deal before he gets to Valdez."

"How could he possibly get to Carla?"

Dyna's eyes glinted. "Blackmail, maybe? Carla's hands aren't entirely clean, Ellie. The cops have been watching her, did you know that?"

The revelation was hardly a news scoop, but she refused to believe that Carla was involved in anything illegal. "Forget it. Carla has nothing to hide."

"Are you sure? How well do you really know her?"

Was her boss implying that Carla was harboring some dirty little secret? No way. Ellie wasn't buying it. "Give me a break. I've read Carla's dossier, and I didn't find one negative thing about the woman."

"That's because I deleted the sordid details. They seemed irrelative at the time."

She searched Dyna's steel gray eyes, but they betrayed nothing. She was cold as an iced martini. One thing was true: in the past, Dyna had never shared one shred of information she didn't wish to share, but two could play that game. "Okay, what do you know about a woman named Carmen Diaz?"

"Is this a pop quiz?"

By the uneasy shifting of her beady eyes, Ellie could see Miss Know-It-All didn't have a clue about Carmen Diaz, or the mysterious hold she had on Carla. From the little she'd overheard, Ellie was truly worried that Carmen might cause their deal to fall apart.

"Listen, Dyna, I'm afraid this Diaz woman is a player. I think she's part owner of the Valdez land."

That tidbit got Dyna's full attention. "Are you saying Valdez needs this woman's approval to sign an Agreement of Sale? That's insane. I know for a fact she has no sisters, cousins, or aunts. Only a family member could interfere in such matters."

Ellie massaged the bridge of her nose, warding off the massive headache gathering behind her eyeballs. "Yeah, but what if Carla and Carmen have a civil union, or secret marriage, or some other legal document binding them together?"

There, she had said it, and the words hurt like hell. For several days, the suspicion had coiled inside her like a venomous snake, but expelling the notion did nothing to diminish its sting.

"Bullshit. Why would Valdez keep their union secret? She was never shy telling the world about Maria, who was, by the way, once listed along with Valdez on the deed to the land. Carmen Diaz is not on the deed, I assure you."

But Ellie was not convinced. Her boss began to pace.

Dyna crossed to the desk, picked up one of Carla's precious figurines and tossed it carelessly from hand to hand. "But I agree. Something is definitely wrong. This Diaz relationship stinks to high heaven, so it's time to activate Plan B."

"*Plan B*?" Had Dyna gone stark raving mad?

Dyna unceremoniously dropped the little figurine onto the desk, where it lay helplessly on its side. "Never mind. Run upstairs and pack, Ellie. We're moving to the Ponce Hotel, as originally planned."

CHAPTER THIRTY-FIVE

Playing games…

Ellie and Dyna sat in the sunny café of the Ponce Hotel as the waitress served an *American Style* breakfast—Dyna's idea—not hers. She wasn't in the mood for anything reminding her of the States, but Dyna had ordered for both of them, which was absolutely infuriating. Since Dyna's arrival, Ellie's life had not been her own.

She'd allowed Dyna to spirit her away from Casa Valdez, because she needed time to rein in her runaway emotions and sift the truth from all the lies. After all, Carla had deserted her, left Casa Valdez with Carmen, so what was she to think?

It complicated matters that Dyna had wined and dined her at a candlelight dinner last night—Dyna's idea—not hers. All of a sudden, she seemed to have romantic feelings for her. Where the hell was that coming from?

Dyna had long ago finished the chapter that included Ellie, and Ellie was long done with it, too. She suspected Dyna wanted something from her. In Dyna's twisted little mind, she likely imagined that by simply having sex with Ellie, she'd get what she wanted. So far, Ellie had deflected her amorous attentions, reminding her again and again that she had a trusting husband waiting back home. In fact, she'd spent so much time deflecting her advances, that she'd not yet learned anything about her secret *Plan B*.

They finished bacon, eggs, and pancakes. Dyna was grinning like a Cheshire, so Ellie hoped she was about to reveal whatever she had up her sleeve. Dyna wiped her mouth with a napkin, shoved away her plate, and lit up a cigarette in the *no smoking* section. The waitress frowned, but did not intervene. Like everyone else, she was intimidated by Dyna's aura of power.

"Enjoying yourself, doll?" She blew a smoke ring at the ceiling fan, then reached across the table and fiddled with Ellie's fingers.

Ellie pulled her hand away and buried it in her lap.

"C'mon, we've been around this block before." Dyna's gray eyes sent an unmistakable message of desire. "Why pretend? You want me, and I want you."

"Back off, Dyna." The woman was definitely playing games, but why? Since Dyna had so brutally ended their affair, Ellie had never given her any encouragement, no mixed messages. She swatted at the disgusting smoke swirling around her face.

Dyna's knee pressed against hers under the table. The stuffy restaurant, the piped-in music, and the noisy chatter of tourists became a deafening din in Ellie's ears, and suddenly she felt ill.

"Are you listening, Ellie? This trip to the island is more than a tax write-off. It's a chance for us to get reacquainted. Don't mean to rush you, but time is limited. You know I'm a patient woman, but in the end, I usually get what I want."

"What about Charley?" She mentioned Dyna's husband by name.

"Charley Who?"

"So, are you guys separated?"

"Of course not, why should we be? He does his thing, I do mine."

Ellie snorted in disgust. She had always been suspicious of Dyna's sudden marriage to a man, when she had previously been Atlantic City's most eligible dyke. It seemed like a marriage of convenience, lending Dyna a measure of mystery and respectability she had lacked before. One thing was certain: she was a big fat hypocrite.

She did usually get what she wanted. But if she thought Ellie was the same naïve girl who'd arrived fresh from the mountains and thought Dyna was a goddess on earth—she had another think coming. That little girl didn't exist anymore, and damn it, Dyna knew it.

"I feel sick," she said, not bothering to hide her revulsion.

Dyna gave a belly laugh, stubbed out her cigarette in a pool of maple syrup. "Indigestion? Has Valdez been feeding you too much rice 'n' beans? That'll teach you to dine with the enemy."

"Carla is not our enemy."

"She's a hard fish to land, though, isn't she? It's one thing to charm the panties off the woman, but getting her to sign an Agreement of Sale is tougher, right?"

"I'm getting the job done. Don't you trust me?"

"Hell, I hired you to acquire Valdez's land, not fuck her."

The crude remark took Ellie's breath away. She jumped up to leave, but Dyna snatched her wrist.

"Slow down, Ellie. Maybe I'm wrong. I know you're an old-fashioned gal, so maybe you wouldn't take a stranger to bed. And don't worry about the contract. I'll make sure you get her signature."

Dyna's attitude made her feel like upchucking her breakfast all over her spiffy tan safari suit. The bitch was in the tropics, so naturally she had dressed like Jungle Jill. "For your information, I am perfectly capable of completing the transaction with Carla on my own, so I'd appreciate it if you'd back the hell off."

"Too late now, doll. I phoned your girlfriend this morning while you were getting your beauty rest, and she'll be here any minute."

Ellie panicked. "Carla's coming *here*? Why didn't you tell me?"

"I was lucky to catch her at home." Dyna smirked. "She agreed to meet us here at the hotel. She also said she was taking us on an adventure."

Adventure? Ellie wilted back down into her chair, suppressing an urge to toss her glass of water in Dyna's smug face. At the same time, she perversely wished she'd worn something nicer than cut-off jeans and a faded India blouse for this occasion.

"Valdez was all keyed up," Dyna continued. "She was pissed because you left without an explanation, and she was very rude to me. I gather she's taking us hiking, as some kind of test, or punishment."

CHAPTER THIRTY-SIX

Old-fashioned pissing contest…

Carla parked in the hotel parking lot, entered the swank establishment, and easily recognized Dyna Collins seated in the *No Smoking* section, defiantly smoking a cigarette. Ellie was not with her. Tamping down her disappointment, she approached the woman, introduced herself, and took a seat.

"Do you mind?" Before ordering coffee, she unceremoniously stamped out Dyna's cigarette on the corner of her empty plate, since no ashtray had been provided.

They were engaged in a stilted conversation, when she saw Ellie enter the room.

"Beautiful country, ideal climate…" Dyna was saying as Ellie walked toward them.

"I agree." Carla was more enthusiastic about Ellie, than the local countryside and climate. She looked fabulous in cut-off jeans and a faded India blouse. The old denims clung to the womanly curve of her hips, while the blouse exposed the blush of sunburn on her lovely arms. *Ay dios mío, mujer, get a grip.* She felt downright dowdy in old blue jeans and chunky hiking boots that had racked up some miles.

She tried to sound casual when she greeted her. "*Buenos días, señorita*, why did you run out on us?"

"I didn't run out, I simply changed my address."

"Was that *her* idea?" Carla jerked a thumb in Dyna's direction.

"What difference does it make?" Ellie countered. "You weren't home, were you? You left with Carmen. Dyna and I decided it was more efficient to headquarter under the same roof."

"*Headquarter?*" Carla mimicked her. "Is that business-speak?"

"Dyna *is* my boss…"

"Yes, but *I'm* your client, and you were staying with me. What could be more efficient?"

"Time out, you two," Dyna intervened in soothing tones. "Point is, we need to wrap things up. Ellie tells me you've worked out some new ideas for the project?"

"Yes, that's why I suggested this little outing. It's more fun to mix business with pleasure, don't you agree?"

As they all walked toward her Honda, she saw Ellie smiling at her from the corners of her eyes and hoped she considered their relationship the *pleasure* part in this difficult business deal. When Ellie prepared to slide into the back seat, Carla restrained her with a strong hand.

"You sit up front with me, Ellie. Dyna can have the back all to herself, so she can play with her laptop."

Ellie slipped in beside her and glanced back at Dyna, who was stone-faced and impassive. At the moment, Carla felt like she had the upper hand.

Once they were on the road, she explained, "Today we're going to El Yunque, our famous rain forest in Luquillo National Park."

"Terrific, I've read great things about it!" Ellie couldn't hide her delight. "Isn't that exciting, Dyna?"

The boss's only comment was a displeased grunt. In the rearview mirror, she saw Dyna hunched down with her laptop, as predicted, oblivious to the exotic scenery unfolding on either side of the car.

"We'll follow Highway 191 into the mountains, then take a little hike to the top when we arrive," Carla continued merrily. "El Yunque is a strange and mysterious place. Legend says that Yukiyú, the supreme Tainos Indian spirit dwells there. We'll discuss our project with our heads in the clouds, isn't that a fine idea?"

"I prefer both feet on the ground when I discuss business," Dyna grumbled.

Undaunted by Dyna's lack of enthusiasm, she continued to describe the day's plans. "After our hike, we will eat at the Rain Forest Restaurant. You'll love it, Ellie."

Ellie seemed skeptical, yet she relaxed into her headrest and listened as Carla delivered an animated description of the jungle they were about to visit, including its colorful legends. By the time they parked and began walking, Ellie said she was really looking forward to their day together. Carla figured if Dyna wasn't breathing down their necks, angry as a storm cloud, perhaps Ellie and she could put their differences behind and rekindle their magic.

"I hate hiking," Dyna complained as they started up the mountain.

"The exercise will do you good," Carla said.

As they traveled steadily upward on an ever-narrowing road, the dark green forest encroached on both sides, thick with verdant vines and foliage. The air was hot and heavy, embracing them in a humid kiss.

"Snakes?" Dyna took careful baby steps, kept to the middle of the path, and peered suspiciously into the foliage.

"Don't worry." Carla laughed. "Puerto Rico has been blessed with many living things—frogs, iguanas, and lovely birds—but no venomous snakes. Remember how Saint Patrick drove the snakes from Ireland? Well snakes can't swim, so they never came from the mainland to join us."

Ellie raised her eyebrows at the statement. Likely she suspected it was a lie, which it was. It was only a folk tale, an Irish one at that. But Carla's father had told it to keep Carla from fearing the forest, and she had loved him for that. In fact, there were snakes on the island, but they were few and harmless, so who cared?

Dyna seemed to relax and began striding with confidence. "You have quality mud here, though." She gazed unhappily at her expensive Italian sandals, and Ellie laughed out loud at her misery.

Carla took possession of Ellie's elbow and guided her along the rustic path at a fast pace designed to leave Dyna behind. The feel of her skin ignited powerful emotions as they traveled up the steep incline. Unfortunately, Dyna kept up, noticed the contact, and glared with disapproval. Carla couldn't be sure, but it seemed the woman was jealous. Whatever. Soon Dyna began puffing, panting, and struggling to keep up. Finally, Carla invited everyone to rest at a stone bench.

"Ready for a nature lesson, Dyna?" Carla asked.

Could Ellie tell she was deliberately baiting her boss? As she and Dyna stood side by side, Carla was gratified to discover that the boss was actually several inches shorter than she. Carla fancied that her own, more athletic build, gave her an animal-like advantage, which she intended to use. When Dyna flopped down on the bench, too close to Ellie, Ellie inadvertently inched away, which enormously pleased Carla.

"El Yunque is four forests in one." Carla remained standing as she lectured. "The first two thousand feet are conventional tropical rain forest, with trees such as the *tabonuco* and *ausubo*. The second phase is thicket, and phase three is palm trees. Finally, at the very top, we have a dwarf forest."

"Do I give a damn?" Dyna yawned.

Carla ignored her. "The path we'll take winds upward for thirty-two hundred feet, and along the way, you'll see giant ferns, orchids, bamboo, and maybe even a rare Puerto Rican parrot."

She hoped her description of the trees, vines, and exotic flowers would bring them to life for Ellie. Her eyes swept the treetops, hoping to spot a parrot, while her ears identified the many sounds of the forest. "Can't you smell the earth? It's so rich, you can almost feel things growing."

Dyna rolled her eyes, while Ellie was obviously enraptured.

"I feel the magic each time I come," Carla continued. "When nature tangles, spreads, and reproduces with absolute freedom, it's like the Garden of Eden."

"Except there are no snakes to tempt us with forbidden fruit." Ellie snorted, clearly skeptical.

Carla winked suggestively at Ellie. "I'm sure we could find something to tempt you…"

"Will you two shut the hell up?" Dyna mopped her forehead and said to Ellie, "Valdez sounds like a bloody tour guide."

"Get up." Carla nudged Dyna's sandal with her boot. "It's still a long way to the top."

"No thanks, I've had enough." Dyna kicked at Carla's boot. "I'm heading back down this fucking hill."

"Sorry you feel that way." Carla took Ellie's hand and helped her to her feet. "As I told you before, Dyna, I prefer to do business at the top of the mountain, but if you're not up to it, Ellie and I will go alone."

Dyna's pale cheeks flushed with anger. "Look, from now on I'm calling the shots, Valdez. You've been dragging your feet too long. It's time to finalize our deal. If Ellie wants to hike with you at her own peril, that's her choice. But I'll wait in the restaurant. We'll sign the damned Agreement of Sale, and then we're done."

Carla knew this behavior was what Americans called an *old-fashioned pissing contest*, and Ellie seemed put off by it. Maybe they should abandon the hike and return to the restaurant with Dyna, because without her as a chaperone, she wasn't sure how to behave with Ellie—all alone, deep in the forest.

"You two are acting like childish rivals on a school playground!" Ellie angrily pointed out. "I'm tempted to leave you both behind!" With that, she strode away, trudging rapidly up the hill on her own.

Dyna stomped back the way they had come, but Carla caught up with Ellie halfway up the next rise. She took her arm. "For God's sake, will you slow down? You're right. I'm an idiot." She loosened her grip, but she did not release her.

She watched as beads of perspiration broke out on Ellie's forehead and upper lip. Her blouse wilted and clung to her body, revealing the details of her lace bra. Carla felt her own tank top clinging to her shoulder blades as they surged ahead. Finally, they stopped in a clearing, which marked the highest point in Puerto Rico.

"Was the climb worth it?" Ellie asked sarcastically.

"That depends…" Carla spun her around so they were face-to-face. She ran her hands around Ellie's waist. "Why did you run off like that?"

"You two were behaving like idiots."

Carla eased Ellie back against the trunk of a tree, stepped against her body, pinning her. "I'm not talking about just now, because yes, I was an idiot. I'm talking about yesterday. You left without a word, Ellie. It hurt to come home and find you gone."

Ellie struggled to free herself. "Think again, Carla. The moment we returned from San Juan, you dropped me at the front door, then left with Carmen. Who the hell is she?" She knotted her hands and shoved against Carla's chest.

But Carla caught her fists and held them tight. She pulled her so close she felt the heat radiating off her hair. "My relationship with Carmen is none of your business. What matters is the relationship between you and me, Ellie."

"What do you imagine is between us?" Ellie countered through clenched teeth. "Define our relationship."

"Our time together in San Juan, did it mean nothing to you?"

"What did it mean to you, Carla?"

She took a deep breath, then pulled Ellie completely off-balance and into her arms. Before Ellie could open her mouth to protest, she covered her mouth with a hard kiss. Their hearts pounded to the same, frantic beat. She could not abide Ellie doubting her passion.

Her kiss deepened and grew more insistent, urging Ellie to give in. She caressed the tense muscles at the back of her neck and ran her fingers through her thick, damp hair.

"I never meant to hurt you," she whispered.

As Ellie relaxed against the tree, Carla cradled her head with one hand, protecting it from the rough bark. With the other, she reached under her clinging blouse and cupped one breast, imprisoned in its bra. With one finger, she gently traced down the warm skin of her belly, igniting the old chemistry between them as Ellie melted to her touch. When Carla leaned into her, Ellie's eyelids grew heavy with desire.

"Please forgive me, Ellie," she murmured thickly. "I want to start over."

Ellie's body communicated a willing response.

Carla was lost. She closed her eyes, and slowly eased her knee between Ellie's legs.

Nearby, they heard a bird's raucous cry.

"Think where we are," Ellie moaned. "We're in a public place." She tried to push away, but her arms seemed limp and useless. "What if Dyna finds us like this?"

"No one else is near us on the trail. I've been watching. Dyna left, and she's not coming back." She paused and searched Ellie's eyes. "What does Dyna mean to you, Ellie?"

Ellie stared into the jungle, a dazed look on her face.

"Is Dyna your lover, Ellie?"

"God, no!" Ellie trembled, seemingly not from anger, but from the abrupt interruption of their intimacy. "You must believe me. Dyna is my boss, nothing more."

"But I've seen how she looks at you. I want to trust you, but..."

She felt Ellie slipping away. Jealousy and anger would surely destroy them both, but she felt powerless to stop it.

"Carla, if you don't trust me after all we've shared, then I can't change your mind." Her pitch was high and unnatural, the voice of a stranger. "You can't have it both ways. You duck my questions about Carmen, but refuse to believe the truth about Dyna and me."

"Are you saying she hasn't made overtures?"

"Borrowing your quote, Carla, the relationship between Dyna and me is none of your business."

The atmosphere between them was charged with the sad fission of unbroken, uncompromising pride. And while the temperature hovered in the low one hundreds, they both shivered. It seemed their frozen impasse would not melt, because even the tropical heat could not thaw so much icy distrust. The sun hid its face behind a cloud, shrouding the forest in darkness. Seconds later, thunder clapped and a torrential rain poured like warm tears from the bruised sky.

CHAPTER THIRTY-SEVEN

On your own...

They spoke not one word climbing down the hill. Instead, they bowed their heads against the pelting rain and entered the Rain Forest Restaurant as miserable, water- logged survivors of their latest emotional conflict.

Inside, the primitively carved teak wood bar, complete with ornate mirror and rum posters, was straight out of a Hemmingway novel, as were the bamboo chairs and slowly rotating ceiling fan. Normally the dim, informal dining area would have charmed Ellie, but at the moment, all she wanted was to hide away in some dry place and lick her self-inflicted wounds.

They spotted Dyna seated comfortably in a private corner, nursing her second beer. When she beckoned for them to join her, she noticed Dyna's clothes were crisp and dry, and the only sign of her hiking experience was a rim of dirt on her shoes.

"Well, look who blew in from the rain." Dyna chuckled. "I saw that storm coming a mile away, so I hope your noble little quest for the top was worth it." She pointedly spread her real estate paperwork out on the table. "I trust we're ready to complete our business now?"

Ellie groaned. She stepped away from Carla and swallowed the painful lump in her throat. "You two get started without me. I'm going to the ladies' room."

Dyna lifted her silver eyebrows and glanced at Ellie's wet blouse. "Don't you want to help Valdez explain her vision for the project?"

"I suspect Carla can express herself without my help, so if you'll excuse me..."

Neither woman tried to stop her as she beat a hurried escape, and then locked herself in a stall with a whole roll of paper towels. As she vigorously rubbed her hair, she controlled her tears, but couldn't ease the ache that originated from her very core.

She figured the women would go ahead and order lunch, and she wanted to join them before they got down to the nitty gritty details of the contract.   She wanted to make Dyna see the project from Carla's perspective. But if Carla didn't trust her, perhaps she'd fare better without her. Yet, Ellie had worked long and hard on this project, and she hated to lose control at the last minute. This was her baby. Call it professional pride, or just plain stubbornness, she intended to be there if Carla signed on the dotted line.

After a quick peek in the mirror, she decided not to waste time combing her tangled hair, and left the restroom. She wanted to support Carla's vision of social equity, architectural harmony, and most controversial of all—the absence of gambling in their DynaCo resort. She feared the fireworks, perhaps the nuclear holocaust, when Carla dropped that bombshell.

As she rushed back down the hallway toward the dining room, she happened to glance out a window overlooking the garden, still steaming from the rain. Ironically, the sun had come out the moment Carla and she reached shelter, and now it mocked her with the cheerful ribbons of a rainbow.

The ribbons wove through the palm trees in the parking lot, where tiny beads of moisture clung to the waxen skin of Carla's Honda. At the same moment, she saw Carla herself stalking across the lot like an enraged panther. She jerked open her car door, but then hesitated and stared toward Ellie's window, an agonized expression on her face. Before Ellie could process this upsetting turn of events, their eyes met and locked as Carla mouthed the word *goodbye.*

For a moment, Ellie was stunned, shocked, unable to move, but then she rushed into the restaurant and confronted her boss. "Carla just left. What the hell happened?"

"You missed all the fun, Ellie." Dyna's hand trembled as she gripped her beer. "Seems like your pal Valdez is playing hard to get."

"What the hell happened?" she repeated. "I was only gone five minutes!"

Dyna shrugged. "You should have clued me in about her unreasonable demands. That bitch is living in a dream world."

Anger practically steamed from Dyna's unnaturally red ears. "Plus, how does Valdez expect us to get back to the hotel? She took the damn car!"

"Then call a damn cab," Ellie countered.

"Do you know how much that'll fucking cost?"

"So put it on your fucking expense account," Ellie hissed, before stomping outside.

They rode back to Ponce in almost total silence. The deal had fallen through, and it was all her fault—at least that was Dyna's take on the fiasco. What if she was right? If she hadn't gotten romantically involved with Carla, would the negotiations have stayed on track? Or were they doomed before she even set foot on Puerto Rican soil? If she had told Dyna what to expect from Carla, could they have compromised?

"So what happens now, Dyna? Do we run back to the States with our tails between our legs?"

"Do as you fucking please, Ellie. But *I* won't give up without a fight."

When they arrived at the Ponce hotel, the cabbie opened Ellie's door and she climbed out. Then, instead of paying their fare, Dyna remained seated in the car. "You're on your own now, doll," she said. "And by the way, you're fired."

CHAPTER THIRTY-EIGHT

Treed coon...

She watched in stunned disbelief as the cab carried Dyna out of her life, presumably forever. Then she dragged herself up to her hotel room for a long, scented bath. As the bubbles filled the tub, the water rising inside the porcelain walls, she felt utterly alone and far from home. She tried to concentrate on her happy childhood, those nurturing hours beside the river in the mountains of North Carolina. She remembered the wonderful stories her grandpa used to tell about life in the Cherokee Nation, and the critters that lived in the woods. What would Grandpa say in this situation?

He would say that Ellie was like a treed coon on a windy night. Yes, that's how Grandpa would assess her situation. She figured the next good breeze would blow her off that tree and into the hound's jaws. But then, she had never been scared of hounds, let alone rats like Dyna.

Still, in one short day, she had been abandoned by the two women who professed to care for her, not a great track record. Dyna fired her because she sabotaged her pet project, and she was right, Ellie blew it. Much worse, she could not drive Carla's hurt expression from her mind. Carla's eyes had been shocked and haunted when she said goodbye, and those eyes would follow her as long as she lived.

When night came, she couldn't face the hotel restaurant, so she had room service send up soup and a sandwich, most of which went down the drain, or into the wastebasket. The gray depression that began at El Yunque deepened to a black shroud that wrapped her in sleeplessness. When she finally drifted off, Carla's accusing eyes trailed her through her dreams.

Then, in the early hours of dawn, a telephone rang. She groped around the unfamiliar room until she found it.

"Good morning, sunshine." Dyna's cheerful voice shocked her awake. "Rise and shine. We have work to do."

What the hell? She jolted upright and swung her legs off the bed.

"You fired me, remember?"

"C'mon, I was only kidding, doll. You know how emotional I get, so let bygones be bygones, okay?"

Sure, why not? Fury burned in Ellie's brain, then raged all the way down to her toes. What was she up to? Was she Dyna's personal punching bag? She jumped up, paced back and forth, which did nothing to put out the fire.

"Go to hell, Dyna!" she shouted into the phone.

"I didn't hear that," Dyna answered cheerfully. "You have exactly thirty minutes to dress, eat, and meet me in the lobby. So if I were you, I'd call for coffee immediately."

She wanted to throw the phone against the wall, but then remembered she had no purse, no money, and she was a long way from home. Mama always warned her not to cut off her nose to spite her face.

"Just like that?" she snapped into the mouthpiece. "I'm supposed to pretend nothing happened?"

"Give me another chance," Dyna pleaded. "The deal is back on track. Valdez has agreed to sign the Agreement on our terms."

No way. She viciously shook her head in an attempt to clear her ears.

"It's true, Ellie. We won."

"What nasty little tactic did you use to make her change her mind?"

"You should be pleased. I told you we'd get this contract."

Ellie took a deep breath. "Good for you, but I want to go on record: I had nothing to do with this turnaround. If Carla signs, you are responsible."

"Don't you want to share the glory? At least reward me with a victory kiss?"

"Hell no, but I will accept a big fat pay raise."

CHAPTER THIRTY-NINE

Beloved enemy...

"So, where are we going?" she asked when Dyna hurried her into a showy Jaguar XKE she had rented for the occasion.

"Casa Valdez, of course. Her Highness awaits our arrival. No doubt she's eager to consummate our deal."

"Carla expects *me* to come?" The familiar sick feeling returned.

"Not only expects you, she *insists* you be present."

No wonder Dyna had hired her back—she had no choice. She couldn't complete the deal without her cooperation, so the reins were temporarily in Ellie's hands. She would gleefully drop those reins, let Dyna gallop out of her life, as soon as she could afford to do so.

But why had Carla summoned her? Surely she could finalize the deal without her help. Did she want to call a truce? Would Ellie have a chance to apologize and begin again? Maybe Carla had also felt the wretched emptiness of being apart.

She knew she was a master of self-delusion, yet her spirits rose as they navigated the heartbreakingly beautiful landscape.

She opened her eyes wide to the tropical splendor, hoping this wouldn't be the last time she traveled this road. But she made a mental memory, just in case.

"Ellie, you look pretty enough to make strong women weep," Dyna commented. "Did you wear that dress for me, or for our client?"

Dyna's observation bolstered her confidence. She had chosen a cool peach sundress, revealing a generous amount of bosom, but had minimized the immodest effect by wrapping a flowing scarf around her shoulders. She wore silver earrings and a wide-brimmed straw hat.

"I bought this hat especially for the island," she explained, wondering if today would be her last chance to wear it.

"In that case…" Dyna watched closely from the corner of her eye. "Maybe we should hang around Puerto Rico after we finish with Valdez? Nothing says we have to catch the first jet back to Atlantic City. That way you can get good use from your hat."

"Thanks, but no thanks." Did Dyna think she was one of those little rubber balls at the end of a rubber string, the ones attached to a paddle? Did she imagine she could knock her away, then she'd bounce right back?

When they turned into the driveway of Casa Valdez, she felt light-headed as they drove between the blooming cacti, toward the blinding whiteness of Carla's house. Her palms perspired and her heart thudded with disturbing irregularity. Although she was desperate to see Carla again, her courage drained away as they neared the wide front porch.

"Please, you do all the talking, Dyna. I'll keep my mouth shut, unless Carla has a question only I can answer."

"Okay by me, doll. I've waited a long time for this victory, and I intend to savor each moment." Dyna took her arm, and they climbed the steps together.

But before they could knock, the heavy door swung open, and Juan Castillo stepped out. "Doña Carla is expecting you." Yet he continued to deliberately block their entry, his arms folded stubbornly across his chest.

Dyna whined, "Do you plan to keep us standing here all day?"

"Only Señorita Birdsong may come in. Doña Carla said you must wait outside, Señora Collins."

"That's ridiculous!" Dyna shook her briefcase in Juan's face. "*I* have all the information for our meeting. Valdez must see *me*."

But he stood his ground. "I am sorry, but Doña Carla was very firm about her wishes."

Dyna pulled her close and stage-whispered into her ear, "What's that bitch Valdez up to now?"

Ellie was painfully uncomfortable when she searched Juan's eyes for a clue, but found only animosity. Rather than prolong everyone's discomfort, she stepped quickly across the threshold. "No problem, I will talk to Carla."

Dyna glared at Juan. "If she's not out soon, I'm coming in after her, *comprende?*"

He widened his stance. "Then I will wait with you, *señora*, to be sure that does not happen."

Ellie slipped into the foyer, closed the door behind her. She was grateful to leave the combat behind. Clearly Juan would make sure her interview with Carla remained undisturbed, but it was upsetting to see the gentle Juan in the role of a menacing bodyguard. It didn't suit him.

Intuition told her she'd find Carla in her study. As she approached, her heart flip-flopped, knees turned to jelly, mouth went dry, and she knew her voice would crack the moment she tried to speak. By the time she crept into the room, the last remnants of her self-confidence were gone, and she stood before Carla, vulnerable as a child.

"Hello, Ellie." Carla was seated behind her big desk. She did not bother to look up when she entered. "What I have to say won't take very long…"

The lower shutters were closed against the sun, but the upper windows allowed golden rays to spill into the room. As morning light filtered into the darkness, it seemed perfectly fitting that Carla's space was aglow with natural light.

As the seconds ticked by, an antique clock kept time with Ellie's tripping heart. Carla's hands and lower body were in shadow, and there were no papers nor pens on the desk's bare surface. Carla remained still as a statue, while sunlight played on the crown of her dark hair, highlighting the silver wings at her temples. Her normally bronzed complexion was unusually pale, her eyes dull from lack of sleep. The corners of her sensual mouth curved down with some unspoken tension, and for the first time, she looked her age.

"I brought the Agreement of Sale." Ellie held up the briefcase Dyna had shoved into her hands. "I don't understand, Carla. Dyna claims you intend to sign."

"You look beautiful today." Carla's words were raw with emotion. "You seem so innocent in that pretty dress, but looks can be deceiving."

She swallowed hard. True, she was not innocent, as Carla well knew, but Carla had made her feel love for the very first time. Ellie was convinced they had shared an almost sacred place, and no amount of sarcasm could make her change her mind about that. "I never meant to deceive you, Carla. I want nothing but total honesty between us."

"But what we *want* and what we *do* aren't always the same, are they?" Carla stood and approached, tense as a dark panther stalking her prey. Ellie drew back instinctively, but not before Carla manacled her wrists and pulled her roughly toward her. "I trusted you, Ellie. You brought me to life again, a miracle."

"Then please tell me what's wrong," she begged, struggling to free herself. "What have I done to hurt you?"

"You have enchanted me, but now I must wake up from that dream. I now understand that you are my enemy, my beloved enemy."

Carla abruptly released her wrists, as though touching Ellie disgusted her. The brutal rejection hurt more than an actual physical blow, and she could no longer stop the tears. "I don't understand…" She reached out to touch Carla's face, but she shoved her hand away.

"Please don't say another word. I want you to leave now, Ellie."

This wasn't happening. Ellie was overcome by grief.

"Tell your boss I'll sign the damned papers, but not here in my own home. I'll meet her tomorrow afternoon, in the bar of Hotel San Cristóbal in San Juan. She'll get what she wants, but she'll have to wait one more day."

"But why did you ask me to come here?" Ellie sobbed.

"I had to see you with my own eyes, hear *you* ask me to sign, before I could believe you'd actually done this horrible thing. Do not come to the meeting tomorrow, Ellie. I never want to see you again."

"I beg you, please tell me what I've done wrong!"

When Carla turned her back, it required every shred of Ellie's remaining willpower to keep from running to her, throwing her arms around her, shaking some sense into her thick skull.

Above all, she needed to know what horrible thing she had done "Please, Carla, will you do one last thing for me?" she pleaded, stalling for time.

Carla's shoulders trembled, but she refused to turn around.

"May I say goodbye to the boys?"

Carla spun to face Ellie, her eyes rimmed with red. "What must I do to get rid of you?" she moaned.

"Are Antonio and Enrique here? I need to say goodbye." She swallowed the last of her pride. If she needed the boys as an excuse to linger, to make sense of it all, so be it. She would cling to any straw she could find.

"Why are you playing this cruel game, Ellie?"

It seemed there was nothing more to say, so before a fresh flood of tears disgraced her even more, Ellie squared her shoulders and turned to go.

"Wait..." Carla called at her back. "Maybe you're not involved in this whole sordid mess, but you are still Dyna's associate, so what else can I think? I will never forgive you, nor will I forget you, Ellie," she said with miserable finality.

"I won't forget you either, Carla," she whispered without turning around.

It was the understatement of a lifetime.

CHAPTER FORTY

Hotel San Cristóbal...

When Ellie retreated through Carla's foyer, for what would definitely be the very last time, Juan cast her a concerned, fatherly look as she pushed past him through the door. Mercifully, her tears had stopped by the time she greeted a sullen Dyna sitting in the rented Jag.

"Well?" Dyna demanded as she climbed in. "Where's the Agreement?"

Ellie waited until she'd started the engine and driven several yards out the driveway before she told her, "Carla didn't sign."

Dyna hit the brakes, killing the engine. "Son of a bitch! You're kidding, right?" She searched Ellie's eyes and confirmed the awful truth. "Damn, what's Valdez think she's doing? She's playing with fire. Does she think she won't get burned?"

She couldn't imagine how Dyna could possibly burn Carla, let alone leverage her decision, but she let it pass. "Look, Carla says she'll meet you tomorrow afternoon at the Hotel San Cristóbal in San Juan. She claims she'll sign the Agreement there, says she doesn't want to do it in her own home."

"Bullshit!" Dyna pounded the steering wheel. "She's stalling. She's screwing with the wrong woman, and she'll live to regret it."

Ellie was weary to the bone. She didn't know what her boss had on Carla to threaten her that way, and she didn't want to know. "I'm quitting, Dyna. I want no part of this filthy deal, so I'm buying a ticket and flying home tonight."

"Valdez gave you your walking papers? Rejection sucks, doesn't it? You can forfeit your commission, if you insist, doll, but I won't give you the money to fly away until the deal is done."

Ellie had fallen into the hound's jaws, after all, and she couldn't escape until the hound spit her out. Dyna had won, and she knew it. "I hear you, boss. I'll hang around, but you best stay on your side of the tree."

Dyna laughed. "We'll stay at Hotel Cristóbal tonight. It will make tomorrow's meeting with Valdez more convenient. I hear it's a first-rate place that caters to Americans."

Ellie slid deeper into her shell and gazed through the car window at a grove of canary yellow flamboyan trees lining the roadway. She glanced back for one last look at the placid, green Caribbean. The scene was peaceful, in direct contrast to her personal turmoil, as she accepted the finality of her situation. Carla and her beautiful homeland had invaded her soul, so no matter where she traveled, or what women might share her life, she would never be free of the lover who now called her the enemy.

She closed her eyes, pretending to sleep, because she simply could not tolerate small talk with Dyna. Nor could she bear witness to the beautiful landscape speeding by. She did indeed feel like the enemy, a vanquished foe banished from her chosen kingdom.

When they entered San Juan, drove along the fashionable Condado and passed the glittering gambling casinos, she suddenly guessed why Carla had suggested this district for tomorrow's meeting. The choice concealed a subtle message, one only Ellie would understand. *Take a good look. Is this the vision you see for my land?*

The modern glass and steel buildings certainly did not reflect Carla's preference for traditional Puerto Rican culture. In fact, it represented a future Carla desperately hoped to avoid, so Ellie was again puzzled by her motive in selling to DynaCo.

They pulled up under the canopied entrance to Hotel San Cristóbal. The structure offered a cold, modern elegance, but she definitely preferred the coziness of El Rincón.

They checked into separate rooms, as promised, then Dyna announced she was taking off somewhere on business.

"Try not to miss me too much."

Ellie rolled her eyes. "When will you be back?"

"Dinner, then *dessert*," she responded suggestively. "I'll meet you in the lounge for cocktails." She gave Ellie some chump change and advised her to avoid tourist traps.

The moment Dyna left, Ellie glanced miserably at her watch. She had three hours to kill before *happy hour*, time guaranteed to pass slowly and painfully. Alone in her expensive, but sterile room, she looked out at the breezy Atlantic, then down at the carefree vacationers lounging under colorful beach umbrellas or congregating at the poolside bar. Their happiness only intensified her misery, so she turned back to the empty room.

Something had gone horribly wrong, and she had to know why.

She located the phone, and called for a taxi.

CHAPTER FORTY-ONE

Her great escape…

The sun was dropping lower in the sky by the time her cab wound its way into an old part of the city, and suddenly she felt nervous about seeing Antonio and Enrique again. But the boys had become precious to her, and she believed they had begun to love her, too, so how could they understand her sudden departure? Carla would be furious, but Carla's anger was hardly an issue anymore, was it?

As they drove through a magical neighborhood, she asked her cabbie, "Why are the streets paved with blue blocks?"

"Those are *adoquines*," the young man explained as he fingered the soul patch in the cleft of his mocha-brown chin. "They're made from slag cast off from the old iron foundries in Spain. In the 1880s, San Juan began using them to make streets, and in ten years some eight thousand tons had been imported."

"You're an awesome tour guide. What's your name?"

"Pablo." The man tipped the red Yankees ball cap set backward on his close-cropped Afro.

"Your English is excellent."

"Yo, I was born in New York City, grew up in the States. I'm what they call a *Nuyorican*."

She decided this guy might prove to be useful.

"This is the Plaza de San José, and that's the statue of Ponce de León, the dude who went looking for the fountain of youth," he continued.

"I could use a sip from that fountain about now," she said.

"No way, girl." Pablo winked. "You look fine as is."

She laughed. Pablo's flirting was harmless. "My name's Ellie Birdsong," She held up her hand, he slapped her a high five. No question, she had finally found an ally.

Pablo squinted into the sun, then searched her eyes. "Excuse me, Ellie, but where are we going? We keep driving round and round, with no destination. Is there a problem? How can I help?"

Her instincts kept telling her that something awful had happened, yet she couldn't identify the precise cause of her panic. She only knew she felt guilty and responsible. People she'd come to love were in some sort of trouble, and somehow she was to blame. As Pablo awaited her answer, she mentally counted the money Dyna had given her.

"Pablo, how much would you charge to drive me to Guanica and back?"

"You jiving me? All the way to the south of the island? How much cash you got?" He invited her to sit up front with him, and she emptied her money between them on the seat. "You're comin' up short, Ellie, but hey, it's a slow day and I got nothing better to do. I'll drive you."

He was doing her a huge favor, and she was grateful. She also realized her great escape would leave Dyna alone with her cocktails, but to hell with her. In two hours, Ellie would be at Casa Valdez, to find the truth hidden in all these lies.

"Thanks, Pablo," she told her new friend. "Floor it, will you?"

CHAPTER FORTY-TWO

Juan Bobo...

She had anticipated a two-hour ride to Casa Valdez, but Pablo took her at her word and kept a heavy foot on the accelerator. She spent most of the trip clinging to the armrest in terror as he spun around hairpin curves and raced through yellow lights.

"Jeez, will you slow down? Are you some kind of speed freak?"

"I learned to drive in New York City, remember?" He grinned. "You said you were in a hurry, right?"

Right. That morning she had traveled this very same road, at a far more sedate pace, in Dyna's rented Jag. During that trip, she'd been too upset to think straight. Now, at least, she was taking action, attempting to make sense of what was happening. So if Pablo in his enthusiasm skidded off an overpass and she wound up like the jelly in a crushed tuna can, so be it—at least she had died trying.

"I freaked when my folks dragged me here from New York," Pablo said. "They had this dream to return to the island, you know? Not *my* idea. I was a badass street punk, a gangsta, you know?"

He had been talking nonstop since they left San Juan, but his ceaseless babble allowed her to zone out and consider her own problems. Her decision to take off to Casa Valdez, leaving Dyna in the lurch, would almost surely guarantee she'd lose her job—for real this time. She pictured Dyna in the lobby of the Hotel San Cristóbal, or stewing at the bar while she waited for her. The image of her boss angrily chain-smoking and downing martinis brought a smile to her lips, the first smile of the day. Maybe for once she had her priorities straight. Certainly her concern for Carla was far more important than a career at DynaCo.

"I felt better once I met some dudes my own age," Pablo was telling her. "Like, the kids in San Juan were cool, you know? Like, they let *me* be *me* without all the bullshit, and for the first time in my life, I felt like I belonged, like maybe this was my country, my roots."

"Will you ever move back to the States, Pablo?"

"No way. I married a local woman, and we have a two-year-old baby girl. We own our own little house with a garden, not some housing project in the ghetto, like where I grew up. Why would I go back?"

"I wouldn't mind living here myself."

"Then why don't you stay, Ellie?"

Good question, but young Antonio had once expressed his hatred for Americans.

"Do you think Puerto Ricans would accept me?"

"They'd welcome you with open arms. Americans are inevitable. Only the *Independentistas* want to break off all ties with the USA, and they're crazy. Uncle Sam feeds us all."

"Pablo, what is an authentic Puerto Rican?"

He laughed. "Ain't no such animal. We're part Indian, part African, part Spanish, and part American, whatever that means. Mama says our blood is mongrel stew. So we have this identity crisis, but we're all *Juan Bobo* at heart."

"Juan Bobo?"

"Yeah, Bobo was this mythical brother who acted like he was mentally challenged, you know? But in truth, his sly, native know-how always brought him out on top in the end. Even a *Nuyorican* like me has a small part of the island imbedded deep in his genes, a quality called *dignidad*."

"So I've been told," she muttered unhappily. Carla had explained that concept of *self-respect* the day they picnicked on the beach, the day they first kissed in the cave. Would she ever truly fit in, or understand the Puerto Rican spirit? A sudden chill shivered through her confidence as they approached Casa Valdez.

"Turn left at that next little road," she instructed Pablo.

But Pablo was looking in the rearview mirror. "Seems like we have a tail, Ellie. That beige Crown Vic's been doggin' us the last ten miles. You know anyone drives a Ford like that?"

Lieutenant Colon, the cop who detained Carla at the Phosphorescent Bay, drove such a car. She hoped she was mistaken. "Just a coincidence, Pablo, and hey, you're going to miss our turnoff."

"But that's a private driveway."

"I know. We're visiting a friend of mine."

"Isn't this Valdez land?" Pablo's dark brows were knit in worry. "Even I know Doña Carla Valdez owns this part of the island, and I don't want to be caught trespassing."

"Friends aren't considered trespassers."

"You know Doña Carla?" Pablo stared with newfound respect.

"I thought I knew her."

She watched with mounting apprehension as Pablo made the turn. In the meantime, the beige Ford flew past without a second look in their direction, and when they reached the house, Pablo parked a respectful distance from the veranda.

"This close enough?" he asked.

"It's fine."

The sun dropped lower in the western sky. Soon they would witness a spectacular sunset, like the one she had shared with Carla her first night on the island.

"Where is everyone?" Pablo wondered. "I don't see any cars. Let's split, no one's home."

"The servants are always here. Someone will let us in."

"Not me, I'm waiting outside."

She flicked the bill of his red ball cap. "You better wait, *compadre*, because if things go south, you'll be driving my getaway car."

CHAPTER FORTY-THREE

Trust, but verify…

She left the safety of the taxi, climbed the grand steps, and wondered if she should expect trouble at Casa Valdez. The notion was preposterous. Mama always said she was a drama queen. On the other hand, when she rang the doorbell, she was overcome with foreboding. The house and grounds were unnaturally silent, like they had been abandoned to the whim of eternity.

She pressed the bell a second time, still no answer. When she knocked on the door itself, it creaked open without resistance to the dark, breezy foyer. Shouldn't they lock up around here? If she pulled this stunt in Atlantic City, the bad guys would rob her blind.

"Anybody home?" Her voice squeaked.

Nothing. *Get a grip.* She put one foot in front of the other and progressed down the tiled hall. Her heart thudded in her ears, her legs were shaky as a guilty trespasser's. Eventually, she heard muffled voices coming from the kitchen, and pulling herself upright to her tallest height, she marched toward the sound with far more courage than she actually possessed. She hesitated only a moment before pushing the swinging door.

"Hello, it's Ellie Birdsong…!" she called out. The kitchen was dark with the coming dusk, and she wondered why none of the three figures seated in the shadows at the table had thought to turn on a light. Although she couldn't distinguish their faces, all three heads jerked up in surprise at her intrusion.

"*Señorita?*" an adolescent voice cried. "Why did you leave without saying goodbye?"

The smallest of the three figures jumped to his feet, flew across the room, and suddenly Antonio's arms encircled her waist.

She hugged back hard, her throat clogged with emotion. "I wanted to say goodbye. That's why I came back, to see you and Enrique. Where's your brother?"

The child untangled himself and seemed puzzled. "I don't know. I haven't seen him all day."

"Maybe he's visiting a friend?" she prompted.

Before the boy could answer, the bulkiest of the seated figures stomped over and roughly took hold of her arm. "I am very surprised to see you again, *señorita*," Juan growled. "I thought we said our last goodbyes this morning. My daughter has packed your things, and Doña Carla told me to deliver them to you, in San Juan."

His strong fingers bit into her flesh, but she vowed to stay calm. "You're right, I didn't plan to return, but it's a woman's prerogative to change her mind, right?" What the hell had gotten into this man? Where was the gentle, easygoing Juan she'd come to trust?

Antonio also seemed disturbed by Juan's weird behavior. He tugged at the older man's sleeve. "Yes, Uncle Juan, where is Enrique? Is he at Pepé Toro's house?"

The third figure rose from her chair and glided toward them with graceful composure. She placed a soothing hand on Antonio's head. "That's right, you guessed it, *mijito*. Enrique went to Pepé's right after breakfast. A few minutes ago, Pepé's mama called and asked if Enrique could spend the night."

Ellie glared at Filo. The woman was lying.

Antonio shoved out his lower lip. "How come *I* wasn't invited? Call Señora Toro and ask if I can sleep over, too."

"No!" Filo shouted. "I need you here with me, Antonio. Your Uncle Juan will be leaving soon, and I don't want to be alone."

What on earth was going on here? She frowned at Filo, then pried Juan's hand off her arm. "What's wrong with you people? Why can't Tony stay at Pepé's? What's the big deal?"

"Señorita Birdsong can stay with Filo and keep her company," Antonio argued. "Why can't I go?"

"You are not listening, Antonio." Juan grabbed the boy's shoulder and squeezed hard. "Señorita Birdsong is not staying. She came to say goodbye. See that taxi waiting for her out in the drive?"

Antonio peeked out the window, confirming Juan's words, then looked back at Ellie. "But why can't you stay until tomorrow? Don't you want to say goodbye to Enrique?"

"Shut your mouth, boy!" Juan shook the child so hard his teeth rattled, then abruptly released him. "Now go outside and play in the garden, you hear me?"

A direct command from Juan Castillo was not to be ignored. Antonio blinked back tears. "Goodbye, *señorita*. When I come to America, can I visit you?"

"You're welcome anytime," she assured him, hoping he couldn't hear the catch in her voice. "Please tell Enrique goodbye for me, okay?"

"Okay." With a weak wave and an attempted smile, Antonio slinked out the door and out of her life.

The adults glared at one another, until Juan broke the silence. "Why did you come back, *señorita*? Doña Carla said you were gone for good."

"Carla sent me away without an explanation," she snapped. "And where is Carla, anyway? Is she hiding? Did she run off when she saw me coming?"

Juan remained stone-faced.

"Did you hear me, Juan? Where the hell is Carla?" she persisted. "I must talk to her."

"*Perdóneme, señorita*, if I knew where she was, this situation would not be so difficult," Juan said.

"*Situation?* Don't tell me you've lost Carla?" Her frustration had reached the boiling point. If someone didn't enlighten her soon, she'd start throwing plates and breaking china.

"This is not your business," Juan warned. "Or maybe it is? Doña Carla said you were involved."

"Involved in what, for God's sake?"

The old man's eyes smoldered with anger. "You know what I'm talking about. Leave now, and do not come back."

"Wait, Father," Filo pleaded. "I think you're wrong about Ellie. Doña Carla is wrong, too. I believe Ellie cares, and we should give her a chance. Can't you take her to Headquarters with you?"

She searched Filo's eyes, surprised by the sudden vote of confidence. Perhaps it was a woman thing, and Filo had glimpsed her heart. "Please trust me," she appealed to them both. This *Headquarters* nonsense sounded like a scene from a bad movie, but she decided to play along. "If you take me with you, you'll know what I'm up to, right?" She turned to Juan. "If you still think I'm involved in some dark plot, at least you can keep an eye on me."

"She has a point," Filo told her father. "Besides, haven't you noticed the change in Doña Carla since Ellie arrived? She's a different person, and I believe her feelings for Ellie are returned, am I right, Ellie?"

Ellie figured she had nothing more to lose. When she nodded in affirmation, she felt the heat of embarrassment flooding her cheeks.

Juan sighed, shrugged his shoulders. "I will never understand women."

Her face burned, but she couldn't take it back. Now both Juan and Filo knew how she felt about Carla, and eventually Carla would hear it from their lips—unless Ellie told her first. "Will you take me, then?" she asked the old man.

"I suppose I will take you," he gruffly conceded. "But you cannot know the exact location."

"Will I see Carla at these so-called Headquarters?"

Juan continued more gently, "I hope so, because if she is not there, God knows what trouble she is in."

"Is Carla in danger?" Ellie demanded.

"Like all Americans, you talk too much. Stop asking questions."

She glanced at the dishes on the kitchen table and again considered breaking things. She was fed up with the whole Valdez crew. All day everyone had been lying, or at least evading her questions. Filo had just claimed Enrique was visiting his little neighbor, Pepé Toro, was that a lie?

"Listen, may I run up to the blue room before we leave?" She kept her voice level as a plan formed in her scattered brain. "I left my sneakers behind."

Filo said, "But I have already packed your suitcase, and I saw no sneakers."

"No, I'm sure I left them here somewhere," she insisted, and before the suspicious father and daughter could interfere, she escaped into the hall and started up the stairs.

As she climbed, she overheard Filo speaking to Juan. "Say hello to Mama and the family for me. Tell Sylvie not to come to work tomorrow, because with only Antonio to cook for, I won't need her."

Ellie ran upstairs, lest she be caught eavesdropping. Apparently Juan was taking her to the Castillo family home in Lares. If they were talking about *family headquarters*, then why all the secrecy? Once inside the blue room, she closed and locked the door. Something smelled fishy, and the stink came from the lie about Enrique being at his friend Pepé's house. One thing life had taught her: *trust, but verify.*

She dropped to her knees and rummaged under the bed for her ratty old sneakers. Luckily, they were right where she'd left them and provided the perfect cover to execute the first part of her plan. With no time to waste, she picked up the princess phone on the bedside table, dialed information, and located the only *Toro* listed in the immediate neighborhood. With the English-speaking operator's help, she quickly confirmed her suspicions.

Pepé's mama got straight to the point: Pepé had not played with Enrique all week.

As she sank the receiver into its cradle, her hands trembled with anger. She'd been spoon-fed so many lies, she felt like gagging, but she snatched her old sneaks and marched downstairs with renewed determination. Juan had said this mess was none of her business, but she intended to make it so. If nobody knew where Enrique was, then what the hell had happened to him?

She poked her head into the kitchen, held out her sneakers for both to see. "I found them…" she called cheerfully. "So I'll be ready to go as soon as I pay the taxi."

CHAPTER FORTY-FOUR

Make it right...

Without waiting for their approval, she dashed outside to where Pablo was faithfully waiting.

"What happened in there?" He stared at her. "You look like an Iraqi war vet who just sidestepped a roadside bomb." He opened the passenger door, and she slid inside.

"Worse than that. I'm afraid the real battle is still ahead. Do you have paper and a pencil, Pablo?"

"What for?"

"Hey, everything is strictly on a need-to-know basis, and you don't need to know. Just give me something to write with."

He quickly produced a pen and notepad, but her hand shook so much, she could barely scribble the message. As the worst-case scenario materialized in her tortured brain—that Enrique had been kidnapped—the awful scene with Carla in her study kept replaying like some insidious horror flick. She couldn't forget the agony in Carla's eyes when she said: "You have enchanted me, Ellie, but now I must wake up from that dream. I now understand that you are my enemy." Clearly Carla thought she had betrayed her, but how?

Next she recalled Dyna's sudden turnabout. She had fired Ellie, then immediately rehired her. But why? Dyna's explanation had been: "The deal is back on track. Valdez has agreed to sign the Agreement on our terms." Then why on God's earth didn't Carla sign those papers unless… Dear Lord, surely *Dyna* was not involved in Enrique's disappearance? If that were the case, then Ellie was also to blame by association, and she had to make it right.

She folded her note into tiny squares. "Do not read this, Pablo, it's private. You must deliver it to Lieutenant Colon at the San Juan Police Department."

Pablo held her note between two fingers. "Are you in trouble with the cops? That's bad news, Ellie. Who says I won't read this the minute you go, and where the hell are you goin' anyhow?"

"You will *not* read it." She confiscated the note and buttoned it into his breast pocket. "And you don't need to know where I'm going."

"If it's so damn urgent, then why not use my cell phone? We do have 911 in Puerto Rico."

"Okay, then give me your phone and leave."

"A cabbie without a cell? No way."

She felt like wringing his neck. "Please help, Pablo! Won't you deliver my note to Colon?"

"Nope." Pablo lifted off his Yankees cap, ran his hand through his dark curls. He fingered the little soul patch under his lip and grinned like an idiot.

"Why the hell not?"

Pablo chuckled. "I can't deliver this, 'cause Colon ain't in San Juan."

"Are you psychic?"

"Not hardly. Your lieutenant's been cruisin' back and forth at the end of this driveway. I didn't recognize him at first, but it's Colon, all right. The dude's been following us. I recognize him because he's given me more speeding tickets than I care to admit."

She took a deep breath. Pablo was right, and she should have put it together sooner. A face swam into her memory—

young blond Latino with a pug nose and pencil moustache—
that night at Phosphorescent Bay, when he arrested Carla. The
beige Crown Victoria was no coincidence, after all.

"Is he still out there?" she asked as her pulse accelerated
with hope.

"Not sure. Haven't seen him pass for several minutes. Maybe
he gave up."

She couldn't picture Colon giving up. "Please try to catch
him, Pablo," she pleaded as she walked away from the taxi.
"Drive fast, will you?"

"Is there any other way?"

CHAPTER FORTY-FIVE

La Borinqueña...

Pablo left her standing in a cloud of dust, and as she walked back toward the house, she prayed that Lieutenant Colon really was out there somewhere. She figured Pablo would break his promise, read her note, and then call the lieutenant immediately. Well, maybe that was okay, even though it would involve Pablo in this mess, perhaps put him in danger, which she didn't want and never intended.

She imagined Colon's boyish face when he read her garbled message about *trouble at the Headquarters in Lares.* Likely he'd think she'd lost what little was left of her sanity, so what would he do? Had she done the right thing, or had she put Carla and Enrique into more danger by alerting the police? All she knew for sure was Carla needed help, so right or wrong, she'd taken matters into her own hands.

Back at the house, they said goodbye to Filo, then Juan and she departed immediately in a rusty black pickup, which had been hidden around back.

"You look out of place in this old truck, *señorita*. It's a vehicle for field hands, not elegantly dressed foreigners."

"No problem." But she had broken a high heel on the running board, rendering her shoes useless. "Lucky I found these…" She stashed her heels under the seat, then laced up her faithful old sneakers.

Those were the last words they spoke for quite some time on their bumpy journey. Juan remained taciturn and preoccupied, with worry lines etched in his face as he concentrated on navigating the ancient truck, which swayed and coughed with each bend in the road. They drove through Ponce and picked up Highway 10 going north out of town.

Ellie suppressed a cheer when she spotted Colon's beige Ford following them at a discreet distance. Her palms sweated with excitement when she realized her plan had worked. But what next? Darkness closed in as she peeked in the side mirror and distinguished the silhouettes of two men in the unmarked car.

"We will have a full moon tonight," Juan commented. "Light at night is sometimes good, sometimes very bad."

She couldn't decipher his cryptic remark. Her mind was cluttered with so many unanswered questions, she didn't even try. Instead, she gripped the armrest as they swayed around a bend and passed the dilapidated beer stand where Juan had stopped for a drink that very first day. This landmark meant they had just turned west onto Highway 111.

"How much farther to Lares?" she asked offhandedly.

"What makes you think we're going to Lares?"

"You introduced me to that intersection. Don't you remember?"

"I should have used a blindfold," he grumbled.

At the same moment, she noticed Lieutenant Colon had missed the turnoff and apparently continued on, oblivious to their change of direction. *Damn.* They traveled the next few miles in silence as she panicked and pretended to take interest in a weird, park-like area on their left. "What is that place?"

"The old Indian Ceremonial Ball Park," Juan explained. "The Taino Indians used the land for religious gatherings and ball games, almost seven hundred years ago. Inside, there are two rows of huge stones standing on end, all with carvings.

Folks in my town believe it is a sacred place, and on moonlit nights like tonight, the Indian spirits wander among the stones."

Ellie shivered at the eerie image, but to hell with ghosts. At the moment, she was more worried about man-made evil, and the fact that the stupid cops had seemingly lost their trail for good.

"We are almost there," he said as the truck's hood pointed straight upward in a steep climb. "We grow coffee beans in these mountains. The hills are good for the crop, bad for my truck."

Sure enough, the pickup choked, wheezed, and barely made it up a sharply inclined street into what appeared to be a town square. The square was typical of any lazy country village. In the twilight, she saw a scattering of benches under the old shade trees, and at the center stood a green-and-cream church with a silver dome. The clock tower displayed four different times—all were wrong, according to her watch—and still no sign of Colon. He had lost their scent, so she was on her own.

Juan cut the engine and the vehicle lurched to a stop. Several men looked and waved to Juan as Ellie climbed from the truck. Everyone fixed on her with a curious eye, and Juan chuckled.

"This is a small town, *señorita*. These men wonder what I, a married man, am doing with a beautiful young *Americana*. We are old-fashioned in our thinking. Even our market has a sign above the door: *bad language forbidden*."

"Well, I'll be careful not to use any four-letter words," she muttered. The townsfolk appeared curious, but not hostile.

"We will visit the church now." He took her arm, dragged her onward.

Strange. First he had professed to be in a blistering hurry, but now he was willing to waste precious time at worship? Two rough-looking young men stopped them at the door to the chapel. Strange again. These thugs were hardly welcoming to a house of God. Juan gave them a signal, mumbled a few words in Spanish, and the men parted like the Red Sea, allowing them to enter.

"What was that all about?" she asked him.

"Never mind." He shoved her across the threshold.

Before she could process this odd behavior, she was stunned by the bizarre scene before her. The pews were packed with rapt participants. They were standing and holding hands as they swayed and sang, but this was definitely not a religious ceremony. Native musicians seated on the floor near the altar provided the background music. They strummed exotic stringed instruments, leading the audience in a hauntingly beautiful melody.

"What is that song?" she whispered, entranced.

"*La Borinqueña*, our national anthem," Juan answered reverently. "The instruments are *tiples* and *cuatros*, made in Puerto Rico. When people sing this, it means the meeting is almost over."

"What kind of meeting?"

Juan refused to answer as he joined in singing with the audience, which seemed to be entirely male: a scruffy-looking bunch of guys in their twenties or early thirties. Many wore soiled work clothes and bandannas, while others were more dressed-up in short-sleeved shirts and loosened ties. From unkempt beards and army surplus fatigues, to rumpled office clothes, they all had one thing in common—hungry eyes and intent expressions.

CHAPTER FORTY-SIX

PIP...

"Who are these men?"

"Not just men, also women." Juan nodded at the pulpit, where a solemn tribunal was seated around a table.

The central figure was indeed a woman, and while Ellie could only see the back of her head, she held it proud and high. "Isn't that Carmen Diaz?" she asked, perhaps too loudly. The singing stopped and several men in the back row turned around to stare at her. They began to whisper, and the whispering spread like wildfire in a sugarcane field, all the way to the front of the church.

Suddenly Carmen spun around and fixed on Ellie with angry eyes. She leapt gracefully to her feet, pointed an accusing finger in her direction. "How dare you bring that woman into this place?"

Ellie's blood ran cold as fear crystallized like chopped ice in the pit of her stomach. The two guards from the front door closed in on either side of her. Carmen motioned to the guards, and then issued an order in Spanish. One guy shoved

Juan aside and grasped Ellie's left arm, while the other captured her right and clamped down hard. Her body recoiled in an odd combination of terror and fury, but she tried to stay calm as she recognized the flag displayed at the front of the church. It was the symbol of the rebel *Independentistas*.

The man on her right saw her staring, tightened his grip like a vise, and smiled through crooked teeth. "We have nothing to hide, *señorita*. *Sí*, we all belong to PIP, the Puerto Rican Independence Party, and we display our flag proudly on the altar."

The flag had a white cross on a green field. While doing her research, she had learned this design represented those who sought total separation from the United States. The group was known to be both dangerous and violent, with many sympathizers among artists and intellectuals. In an odd way, she had been moved by their sentiments.

"Why are you meeting here, in this church?"

"Lares is the birthplace of our independence from the Spanish, so this holy place is the hub for our movement against you Americans." The man gave her arm an ugly twist, causing her to cry out in pain.

Juan tried to come to her rescue, but the guards shoved him roughly to the floor.

"Leave him alone!" she shouted, giving her tormentor a vicious kick in the shins. He grunted and loosened his hold on her.

In the meantime, Carmen continued to bark orders, demanding the church be cleared. The members stampeded out in a mass exodus, and soon the room was virtually silent. She squirmed between her two guards, while Juan sat on the floor with his face between his hands. Carmen restlessly paced in the nave, complaining to the two other members of the tribunal, whose faces remained in shadow.

"Lock the doors!" Carmen shouted. "And bring Ms. Birdsong up here where we can talk."

The sadist on Ellie's right released her, rubbed his sore shin, and then signaled for his partner to move her forward. As they stumbled up the aisle, she wondered about Lieutenant Colon. Where were the damn cops when you needed them? When they arrived at the first pew, her escort shoved her down onto the hard seat.

"Stay with her," Carmen told him.

When the man's hands clamped down on her shoulders, she inadvertently cried out in fear, causing one of the figures at the table to stand. Even in the shadows, something about the figure was intimately familiar. Her heart seemed to stop, and she could hardly get her breath. "Carla, is that you?" she screamed. "Don't let them do this!"

"Speak only to me," Carmen snapped. "You have some explaining to do, Ms. Birdsong, and your explanation better be good."

"Go easy, Carmen," Juan pleaded from the floor. "I don't think she is to blame."

"What do you know, old man? Frankly, I'm shocked you brought her here. What were you thinking?"

"*Lo siento.* I am sorry," Juan apologized.

"You should be sorry. Why don't you go home where you belong?"

Juan quickly accepted Carmen's offer. He struggled to his feet and shuffled away like a whipped hound. With his departure, Ellie felt like she'd lost her last friend on earth.

"What do you want?" she shouted at the obnoxious woman.

"Now we can talk openly," Carmen answered calmly. "Tell me everything, Ms. Birdsong"

A single beam of light shot down from the rafters, illuminating her interrogator. Raven black hair glistened around Carmen's hard, handsome face. Even dressed in army fatigues and heavy boots, she was a strikingly beautiful woman, but her attitude left something to be desired.

"What the hell are you talking about, Carmen?"

Carmen stormed down off the platform. "From now on, you must call me Mrs. Valdez."

Carmen and Carla were *married*? The idea was preposterous. If the Carla Ellie knew had taken marriage vows, she would be faithful. But how well did she really know Carla? Bowing her head in shame and defeat, she realized she had better tell these monsters whatever they wanted to hear, if she intended to survive.

CHAPTER FORTY-SEVEN

The black sheep…

A deep voice said, "It never helps to lose your temper, Carmen."

The voice was heartbreakingly familiar. Ellie lifted her face, hoping to find Carla somewhere in the shadows.

"I got carried away, darling," Carmen responded. "But you're right, it never helps." She faced Ellie again, ready to proceed with the interrogation, but then she caught Ellie staring at the figure seated at the table. "Ah, Ms. Birdsong, would you prefer to have my husband question you?"

Ellie was lost and confused, stuck somewhere between the bumper hitch and the trailer tongue… Either way, she was being dragged along for a ride that made no sense. She moistened her lips, steadied her voice, and spoke to the person at the table she hoped was Carla.

"Who the hell are you?"

The man's sudden movement away from the table toppled his chair, and his laugh was harsh and derisive. Before she could prepare herself, he was standing squarely before her, his legs planted like oak trees. "Hello, Ms. Birdsong, who the hell do you think I am?"

The man bore an uncanny resemblance to Carla, but he was slightly taller and thinner. He had the same glossy black hair, but his was cropped short and untouched by gray. He lacked Carla's grace, her smooth bronzed skin. And while his full lips were sensuous like hers, they twisted up at the corners in an unpleasant, sarcastic smile.

"I look like her, don't I?" he said.

She couldn't tear her eyes away.

Carmen said, "Allow me to introduce my husband, Roberto Valdez, Carla's brother."

Ellie was stunned. "But Carla has no brother!"

"How can you look at me and not believe?" Roberto arched his raven's wing eyebrows above eyes as deep brown as Carla's, but that was where the similarity ended. While Carla had a haunted, questioning expression, this man had the focus of a ruthless hunter.

Still, she sensed that in a day filled with lies, she had finally stumbled upon one truth. Carla's dossier included no information about a brother, but she had already discovered that the materials Dyna had given her were woefully lacking. "Your voice is like Carla's…" she reluctantly conceded. "But you speak English like an American."

"Well, I've lived in the States most of my life," Roberto explained. "Carmen and I met there when we were students."

As she gaped at this stranger, so achingly like Carla, she was stricken by a memory. That day at the beach, an angry young Antonio had said, *all Americans should be driven from our country.* When she asked him where he'd gotten such hateful ideas, Antonio said, *Roberto told me.* When she asked who Roberto was, he refused to share the fact that he had an uncle.

Another truth, more emotionally stunning than the fact of Roberto himself, was that Carla and Carmen were not lovers, they were sisters-in-law. Ellie had been wrong about so many things, and this new development perhaps explained why Carla had been unable to finalize the real estate deal on her own.

"If you're really Carla's brother, do you own rights to the land my company wants to buy? Do we need your signature to close the deal?"

Roberto sneered. "What makes you think I'd agree to any deal with the American devil? You see, I've always been the black sheep of the Valdez family, the forgotten man, and only recently has my sister invited me back into the fold."

"Shut up, Roberto!" a new voice shouted as the third member of the tribunal joined them. The short, powerfully muscled young man resembled a prizefighter, and his battered face testified to a lifetime of brawling. "You've said too damn much already."

"Meet Manuel Castillo." Roberto spat out the words. "He's our leader, the spokesman for PIP. He's also Juan Castillo's eldest son.

Ellie did another double take. How on earth could a seemingly gentle man like Juan have given birth to an outlaw like Manuel?

"*Buenas tardes*, Señorita Birdsong." Manuel frowned. "I wish I could welcome you to our little gathering, but one rarely welcomes the enemy." An unpleasant wave of nausea washed through her as Manuel playfully knocked the straw hat off her head. He retrieved it, tossed it atop a pole where a United States flag was hung upside down. "What a silly hat," he continued. "Now I can see your eyes."

Roberto intervened. "This is a Valdez family matter, remember? I will do the talking."

"Be my guest, but don't forget the fate of the Valdez land becomes a *political* matter when it appears to be falling into the wrong hands."

Roberto nodded to Manuel, and then focused on her. "Ellie, you were about to explain your role in this mess…?"

Why should she trust him? For all she knew, he could be plotting against his own sister. "Where is Carla? I thought she'd be here," she demanded.

Ignoring the question, he winked at Carmen. "The girl's got attitude. She's not only beautiful, she's also an accomplished actress." He casually lifted several strands of Ellie's hair, then dropped them into her face.

She balled her fist, but the guard caught her wrist and pulled her off-balance. "What's wrong, Roberto, can't you fight your own battles?" she taunted.

"Oh, for Christ's sake." Roberto sighed. "I promise not to touch you, if you promise not to punch me, agreed?" He paced back and forth, then confronted her again. "How well do you know Diego Martinez?"

The blunt question took her by surprise. "We've never been formally introduced, but I witnessed him in action at the Ponce market, when he fought with Carla."

"Tell the truth, Ellie."

"I told you, I don't know him."

"But you seduced my sister at El Rincón. I met with Carla when she returned home, and she was as lovesick as a schoolgirl. Is that how you convince all your clients to sign on the dotted line, Ellie? By luring them into your bed?"

Maybe Roberto thought they had a nonviolence agreement, but after that remark, all bets were off. She executed her famous two-handed shove, the one guaranteed to knock any bully off-kilter, the one she had practiced on her three older brothers. Sure enough, he staggered backward like a punch-drunk boxer.

"You may be Carla's flesh and blood, but you have no right to disrespect Carla and me!"

"Peace, Ellie..." He held up both hands. "Sorry, I was way out of line with that remark. Truth is, I don't know the whole story, but I do know Carla. Different as we are, I love my sister and don't want her to get hurt. She hasn't cared about any woman since Maria died. Then you come along, she trusts you, maybe even loves you, and then you betray her."

Ellie dropped her arms, weary to the bone. Good as it felt to hear that Carla might love her, she feared their relationship had been utterly destroyed by misunderstanding and distrust. At the same time, she was slowly beginning to understand exactly where Roberto was going with his wild accusations. She laid her cards on the table and played her hunch. "You think I kidnapped Enrique, right?"

The church got as silent as the cemetery next door. With all eyes on Ellie, Roberto slowly pulled himself erect. "Yes, we all thought you were involved. I was convinced you were guilty, but now that we've met, I'm not so sure…"

Carmen interrupted, "Don't let her fool you. Remember, we're talking about *your nephew*. Enrique is only seven years old. He's in danger, so we must convince Ms. Birdsong to cooperate."

Ellie's throat constricted with a sorrow more debilitating than fear. Now that her suspicions had been confirmed, she was no longer worried about her own safety. Rescuing Enrique was all that mattered. "If Enrique's been kidnapped, what the hell are you doing about it?"

CHAPTER FORTY-EIGHT

Criminal offense…

"We're working on it." Roberto scowled.

"All I see is a bunch of big, strong men sitting around on their hands," she said.

Roberto turned to the leader of the *Independentistas*. "Tell her, Manuel. We have agents stationed all over the island. We always look out for our own, and we are already using those guys to locate Enrique."

Manuel responded in a gruff monotone, "What else do you need, *compadre?*"

"Put a tail on Ms. Birdsong's boss, Dyna Collins," Carmen interrupted. "After all, Collins and Ms. Birdsong arranged for Enrique's abduction."

"Are you deaf?" Ellie screamed. "I told you I had nothing to do with it." She also refused to believe Dyna would do such a thing. She was a womanizing, arrogant shit—but a kidnapper? Never.

"Someone told Collins that Martinez was after the Valdez land," Carmen continued. "Martinez has strong ties to illegal gambling in San Domingo and San Juan, so why wouldn't he want a piece of the action? If casinos are built at our end of the island, he would benefit big time. Collins probably kidnapped Enrique in order to blackmail Carla, and to give DynaCo an edge."

Ellie almost confessed that she was the "someone" who told Dyna that Martinez was competing, but what good would such an admission do? This crowd already thought she was capable of kidnapping.

"Listen, you're wrong about my boss. DynaCo can afford to buy the Valdez property at any price, without resorting to criminal activity."

"What makes you think we'd sell at any price?" Roberto said. "I know for a fact that your precious Dyna pressured Carla by threatening to expose *me*. I'm on Puerto Rico's *Ten Most Wanted* list. I'm guilty of nothing, but they don't see it that way."

Ellie had suspected Dyna had some sort of leverage over Carla, which apparently involved Carla's brother, Roberto. Had Dyna really threatened to turn him in?

"When Dyna Collins discovered I was wanted," Roberto continued, "she had Carla followed, and Carla unwittingly led her investigator right to my door." He began to pace. "My sister is not skilled in the art of deception, so she was devastated to realize she'd put my freedom in jeopardy."

Ellie reasoned that if Dyna knew about Roberto, her investigator had likely tailed Carla the morning she left before dawn with Carmen, the morning after the incident at the Ponce Market. She pictured Dyna's spy hiding near Casa Valdez, awaiting an opportunity to follow Carla to her brother's hideaway.

"Do you know for a fact that Dyna's involved?" Ellie demanded.

"Once your boss found out where I was hiding, she told Carla point-blank that if she did not sell to DynaCo, she'd call the cops. Carla almost agreed, but I went underground to safety and convinced her not to cave."

"Carla told you this?"

"Absolutely," Roberto said.

"So where is Carla now?"

Again, everyone refused to answer. Either they were hiding something, or Carla, like Enrique, was also missing. "Look, have the kidnappers made a demand? Asked for ransom?" Silence. "You don't know, do you?"

Carmen cleared her throat. "As soon as Roberto went underground, where the cops couldn't find him, Enrique disappeared. We figure Collins arranged it. With your help, Ms. Birdsong, they snatched Enrique and brought Carla to her knees. If you don't lead us to Enrique, I can't guarantee your continued safety."

Ellie was sick with fear for Carla, Enrique, and herself, but she still couldn't believe Dyna would stoop so low as to kidnap an innocent young child. She collapsed onto the nearest pew. She swallowed hard. Recently she'd come to believe her boss could sink to almost any depth, but not that far. "Sorry, I still don't buy it."

"Use your head, Ellie," Roberto urged. "Yesterday at El Yunque, Carla told you she wouldn't sell. Later Collins dropped you at the hotel in Ponce, then she left. Within an hour, Enrique was missing, and suddenly Carla was willing to sign her life away. Doesn't that convince you?"

The evidence was damning, to be sure. She dropped her head between her knees. "Okay, consider this…" she began. "This morning I met with Carla at Casa Valdez and took her the papers to sign. If Enrique had been kidnapped, if Carla was so damned worried, then why didn't she sign when she had a chance?"

"That was my fault, *señorita*," Manuel Castillo admitted sheepishly. "This morning my men thought they knew where to find Enrique, so we convinced Carla to give us time to retrieve him. Unfortunately, we were wrong."

"Asshole," Roberto muttered.

The situation was intolerable. She was determined to find Carla and the child she loved so dearly. Had she saved Enrique from drowning, only to lose him again?

"How can I help?" she pleaded.

"You're a great actress, but save it for the curtain call," Carmen said, then returned to the platform and picked up a heavy gavel. "Tell us what you know."

"I know nothing!" Did the crazy woman intend to pound her to death?

Manuel attached his beefy paw to her shoulder. "When you came to the church tonight, you must have known about the kidnapping, so where did they take the boy?"

"I had *guessed* about the kidnapping!" She shook him off. "Juan and Filo kept lying about Enrique's whereabouts, so I put it all together."

Carmen smacked the gavel into the palm of her left hand.

The menacing gesture enraged Ellie. What was wrong with these people?

It was dark outside, and Enrique was out there somewhere. He was surely scared and hungry. "For Christ's sake. *Carla* wouldn't waste time questioning me. She's already on the trail, isn't she?"

From their sheepish expressions, she knew that she'd hit a nerve. Carla was out searching for Enrique, while everyone else planned and postured. The thought of Carla single-handedly tracking the criminals was terrifying. What if she'd been captured?

She stood up and confronted Carla's brother. "Shame on you, Roberto Valdez! You're worried, angry, and full of guilt because you've let Carla go it alone. Why don't you get off your ass, organize these men, and go after the shits who really did this thing?"

He blinked rapidly, with eyes remarkably like Carla's. She sensed a subtle relaxing of tension at the corners of his mouth and suspected he was softening. Seconds later, he smiled and self-consciously cleared his throat.

"I'm impressed, Ellie. You're quite convincing when you're all riled up. I understand why my sister found you so... challenging." He gently removed the gavel from Carmen's fist. "Maybe Ellie knows more than she cares to admit, but what the hell? If she wants to tag along and help us find Carla and Enrique, it's okay by me."

Carmen said, "Have you lost your mind? We should tie her up and stash her in the church cellar. She's nothing but trouble."

"Think again, darling. If it's true, as *you* believe, that Ellie is helping the bad guys, then we have a live hostage. She enhances our bargaining power."

Carmen Diaz Valdez gave Ellie the evil eye. "My husband is right. Maybe you'll be more valuable at the end of our leash. We'll find you some suitable clothes and take you along. But I warn you, bitch, if you bark or bite, then I will personally take you to obedience school."

CHAPTER FORTY-NINE

Fugitives' hideaway...

Manuel warned, "Very well. If you take the *Americana* along, you must guard her at all times. And keep a close eye on the traffic. Although my men have seen no new activity on the road to the observatory recently, Diego Martinez's black Hummer drove in this afternoon."

"Did anyone tell Carla about Martinez's location?" Roberto asked.

"I'm afraid so. When your sister called several hours ago, one of our brain-dead operatives gave her all the details."

Ellie breathed a sigh of relief, because it seemed Carla was still a free agent, likely out hunting for Enrique. Or at least she had been free several hours ago.

"Where is this observatory?" she asked.

Everyone ignored her.

"Damn!" Carmen cursed. "So Carla has a head start. I hope she doesn't do anything stupid."

As Ellie tried to make sense of it all, Manuel's cell phone rang and he answered. Unfortunately, she couldn't follow his rapid Spanish, but his words clearly upset everyone in the room.

Carmen moaned. "They found Carla's car abandoned on the access road, but where the hell is she?"

Manuel squared his shoulders, strode toward the exit. "We must move quickly. Roberto and I will lead with two other men. Carmen, you follow with Ms. Birdsong, and bring my father. I don't want the old man left behind to shoot his mouth off."

Carmen grasped Ellie's wrist and dragged her quickly from the church. They all ran through the plaza, where townsfolk still lingered on benches and didn't even glance up. They seemed accustomed to such disturbances, or else they were too scared to interfere.

Carmen and she walked onto a rocky lane leading away from the center of town, while the men went toward their cars. Carmen urged Ellie to jog faster. As they ran, the shadows of tall foliage loomed on both sides of their path, and the plaintive cry of a bird calling to the night precisely reflected Ellie's fear.

"Where are we going?" she asked when Carmen steered her onto a steep dirt path leading down into a dark valley. She saw a ramshackle hut built on stilts. The house was perched precariously on the mountainside, and she estimated the structure contained only two or three rooms.

"This is the home of Juan Castillo," Carmen gruffly explained.

"But Juan has six children," she panted. "How does he fit them all in?"

Carmen slowed to a sedate trot. "We call this style cabin a *bohío*. Many of my countrymen are born in such places, and grow up in them as well. You rich Americans never understand this."

As they continued their breakneck descent, she was annoyed by Carmen's holier-than-thou attitude. "*You* weren't born in a *bohío*, were you, Carmen?" It was a wild guess, but Ellie had a hunch. When her escort didn't respond, she tried again. "You were born in the States, and *you* are a rich American, am I right?"

The woman came to such an abrupt halt, that Ellie bumped smack into her. Carmen's eyes sparked like hot coals as she tensed for a fight, but Ellie refused to let her off the hook.

"Admit it, Carmen, you fit the profile. They say the privileged classes make the best rebels. They're sick with guilt over their own good fortune, so they bend over backward to make up for it. Is that Roberto's problem, too? No wonder you two make such a good couple."

She had gone too far and was sure Carmen would strike her, but instead, the woman started to laugh. Her hysterical outburst shocked the stillness. A small boy emerged from the bowels of the shack to discover what all the commotion was about, and then, Carmen got hold of herself and placed a friendly hand on Ellie's arm.

"I hate to say it, Ellie, but your analysis is dead-on. It's true I was born in America, to wealthy parents, and as you can imagine, Roberto has never wanted for money, either. You should have been a shrink. Maybe my husband and I are *both* out to prove something."

The child crept near, his enormous dark eyes wide with suspicion. "Doña Carmen, is that you?"

"*Sí*, tell your mama she has company."

Carmen's laughter had thawed the animosity between them, and they climbed the front steps in surprising harmony.

"I've seen that boy before," Ellie told her. "His name is Luis, and I saw him at a beer stand."

"Yes, he is Juan Castillo's youngest son."

They entered a dim hallway that smelled of fried cooking. Surely this poor dwelling was the *country place* where Carla and Carmen went the day Ellie had assumed they were leaving for a romantic tryst. It was the perfect fugitive's hideaway.

Their sudden disappearances from Casa Valdez now made sense. Carmen wanted to be with her husband, and Carla needed to confer with Roberto regarding DynaCo's offer. Yet understanding these likelihoods did not make Ellie's current predicament any more bearable. Indeed, the knowledge made her furious. The needless jealousy, suspicion, and outright mistrust had ruined everything.

"Ellie, is that really you?" A shy female voice greeted her from the shadows. "I did not know you were coming to our house."

"Neither did I, Sylvie," she answered cautiously. Likely Filo's younger sister knew nothing about the disaster that had befallen the Valdez family. Ellie noticed a heavy, middle-aged woman rocking in the dark corner. "Is that your mother?"

"*Sí, mi madre*, with one of my brothers."

Ellie almost tripped over a boy slightly older than Luis. He was seated at his mother's feet, reading an American comic book in the dim light. She briefly wondered why someone didn't turn on the lights, ignite the candles, or whatever these folks did for illumination, but then she remembered they were keeping a low profile. The family of a fugitive lives in fear and whispers.

"We need to borrow some work clothes for Ellie," Carmen explained.

"Mine are too small," Sylvie replied. "But she can wear something of Roberto's."

Carmen stayed behind to talk with Mama Castillo, while Sylvie led Ellie into a long room behind the communal area. The children's dormitory had cots lined up at right angles to the walls. By the looks of it, boys slept on one side, girls on the other. Sylvie reached under an unmade bed and pulled out a box containing men's clothing. She handed Ellie wrinkled jeans and a T-shirt, which she quickly accepted, and then began to undress.

"How long has Roberto been living here?" she casually asked the girl.

"Two years, ever since the trouble. Doña Carmen comes every weekend, and my parents let them use their bedroom, so Roberto and Carmen can sleep together." Sylvie giggled.

So her original impression had been correct. This was a three-room shack with an outhouse hidden somewhere out back in the palm trees. The arrangement was pathetic. If Roberto was truly innocent of committing a crime, as he claimed, then husband and wife should not be living apart. He was like a prisoner on house arrest, receiving conjugal visits from his wife.

"Don Roberto helps Manuel in the fields," Sylvie continued. "And he's a hard worker. Since he came to live here, our coffee crop has doubled, but neither he nor my brother can show their faces in the light of day."

"How do they manage that?" She zipped Manuel's jeans over her too-wide hips, making a mental note to avoid deep-knee bends.

"They always wear the *pava*, a big straw hat, when they work. When strangers pass through the village, they bow their heads and hide."

"It's not fair, is it, Sylvie?" Ellie held her breath, hoping the girl would take the bait. If she gained her trust, maybe she would tell her the whole story.

"Not fair at all!" Sylvie violently agreed. "Manuel and Roberto had nothing to do with the bombing. Just because PIP took credit, does not mean *they* were to blame."

"What bombing?"

"The Gomez brothers did it. They are loco, not at all like my brother and Don Roberto. Everybody in Lares knows the truth, but the police will not believe it because the Gomez brothers signed the names *Manuel y Roberto* in their letter to the newspaper."

"Why would the Gomez brothers do that?"

"Manuel and Roberto believe the *Independentistas* can only win support through elections and talking to people, but the Gomez brothers do not. They think violence is the only way to get attention, and they wanted to punish my brother and Don Roberto. We still pray the Gomez boys will be captured and tell the truth, but no one knows where they are hiding. Maybe they left Puerto Rico, or maybe they are dead."

Ellie quickly finished dressing as she processed the information. If Sylvie's account was accurate, then the Valdez and Castillo families were the victims of injustice, and she wished she could help. She combed fingers through her unruly hair, tied it back in a no-nonsense ponytail, and then checked her image in a tiny mirror. Well, no one was likely to recognize her now, because she looked more like a boy, than a woman.

"Thanks for the clothes, Sylvie. I guess I'm ready now."

"It's about time." Carmen opened the door. "I overheard your little chat…" She scowled at the girl. "Go find your father, Sylvie. Tell him it's time to go."

Sylvie scuttled away, and Carmen said, "You have an interesting interrogation technique, Ms. Birdsong. You showed Sylvie a little sympathy and tricked her into airing the family's dirty laundry."

"Was Sylvie telling the truth?"

"When the American Bank in Ponce was bombed, PIP claimed responsibility. Remember the headlines? It made front page in the States, giving the Independence Movement a bad name."

"Yes, I remember. The bank's night watchman died in the explosion, so if your husband *is* guilty, then he's a murderer as well as a terrorist."

"If you knew him," Carmen said, "you'd realize he'd never resort to those tactics. Neither would Manuel. They became friends while serving the US Army in Iraq, where they both learned to hate violence for any cause."

She stared at Carmen in disbelief. "You say they met in *Iraq*? But they grew up only a few miles from one another in Puerto Rico. Manuel's dad worked for Roberto's dad, so they must have known one another as children."

"You still don't get it, do you, Ellie? Don Carlos, Roberto's father, was a self-important tyrant who didn't allow his children to play with the hired help. His imperial attitude was the main reason Roberto ran off to America, to escape his father's old-fashioned credo of *noblesse oblige*.

"Manuel took off for the States to escape this crushing poverty..." Carmen's sweeping gesture encompassed the poor little room where they stood. "Roberto joined the National Guard while he was at university, while Manuel signed on in the regular army to make a better life for himself. Neither expected to land tours of duty in the Middle East, or to meet a fellow Puerto Rican in Baghdad."

Ellie tried to imagine Carla's father as a feudal plantation lord. "Why didn't Carla leave home?"

Carmen laughed bitterly. "In case you haven't noticed, Carla Valdez is a woman of great principle and sacrifice. She stuck by her obnoxious old father until the bitter end, and since then, she's worked to eliminate the hurtful class distinctions that divide our people. She has devoted her life to being a good daughter, good mother to Maria's children, and a responsible steward of the land she inherited."

"And you resent her for that?"

"Hell, no, Ellie, I respect her more than I can say. In fact, I believe Roberto would have been better off if he'd stayed right here with his sister. Iraq changed him. All the killing, the political hypocrisy, and frankly, the discrimination against Puerto Ricans in the US Army, drove him right into the arms of PIP. It didn't have to be this way."

Next, Carmen pulled a green metal trunk out from under one of the cots, unlocked it with a key from her backpack, and lifted out a gun.

Ellie recoiled in surprise. "Apparently you and Roberto hold different views on nonviolence."

"Apparently so." Carmen smirked as she checked the safety, stashed the pistol in her pack. "This is Roberto's army-issue M9 Beretta. He hates the weapon, but I love target shooting. I did it for fun with my girlfriends in Miami."

Who the hell was this woman, Latina Rambo? Sure, Ellie had shot a few cans off the fence with her brothers, but Carmen seemed to take marksmanship a bit too seriously.

"Manuel told you to guard me," Ellie said. "Do you plan to use that thing on me?"

"Not if you behave yourself."

CHAPTER FIFTY

The far side of the moon…

Juan was waiting for them in his truck, with the engine running. He had a Havana cigar clamped between his teeth and his eyes reflected his determination. "What did I tell you, *señorita*, see the full moon?"

As they began the bumpy descent from Lares, the moon illuminated the rugged mountain landscape and cast long, eerie shadows across the highway. All three were sandwiched up front—Ellie in the middle, Carmen hugging the window—and the cab was tense with fear and anticipation.

"Where are we going?" Ellie asked.

"Not far, but it is very hard to drive into there," Juan said. "You will see some strange sights tonight. Some say the Karst Country is the oddest place on earth, like walking around on the far side of the moon."

"What's he talking about?"

Carmen responded with a strange smile. "It's definitely a weird place. Years ago, the limestone shelf under the island got exposed, leaving enormous white craters everywhere and little conical peaks in between. The sinkhole where they built the Arecibo Observatory is thirteen hundred feet wide and three hundred feet deep."

"What does this observatory observe? Space aliens?" Ellie joked. She knew better, but her nerves were on edge.

Carmen laughed. "Space aliens? Yes, that is what the locals thought. But in fact, it was a radar telescope that watched the ionosphere, according to the geeks who used to run it from Cornell University and the National Science Foundation."

"Right, I knew that, but you're describing it in the past tense. What happened to it?"

"Don't you follow the news? In December 2020, its mammoth radio telescope collapsed. Several cables that supported the 900-ton reflector dish broke, and the disc crashed into the valley, like a giant Frisbee."

"It was the end of an era," Juan sadly added. "They will not repair it, so they no longer have visitors or security guards at the facility."

Carmen said, "The PIP men spotted Carla's Honda on an isolated road leading into the hills. If Martinez lured Carla off the road up there, they could hide, or wander unnoticed, for days."

Not good news. Ellie stared at the landscape, which was more like a set from a science fiction movie than a resort island. She couldn't understand the players' motives. Hadn't Carla already promised to sign over her land to Dyna, to prevent Dyna from turning Roberto over to the police? If so, why was she wandering around in these hills after Diego Martinez? Was he responsible for the kidnapping?

"What if this is a trap? Did Martinez lead Carla here to pay a ransom? To sell her land to him, instead of to Dyna?"

"Who knows?" Carmen massaged her forehead. "Anything is possible. I expect by the time we arrive, Roberto and Manuel will have the situation well under control. After all, we gave them a good head start."

From her mouth to God's ear, as Ellie's mama used to say when she hoped for divine intervention. Perhaps Roberto and Manuel would locate Carla and Enrique, then capture Martinez, but she had her doubts. Her dark angels told her something was terribly wrong with the whole scenario, that they were missing some vital piece of the puzzle.

Suddenly, a police siren sounded behind them. The squad car's spinning red cherry illuminated their cab like a harbinger of doom.

"What should I do?" Juan panicked.

"Pull over," Carmen snapped. "What else can we do?"

The old truck sputtered to a stop, and they all sat in agitated silence as a tall policeman sauntered up to Juan's open window.

"*Qué pasa?*" Juan asked with a wide, unconvincing grin. The cop peered in at Carmen and Ellie, checked Juan's driver's license, and then asked for their names.

"*Ellas son* Señorita Diaz *y* Ellie Birdsong, *una Americana*," Juan responded in a nervous falsetto.

Ellie noticed Juan had introduced Carmen as *Diaz*, her maiden name, and now she understood why. In Carla's case, the name *Valdez* was a badge of honor. In Roberto's case, it was cause for shame.

"*Una Americana?*" The officer eyed Ellie good-naturedly. "I speak English. Welcome to our country, *señorita*."

"Thanks," Ellie mumbled as the officer lapsed back into Spanish and began scolding Juan. She turned to Carmen. "Did we do something wrong?"

"Believe it or not, he stopped us for a faulty taillight."

Ellie exhaled in heartfelt relief. This delay was unfortunate, but not fatal. Under different circumstances, she'd have latched onto this cop and begged for his help. But as things were, she didn't want to get Roberto arrested for a crime he maybe didn't commit. Did that make her an accomplice, or just plain stupid?

The officer handed Juan his license, and then smiled at Ellie. "I love it when Americans visit our country, but some folks on this island don't share my affection. Have you ever heard of our Independence Party, Ms. Birdsong?"

She nodded and twisted her sweating hands.

"Well, we captured two PIP leaders tonight, right here on this road," the cop bragged. "They were dangerous criminals, who bombed an American bank and killed a man." He paused, preening like a peacock.

Even in the dark, Ellie saw Carmen's face blanch white. She reached across the seat and held the stricken woman's icy hand. What terrifying thoughts were racing through her mind? Her husband had hidden in safety for so long, so why now, of all times, must he be caught?

"How did you know where to catch these outlaws?" Juan asked. Ellie marveled at the old man's calm when the cop shoved his head all the way into the cab.

The officer dropped his voice to a whisper. "Someone tipped us off. The informant told a lieutenant from San Juan to be on the watch, so this lieutenant followed the criminals all the way from Lares. You will read all about it in tomorrow's papers. Look for my name." The cop touched his nametag.

"Where did they take the PIP men?" Carmen's voice trembled.

"They are being held at the Ponce jail. I expect the trial will be in Ponce also, since that's where the bombing occurred."

"Congratulations, officer," Juan squawked, then started the engine.

The policeman withdrew and stood aside. "Don't forget to get that taillight fixed…" he called as they drove away.

They had moved only a few yards, when Juan began to curse and Carmen began to cry. Ellie was speechless with misery and guilt, because the arresting lieutenant was surely Colon, and she was the Judas who had supplied the tip, via her cabbie, Pablo. Her plan had backfired, and now they had no advance guard to confront the bad guys. Eventually, everyone would discover that she was the traitor, and she'd be screwed for all time.

"Turn around, Juan," Carmen wailed. "Take me to the Ponce jail."

Juan shook his head. "I'm not sure…"

Ellie pounded her fist on the dash, surprising everyone, including herself. "Carla and Enrique are in danger, and you want to quit? We can't help Roberto and Manuel now, but we can help Carla. Keep going, understand?"

Both seemed startled by her outburst. Juan mopped his face with a large handkerchief, while Carmen dried her eyes.

"She is right," Juan said at last. "Your husband and my son aren't going anywhere, Carmen. We must pray for them, and then hire good lawyers. Right now, Doña Carla needs us, and I have a pretty good idea where the PIP men spotted her car."

"But what can we do without the men to back us up?" Carmen asked.

"In case you haven't noticed, *I* am a man, Doña Carmen, and I am a good fighter!" Juan bristled. "And from what I have seen, Señorita Birdsong will be a formidable ally, too."

Juan floored the gas, and Ellie appreciated his vote of confidence as they sped into the night. Even Carmen offered her a grudging smile, so she figured she'd earned a measure of acceptance. On the other hand, the final ordeal still lay ahead, and the respect she'd won could easily be lost. She closed her eyes and said a frantic prayer.

CHAPTER FIFTY-ONE

The pit...

"This is it!"

Juan's deep voice jolted her back to reality, and she realized she'd been petrified in a daze of fear. She was exhausted, confused, and hoped to God she'd be of some help when the shit hit.

Carmen said, "Are you okay, Ellie?"

When Ellie scooted upright, her bruised ribs protested, her head throbbed. Had it been only that morning when Carla faced her in the study, told her to leave her house forever?

"I'm fine," she lied.

She gazed out the truck window, where the moonlight revealed breathtaking views of the odd karst hills, silhouetted against a midnight blue sky. Judging from how the old pickup lurched and swayed, they had left civilization far behind. Making the setting spookier still, Juan turned off their headlights.

"The observatory is down in that valley," he explained. "We are now officially trespassing."

In the eerie glow, she saw three tall towers, with a crooked platform suspended between them on cables. The enormous dish that once received radio signals lay like a broken platter hundreds of feet below. At the same time, she noticed something glistening from the bushes at the side of the road.

"Stop, Juan!" she shouted. "Back up, I think I saw Carla's Honda."

Sure enough, the car was barely concealed, as though Carla had left it in a hurry. The three stepped cautiously across the rocky ground, approached the vehicle, found it unlocked, and unoccupied. Ellie smelled a trace of Carla's cologne, which triggered a fresh onslaught of emotion.

Weird limestone pits surrounded them, while the cone-like hills cast illusive shadows on the ground. Juan pointed to a natural pathway through the limestone. "Let's try that direction," he said.

Forming a single file, they began the arduous climb. Ellie's body rebelled, and several times she almost lost her balance, making her grateful for her trusty old tennis shoes. They piled into one another when Carmen pointed out Diego Martinez's shiny black Hummer. It was garaged in a natural cavern, where a shallow rushing stream washed the undersides of its white-walled tires.

"*Madre Maria!*" Juan exclaimed. "It took some skill to drive onto that rock shelf, unless there's another route into this place. Maybe Martinez knows a different entrance?"

"You got that right, my friend..." The deep voice startled them from behind. "I am one of very few who knows the secrets of the Karst Country. In fact, my mother's family owns this part of our little world."

Ellie's heart contracted in terror as she recognized the voice, the same slimy tenor she'd heard that day in the Ponce market. Taking Juan's arm for moral support, she turned to confront the speaker. "Mr. Martinez, I see we've come to the right place."

"Indeed you have, Señorita Birdsong. What took you so long?"

Carmen stiffened at her side, and Ellie hoped that for once, Carmen would keep her fiery temper in check. Juan, too, was shaking with anger, but in reality, they were all helpless as they stared at Martinez's Ruger automatic handgun.

"I thought you were from the Dominican Republic?" Ellie absurdly asked the man. "How come your family owns land here in the Karst Country?"

He laughed. "You are correct. I was born in the Dominican Republic and grew up there with my father's family. But Mother is as Puerto Rican as Mr. Juan Castillo here. What does it matter, my dear Ms. Birdsong? We are all citizens of the same planet, no?"

"You were expecting us?" Carmen was incredulous.

Just then, another man stepped from the shadows, and Ellie's stomach lurched as she recognized the thug who attacked her in the garden. He moved closer, smiling through his dead fish eyes.

"Nice to see you again, Ms. Birdsong." He tipped his ball cap. "Yes, we knew you were coming. We have a special radio, and our favorite channel is the police frequency." He waggled a rude finger in Juan's face. "Shame on you, Castillo. How careless to drive with only one taillight."

"How do you know our names?" Carmen asked.

"We make it our business to know everything that concerns us," Martinez said.

"Carla and Enrique are *my* only concern," Ellie interrupted. "Where are they, you bastard?"

"Mind your manners!" Fish Eyes rammed his knuckles into her ribs, causing them to vibrate with the pain inflicted the last time this asshole hurt her. "My boss asks the questions, bitch, and you supply the answers, *comprende?*"

Juan sprang forward like an enraged bull, shoving at Martinez's gun hand, then going for his throat. When Fish Eyes interceded, Ellie heard a sickening thud, followed by a groan. Carmen screamed when Juan toppled to the ground.

"What have you done?" Ellie cried.

"Relax, lady, it was only a love tap." He wiped Juan's blood off the butt of his pistol with a large handkerchief. "The stupid old man will recover, but he'll have one hell of a headache in the morning."

Carmen yanked at the handkerchief in the man's hand. "Please let me make Juan a bandage."

Fish Eyes held the handkerchief aloft, laughing.

"Let her do it." Martinez snorted with disgust. "When she's done, tie Castillo up in the back seat of my Hummer. I prefer the old fool's wound be covered, otherwise he'd bleed on my white leather upholstery."

Once Carmen completed her nursing, they watched Martinez's bodyguard haul Juan's sack-like body down into the cavern. The episode resembled a scene from a Hollywood thriller, with gruesome special effects heightened by the haunted setting.

Martinez waved his Ruger at them. "Stay on this path and move, ladies," he directed. "I'll be right behind you. When you see a cave up on the right, go inside."

"This cave is your personal mountain retreat?" Ellie inquired snidely. "I've had more hospitable welcomes."

"Don't complain, *señorita*. Under the circumstances, you are lucky to be invited at all. Perhaps you would prefer an engraved invitation to the bottom of the river?"

The entrance to the cave was lit by a series of acrid-smelling kerosene lanterns set on the rocky floor, and as they moved deeper into the pit, she heard a scratchy radio broadcasting from the damp depths.

"Take the next left." Martinez prodded them with the barrel of his gun.

Carmen said, "You guys don't maintain a very low profile. Aren't you afraid someone will discover your little hideaway?"

"As you Americans say, we have covered all our bases. If an uninvited guest comes within one hundred yards, we'll see him before he sees us."

"What about Carla Valdez?" Ellie interrupted. "Did you see *her* coming?"

"Why don't you ask her yourself?" Martinez snickered. "Doña Carla is always a lady. I am sure she will answer all your questions."

CHAPTER FIFTY-TWO

The wolf's clothing...

They stooped low, passed through a cavity in the cave wall, then entered a small, natural chamber. Ever since Martinez mentioned Carla's name, affirming that she was indeed being held there, Ellie's stomach had churned with an upsetting mixture of fear and anticipation, both aggravated to the point of nausea by the potent kerosene fumes. Two more lanterns hooked to the wall illuminated the space, and as her eyes adjusted to the shadowy interior, she saw a metal table and chairs set up at the center of the room. A new guard armed with a rifle stood behind one of the chairs, where a forlorn figure sat with her head buried in her hands.

"My God, Carla, are you all right?" Ellie bolted, hoping to reach her, but Martinez grabbed her wrist.

Carla still wore the same white blouse and tan slacks she'd worn that morning, now filthy with mud. As she slowly lifted her head, Ellie saw a flicker of hope in her eyes, which immediately changed to despair.

"I've seen better days, Ellie. But I guess you and your associates already know that." She then turned to her sister-in-law. "Carmen, why did you bring her? Don't we already have enough trouble?"

"For a smart woman, you can be downright ignorant, Carla Valdez!" Ellie cried, her heart breaking.

Martinez shoved Ellie and Carmen down into chairs. "Keep your big mouths shut while Doña Carla and I complete our business."

Carla said, "I am so sorry, Carmen. Martinez knew I would follow him here, and I walked right into his trap. But I never meant to involve you and Roberto."

Martinez said, "I knew you were up to something when you refused to sign this morning, Doña Carla. I figured you'd bring your outlaw brother and his pathetic band of rebels into the mix."

"Leave Roberto out of this!" Carmen hissed. "You aren't fit to speak his name."

"Will you shut her up?" Martinez shouted.

The new guard, with long black hair tied back in a ponytail, put down his rifle and lurched across the room. He hit Carmen across the mouth with the back of his hand.

Carla sprang to her feet, but Martinez buried his gun in her ribs, while Ellie sat helplessly by.

"Congratulations, Diego." Carla's voice was thick with misery. "Now you can add attacking women to your résumé of accomplishments."

"I asked Carmen politely, but the lady chose not to listen. If she interrupts again, she'll get more than a harmless slap."

Martinez eased Carla back into her chair at gunpoint, while Carmen's eyes overflowed with tears. Ellie knew the disgusting man would not tolerate another outburst, so no matter what happened next, she had to come up with a plan that would keep them all safe.

Martinez fished an expensive cigar from his pocket and lit up. Its ghastly stench, combined with the kerosene fumes, made her more nauseous as he propped his fat rump on the edge of the steel table.

"We made our retreat into the Karst Country as obvious as possible," Martinez continued. "Manuel's men could not miss seeing my Hummer. I took a chance in assuming that you would follow, Doña Carla, but I'm a gambler by profession."

"Is Enrique here?" Ellie asked, swallowing the bile in her throat.

"No, he's not here," Carla interjected angrily. "If he were, I'm sure these assholes would drag him out to apply additional pressure."

Ellie knew the pressure on Carla was intolerable, as long as the child's whereabouts remained unknown. She prayed for Enrique and tried to think clearly. How could she gain Diego Martinez's trust? Mama always warned her against *wolves masquerading in sheep's clothing*. Well, so far, she had behaved like a helpless lamb. It was time to be one of the bad guys and fight like a wolf.

She turned to Martinez. "I still don't understand why you lured Carla here. Couldn't we have gotten her signature some other way?"

Diego lifted his eyebrows. "Whose side are you on, Ms. Birdsong? My sources tell me you quit your job."

She looked squarely into his beady eyes. "You're wrong. I left San Juan because Dyna tried to seduce me. She's my boss, but she's also a married woman."

"Ah yes, you are both lesbians." Martinez smirked.

Ellie was mortified as she glimpsed Carla listening in stony disgust.

"Dyna is a persistent woman," Ellie muttered.

The gorilla with a ponytail whistled and grabbed at his crotch.

"So you were running away from an *amorío*?" Martinez winked at the guy. "But tell me, Ms. Birdsong, why should I believe you have my best interests at heart?"

She sat up straight, wiped her sweaty palms on her jeans. "My career is down the crapper, and I've worked too hard to blow this. Let me help you. I'll share DynaCo's blueprints and research. I'll do everything I can to facilitate the sale. I share your interests, Mr. Martinez, because you are the only game left in town."

Carla laughed bitterly. The cold, heartless sound twisted a knife in Ellie's heart as she turned back to Martinez. "Why *did* you bring Carla here?"

"When Doña Carla refused to sign, we couldn't understand why she wasn't cooperating. Her brother had been threatened and her son had been kidnapped. She was desperate, and we feared she might contact the cops, or the FBI."

"Would I go to the police and endanger Enrique's life?" Carla cried. "You're an idiot, Diego, and don't forget, I'm not the only one who cares about Enrique and the fate of the Valdez land."

"You mean Roberto and his PIP buddies? If you were counting on them to act as your private army, I regret to inform you that they won't be coming to your rescue."

Before anyone could restrain her, Carmen lunged. "You tipped off the cops? I'll kill you, Martinez!"

She almost connected with a swift jab to his jaw, but Ponytail was fully alert. He tripped Carmen and caught her in his strong hands. Ellie watched in stunned disbelief as the man squeezed the back of her neck between his thumb and index finger, and she wilted to the ground, unconscious.

"I did warn her…" Martinez blandly commented and relit his cigar.

At the same time, the bodyguard with dead fish eyes appeared at the opening to their room. "You okay, boss? The old man is secured in the Hummer, now what?"

"Get Señorita Birdsong and Carmen out of here. Tie them up with Juan Castillo, and I'll deal with them all later."

CHAPTER FIFTY-THREE

A mouthful of lies...

Ponytail took hold of Carmen's shoulders, while Fish Eyes lifted her ankles. Much to Ellie's relief, Carmen stirred when they started to move her. She looked up at Ellie with a drugged, uncomprehending stare.

It was now, or never. Ellie appealed directly to Martinez. "You're making a big mistake. Let me stay, and I will help you get what you want."

"Leave now, Ellie," Carla seemed to urge through bloodshot eyes. "I hate the sight of you."

The cruel words hurt, yet she persisted. "Listen, Martinez, *I* was the one who tipped the cops about Roberto and Manuel. *I* alerted Lieutenant Colon and told him where to catch them. Thanks to me, they're behind bars and out of your way. Doesn't that prove I'm working for your team?"

She couldn't bear to look at Carla, who was cursing under her breath. At the same time, Carmen's eyes fluttered open and focused, accusing Ellie with silent hatred. She now knew Ellie was responsible for her husband's imprisonment.

Martinez stared long and hard. "Okay, I am impressed, Señorita Birdsong. The Puerto Rican police have been after Manuel and Roberto for two years, and you claim to have ended the search with one phone call?"

"Not a phone call, a note."

"You expect me to believe that?"

Ponytail bent over, whispered something into Martinez's ear, and the next time Martinez faced her, she saw respect in his eyes.

"Perhaps I spoke too soon," he said. "Take Carmen Valdez to my car, but Señorita Birdsong can stay. Maybe she'll be of help, after all."

Only after the guards had carried Carmen from the cave, did Ellie dare look at Carla. Her face was ashen with defeat.

"Is this true, Ellie? My brother has been captured, and you are to blame?"

In the past few minutes, Ellie had told a mouthful of lies, but Carla's accusation stood alone as the gospel truth. She never meant for Roberto and Manuel to be the victims of her note, but it happened anyway. She nodded at Carla, confirming her complicity.

Martinez smiled. "She has done well. I understand the police radios have been buzzing with the story. She has done me a great favor, and I'm grateful. May I call you Ellie?"

He pointed at a briefcase on the table. "I have drawn up an Agreement of Sale, and now that Doña Carla understands that no one is coming to her rescue, she will sign willingly, right, Doña Carla?"

Carla lifted her face and stared at Ellie, her eyes filled with pain and confusion. "Roberto and Carmen tried to warn me about you, Ellie, but I refused to believe them. Even this morning, when I forced you to leave my home, I still hoped that you weren't involved."

She stopped to clear her throat, as though her next question was too painful to ask. "Tell me, did you also help plan Enrique's kidnapping?"

Ellie might win points by saying *yes*, but the gangster already knew she'd not been party to his horrendous plot.

"No, Carla, I had nothing to do with Enrique's kidnapping."

Martinez nodded approvingly, as though she had passed some test.

He said, "For once Ellie is telling the truth, Doña Carla. Now that that's settled, I hope she will help me execute this Agreement—after all, she is a real estate agent."

"I will gladly help you with the papers," Ellie said.

She noticed Carla was watching her, with an odd expression on her face.

Ellie played along as Martinez fetched his briefcase and extracted the legal documents. Finally, he tucked his pistol into its shoulder holster in order to shuffle the papers.

"Listen to me, Ellie," Carla said. "If I sign the Agreement, will Martinez honor his end of the deal? What makes you think he'll release Enrique, Carmen, and Juan once he gets what he wants?"

She glanced at Martinez, who said nothing.

"You see?" Carla pressed. "He'll kill us all, we know too much."

Her blood froze as the truth of Carla's words hit home. "No, Martinez won't hurt us, Carla." She struggled to keep her voice steady.

"How will you stop him?" Carla persisted.

She felt trapped and desperate as Martinez went about his business, calmly spreading pages out on the metal surface. He was bent over the table, already counting his profits, when she realized that Carla had been right all along. Whether she had signed this morning, or now, Carla could not guarantee the safety of her loved ones. Martinez could not be trusted, so Carla's only option had always been a violent reversal of fortune. She had hoped Roberto and his men could fight and win, but thanks to Ellie, that hope was gone.

"You should sign, Carla," she urged unhappily. "Martinez *might* honor his word."

"The man doesn't know the meaning of honor." Carla was still watching her with an odd intensity. "But do I have a choice?"

Before Ellie could answer, Ponytail burst into the room, weapon in hand. "Mr. Martinez, I hate to disturb you, but I've lost your bodyguard. We locked the woman in the Hummer, then headed back. He was right behind me on the trail, but now he is gone."

"How can he be gone?" Martinez's fat lips puckered with displeasure.

"A car was parked in the bushes near Doña Carla's Honda: a beige cop car, with a radio transmitter and a magnetic cherry light on the front seat."

Martinez removed his pistol from its holster and cautiously edged toward the doorway. Ponytail swung his rifle to ready, while Ellie held her breath, hardly daring to hope as a burst of sharp, crackling gunfire exploded somewhere out in the night.

"It's the police!" Ponytail shouted, flattening himself against the stone wall.

"Shit." Martinez waved his gun toward the exit. "You go have a look, while I keep my eye on these two."

Ponytail departed, leaving Carla and her alone with Martinez, whose flushed face was beaded with perspiration. Ellie didn't like the way his gun hand trembled.

She said, "Mr. Martinez, Carla should sign the Agreement now. Just in case…"

He frowned, but walked resolutely back toward the table. He shifted the gun to his left hand, then patted his shirt pocket with his right. "Damn! Where's my pen?"

"Just a minute, I have one…" Ellie told him.

The time had come to make her move.

Her fingers felt stiff and lifeless as she reached down to retrieve the backpack Carmen had left sitting on the floor between their chairs. She bit down hard on her lower lip, hoping the pain would keep her focused as she unclasped the bag and searched inside. The M9 Beretta felt cold and slick as she rapidly released the safety, and gave silent thanks to her brothers, who had taught her to shoot all those years ago. Then, like a sleepwalker in a nightmare, her numb fingers tightened on the weapon.

"Where's the damn pen?" Martinez whined.

"I'm sure it's here somewhere…" As she pretended to search, building her courage, another round of gunfire ripped through the stillness.

Carla noticed what Ellie was doing and staggered to her feet. "Give up, Martinez," she said in a low, threatening voice. "The police are here."

As Martinez spun to face Carla, his little pig eyes were wild with fear. He pointed his pistol at her chest.

Carla held out her hand. "Give me the gun. Can't you see it's over?"

Another burst of gunfire shattered the night, and Martinez's finger trembled on the trigger.

"I'll kill you before I let them arrest me!" he screamed at Carla.

"Don't do it, Martinez!" Ellie pulled out the Beretta, took aim, and braced her wrist with her left hand.

She couldn't tell which shot came first, but their small space exploded. Her hand and forearm vibrated with the impact of firing, and she froze in fascination as a small round stain blossomed like a rose on Martinez's white sleeve. His eyes expanded in surprise as he buckled, then toppled to the floor.

At the same time, she sensed movement to her left and lowered her arm in time to see Carla's hand lift to a place above her heart. Her fingers were red as a sunset. She lurched forward, then dropped to her knees. Moments later, she was lying face down on the floor.

CHAPTER FIFTY-FOUR

Cop for a day…

Dear God! Her ears rang as she fell to her knees and stroked the warm skin of Carla's cheek. She kissed the soft fullness of her lips. "I love you," she whispered.

"She can't hear you, Ms. Birdsong," a man's voice gently intruded.

She looked up into sad blue eyes, then looked down to brush a lock of thick black hair from Carla's forehead. But when she tried to cradle Carla's head on her lap, strong hands pulled her away.

"Let me help," the man said.

She blinked uncomprehendingly as his lips moved below a pencil-thin moustache. "Lieutenant Colon?" She watched in a daze as the lieutenant carefully rolled Carla onto her back. He unbuttoned the blood-soaked blouse, examined the wound.

"Doesn't look serious, thank God. The bullet missed her heart and lungs. It entered the fleshy part of her shoulder. One inch lower, and Doña Carla would be dead."

In this night of horrors, she could not believe the hopeful news.

He continued, "She'll be mighty sore for a couple of weeks, and she'll have to wear a sling, but Doña Carla should be out of the hospital in a day or two."

"Call an ambulance!" Ellie cried.

"Already on the way." A second male voice approached through the shadows. "It's coming from Arecibo. It'll be here in a matter of minutes."

She squinted up at a red Yankees baseball cap. It was turned backward above a close-cropped Afro. "Pablo?"

"Who else? Your personal cabbie, reporting for duty."

"But how did you get here?" Her mind was playing tricks.

"Gotta confess, Ellie. I read your note the second I left Casa Valdez and figured my CB radio would be way faster than hand delivery. The good lieutenant was already in the neighborhood, so we hooked up ASAP. Once he realized how invaluable I was to the operation, he let me play cop for a day."

Colon grunted. "Actually, Pablo blackmailed me. He wouldn't fill in the blanks until I agreed to let him tag along."

She held Carla's hand, as Colon and Pablo bantered back and forth.

"Yeah, but *I'm* the paramedic." Pablo knelt and opened a First Aid kit.

"Maybe we should wait for the ambulance," Ellie said.

Pablo playfully jabbed her elbow. "Oh woman of little faith, I was a medic in the National Guard. The enlisted women thought I was hot. I should have been a doctor, but after tonight, I'd rather be a cop."

"God help the police force," Colon muttered as Pablo cleaned and bandaged Carla's shoulder.

Their chatter made Ellie dizzy, while the stench of kerosene, cigar smoke, and sulfur from the gunshots made her light-headed. "What about Diego Martinez?" she asked as the implications of her own actions finally hit her jumbled brain. "Did I kill the bastard?"

Colon chuckled, then gestured to where Martinez was propped in the corner like a beached toad. He whimpered and picked at his sleeve, while a policeman she hadn't noticed before stood beside him, looking on in disgust. "Martinez will recover to enjoy a long life in jail, and I won't have to arrest you for homicide, Señorita Birdsong."

"That was some righteous marksmanship, Ellie," Pablo said. "Where'd you learn to shoot like that? Carla Valdez will be mighty grateful when she wakes up. If you hadn't shot Martinez's gun arm, then she'd be a goner."

She squeezed her eyes to force back tears. God, what if she had lost Carla? She couldn't claim to be a marksman, but her lucky shot had prevented the unthinkable. Still, nothing had changed. When Carla regained consciousness, she'd still hate her, never forgive her for putting her entire family in jeopardy.

"When Carla wakes up, she'll be grateful if I'm a million miles away," she told the men. They gave her quizzical looks, but eventually they'd understand that she was no heroine, not by a long shot.

"You're wrong. She will thank you." Pablo insisted. "The cops know you helped them catch the PIP outlaws."

She dropped her head between her knees. "Don't you guys get it? Why would Carla thank me for putting her brother behind bars? And even if she believed I wasn't directly responsible for his capture, she thinks my boss helped kidnap her son."

"Did she?" Colon frowned.

"You've found Enrique, right?" she demanded.

The officers' dead silence said it all. Enrique was still missing.

Ellie felt like she was going to throw up. "I honestly don't know if Dyna Collins was in on it," she told Colon.

He spread his hands. "It's not as bad as you think, *señorita*."

"Then where is Enrique?" she wailed.

"Señor Martinez does not deal well with pain. He just told us where to find the boy." Colon rocked proudly on his heels. "He says Enrique is safe…with his father."

CHAPTER FIFTY-FIVE

Only the good times...

Ellie felt gut-punched. "Oh my God, he can't be with his father! The man wants to steal Enrique and his brother from Carla. He has no custody rights."

Colon shrugged. "He's still their father."

"No, you need to get him back right now. What are you waiting for?"

The men in the cave stared at her like she'd lost her mind.

When she climbed up from the floor, the blood in her head rushed to her feet and the room started to spin. The guys must have figured she was about to faint, because two pairs of hands eased her back down. She lay flat and reached again for Carla's upturned hand. Although it seemed lifeless, its warmth was comforting. "Did you hear that, Carla?" she whispered. "Enrique is okay."

Carla's lips moved, but her voice was nearly inaudible. "He's not *okay* if he's with Joey Arroyo." She squeezed Ellie's hand. "I need *you* to find him, Ellie."

"Joey Arroyo? The basketball star?" Pablo was thrilled. "That's fucking awesome! I wanna meet him."

Colon gave Pablo an exasperated look, then turned to Ellie. "I don't need assistance from a cabbie with attitude."

"Please let me help," Pablo begged.

Colon sighed. "Look Pablo, since you're already playing doctor, wait here for the ambulance. Once they've transported Doña Carla and Martinez, then you can help the paramedics tend the old man and the woman who were locked in Martinez's Hummer."

She had almost forgotten about Carmen and Juan. "Are they okay?"

"They are unhurt, *señorita*." The cop guarding Martinez spoke up. "I checked on them coming in. Both were coherent, and said they had no life-threatening injuries."

"Did you hear that, Carla?" Was it her imagination, or had Carla's eyes shifted under her lids?

"She can't hear you," Colon said. "She's out cold again. Doña Carla won't wake up anytime soon, and when she does, she'll be grateful for a Demerol drip in her vein."

"I'm coming with you to find Enrique," she said.

"That's not happening," Colon said with finality. "What you must do is take Doña Carla's car back to Casa Valdez. Do you think you can handle that?"

Suddenly both Pablo and Colon hauled her to her feet.

"Don't worry, Ellie, I will take good care of Doña Carla and the others," her cabbie said.

"Thanks, Pablo, how will I ever repay you?"

He tipped his red ball cap. "Don't worry, I'll think of something..."

She turned to Colon. "But how will you locate Joey Arroyo? He could have the boy on a flight to Philly by now."

"No, we have already alerted the airlines. He's on the island, and we will find him."

She stole one last look at Carla's face, which was strangely peaceful, almost like it had been when she was sleeping beside Ellie, on her pillow at El Rincón. The memory caused a sharp pang of sorrow, and she promised herself that in the lonely years ahead, she would remember only the good times with Carla.

CHAPTER FIFTY-SIX

Into the night…

While Colon's partner and Pablo stayed behind with Martinez and Carla, she and Colon navigated through the rocky passages and into the night. The full moon had risen high in the sky. She filled her lungs with fresh air and gazed at the heavens, swearing she would never venture into a cave again.

Her foot bumped against a log. When she glanced down, she saw dead fish eyes staring up at the stars. The back of the man's head had been blown away, and gooey bits of brain matter clung to the bushes.

"Jesus Christ!" Her stomach turned inside out. She stepped away from the corpse, leaned on a rock, and lost what was left of the American-style breakfast Dyna had bought her that morning, a lifetime ago.

"You okay?" Colon asked, steadying her.

"Where's the other one, the man with the ponytail?"

"Alive, but wounded. He and Martinez will share a secure ambulance."

She caught her breath. "Sorry, it's just that I got mugged by that guy, and now he's dead."

"Very much dead." Colon shook his head and guided her to the road, where three ambulances were arriving. One for the bad guys, one for Carla, and one for the corpse, she figured. So much violence. How had it gotten so out of control?

She saw Carmen and Juan seated on a rock down near the Hummer, both with their heads buried in their hands. "How will they get home?"

"They won't be going home right away. We're taking them to the station for statements. Another officer will drive Mr. Castillo's truck to Casa Valdez, but we still need you to return the Honda."

She watched as two other squad cars parked. A female officer got out and began stringing crime scene tape around the rocky outcroppings. Absurdly, it looked like festive yellow ribbon on a dark and dusty cake.

Colon said, "You will do that for us, right, Señorita Birdsong? Drive the Honda back?"

"Yes, of course," she lied.

"Thank you very much." He smiled under the pencil moustache and ran his fingers through hair that looked like spun corn silk in the moonlight. "And I hope you have a pleasant trip back to the States."

He gave her the keys, helped her into Carla's car, and watched intently until she drove away.

She retraced their path into the Arecibo Observatory, but pulled off at the first opportunity. She backed into a little cranny between boulders and cut the lights. From this hidden vantage point, she could watch the procession of official traffic coming and going from the cave. Not long into the caravan, two of the ambulances passed with lights spinning and sirens burping. One was clearly transporting a very precious passenger.

Easing back onto the road, she followed Carla to the hospital.

CHAPTER FIFTY-SEVEN

Hiding in plain sight...

Carla swam in and out of consciousness. She knew she was at Hospital Pavia Arecibo and had just left the emergency room. The recovery area was somewhat private, hung with pale blue partition curtains. She was hooked to an intravenous drip, machines beeped, staff chattered beyond her curtain, and the lights were too bright.

In other words, it was much like every hospital she'd visited, and all those memories were bad. The last year of Maria's losing battle with cancer had been a nightmare of successive hospital rooms, a blur of doctors, and a time she desperately wanted to put behind her.

"Ms. Valdez, are you able to talk to me now?" The man had an American accent and spoke to her in English. He smelled like heated cotton from a clothes dryer.

Dragging her eyes open, she saw a crisply uniformed cop loaded down with a gun belt, handcuffs, and a clipboard. He introduced himself, said he'd been with her in the cave, but she promptly forgot his name.

"You talk, I'll listen," she managed through parched lips.

"You were lucky, ma'am. Mr. Martinez's weapon was a little Ruger SR22, so the bullet was small. The docs tell me you suffered a flesh wound, a through-and-through in the muscles of your upper left arm. It didn't hit any bones, arteries, or nerves, so you're gonna be fine."

She felt neither lucky, nor fine, but the officer's words brought back the carnage in the cave in living color. She had been there with Martinez, and Ellie.

"Oh God, is Ellie hurt?" Her panic triggered one of her monitors. Its crazy beeping brought an anxious nurse running into her room.

The nurse cursed the cop in Spanish until he promised to leave the room.

"I see now is not a good time," he said. "I'll come back tomorrow, ma'am."

"What about Ellie?" she pleaded to no avail as he made a quick retreat.

The nurse, who had kind blue eyes and wore scrubs printed with colorful little jungle animals, told her to calm down as she dimmed the lights. She offered more morphine and fussed with the bandage that felt like a giant diaper on her upper left body.

"No, *gracias*." Carla refused the pain meds. Now that she'd recaptured the scene from the cave, she needed her wits about her to sort it out. But unfortunately, the nurse ignored her refusal, for she saw her inject something into her IV.

Poor, dear Ellie. The pieces were jumbled like a jigsaw puzzle, where past collided with present. Images from Maria's hospital rooms, when Carla believed she would never again find happiness, to now, when Ellie had changed all that.

What had happened to Ellie? She recalled the gunshots, the pain, and Ellie holding her as she lay on the cold, rocky floor. Long before the violence, she had realized that Ellie had not betrayed her. She was trying to save them. She remembered her lifting the gun from Carmen's backpack, but then what?

Something about Enrique? She couldn't make the image clear, and as the drugs took her, she drifted back into a troubled sleep.

Someone was holding her hand. Soft, cool fingers stroked her forehead and called her name.

"Carla, can you hear me?"

The voice was gentle and loving. "Ellie?"

"Yes, I'm here."

Pulling herself out of the depths, she opened her eyes and found her visitor was real. With her right hand, she touched Ellie's face and felt tears.

"Ellie, were you hurt?"

"No, dear Carla, I'm fine. But how are you?"

She didn't have the strength or desire to talk about herself. Instead, she begged for a full recap of their night of horrors, and Ellie obliged. Though still foggy, she understood two important details: Ellie was unhurt, Enrique was still missing.

"They said he was with Joey Arroyo. Oh, Ellie, he can't be with that man!"

"No, he can't. How can I find him?"

She clung to Ellie's hand and tried to picture where Maria's scumbag of an ex might hole up with a little boy. She couldn't stop blaming herself. She should have been more careful with both her sons, once she knew the asshole was on the island.

"I was a fool, Ellie. Enrique had never met his father, but he'd seen pictures. He might have gotten into a car with him…"

"Stop! Don't even go there. It's not your fault, Carla. Please try to think where Joey would take him."

Knowing the lazy son-of-a-bitch, Arroyo would take the path of least resistance. Being a creature of habit, he would do what he always did.

"He's staying at the Condado Vanderbilt Hotel in San Juan," she said with certainty. "He always stays there. It's a flashy place with a cigar lounge, and he loves to smoke those filthy things."

"Hiding in plain sight," Ellie commented.

"Exactly. A guy with his son, who would question it?" She reached up to touch Ellie's face again. She longed to pull her down beside her in the narrow bed, and together sink into oblivion, but she said, "Promise you won't go there, Ellie. Call the police."

But Ellie did not answer. Instead, she bent down and kissed her lips. She tasted like salty tears, like the ocean. As the kiss deepened, Carla felt herself slipping away into a good place. By the time Ellie said goodbye, she was drifting in space.

CHAPTER FIFTY-EIGHT

Irony of ironies…

As Ellie left Hospital Pavia Arecibo and walked toward Avenue San Luis, where she had hastily parked the Honda, she wasn't entirely surprised when Lieutenant Colon whistled and beckoned her over to his unmarked Crown Vic. She was surprised to see two more squad cars parked nearby.

"I should have known you would not do as I asked. Why didn't you return the car to Casa Valdez?" he said.

"You never said I should go *directly* there."

He sighed. "How is Doña Carla?"

"Hanging in. But if you'll excuse me, I'm in a hurry."

"Buenas noches, señorita," A very tall, uniformed officer detained her. "Remember me? Have you had that taillight fixed yet?"

"You're the one who stopped Juan's truck on the way to Lares!"

"Sí, what a coincidence." He smiled.

"No coincidence," Colon said. "We were stopping all motorists leaving Lares last night. I had followed you into the village, Señorita Birdsong, and I wanted to be sure you would not slip out unnoticed.

"When I saw you leave the town in that rusty old truck, I asked this officer to stop Juan Castillo and confirm your identity. It was a bonus when we captured the two PIP outlaws in the same general sweep."

The statement stopped her in her tracks. "Run that by me again. Are you saying you caught Roberto Valdez and Manuel Castillo *by mistake?*"

Colon laughed. "I'm afraid so. Pablo would like to take credit, but by the time he contacted me on his CB radio and read me your note, the criminals were already in custody. Normally Roberto and Manuel would not be careless, but I now realize they were distracted by their eagerness to find Doña Carla and Enrique. They fell into my dragnet, and none of us could believe our good fortune."

"So you were following *me?* But why?"

Colon chuckled again. "Mainly due to your connection with Doña Carla." Colon reddened and cleared his throat, causing her to wonder if his men had been spying when Carla and she spent the night in El Rincón. "Not only were we concerned about Diego Martinez's sudden appearance in San Juan and his meetings with Doña Carla, we also sensed that Doña Carla was getting careless. She was making trips into the country, and we had a hunch she was meeting with her fugitive brother."

"Were you also looking for Carmen Diaz?"

"Yes, of course. She has been aiding and abetting those criminals for years. That's why I stopped Doña Carla the night you two rode in the glass-bottomed boat. I had heard rumors that Carmen was staying at Casa Valdez, and we figured she would eventually lead us to her husband."

"So you knew nothing about the land sale, or the kidnapping?"

Colon blushed three deeper shades of crimson. "No, I'm ashamed to admit I knew nothing of those problems until tonight."

Irony of ironies. Carla would never believe that in the end, Ellie was not responsible for Roberto's arrest.

"Believe it, or not, Roberto has been very cooperative from behind bars. He is extremely worried about the boy who is missing."

"What did you expect? Enrique is his nephew. He loves him."

The lieutenant's ears glowed with embarrassment. "You are right, he is a loving uncle."

"I'm also sure that he and Manuel are not guilty of bombing the American Bank," she snapped.

Colon stared straight ahead. "Right again. We now know they are almost certainly innocent. After listening to their stories, my investigators made inquiries regarding two local hoods called the Gomez brothers. The international terrorist database confirmed that the Gomez boys left the island two years ago. They were recently arrested for anti-American activities, including a bank bombing in Miami. Although they have not yet confessed to the bombing in Ponce, I believe they will. So it's just a matter of time until your friends are released with apologies."

"You should release them tonight, damn it!" After two years of living in the shadows, of looking over their shoulders in fear, she figured it was high time justice was served to Roberto and Manuel, hopefully on a silver platter.

"No can do, señorita," Colon said. "But I do have a consolation prize..." He reached into his car and dragged out a plastic evidence bag. "I brought this along in case our paths crossed again tonight. Go on, open it."

Inside were the ragged remains of what used to be her purse. She located her wallet—minus all her cash—but inside the secret pocket, she found her driver's license and credit cards.

"Where did you get this?"

"The maid who works in the kitchen at the Parguera Hotel discovered it in the bushes the morning after you were attacked. Seems the girl took quite a liking to you, so she turned it in right away."

Suddenly she remembered the beautiful necklace Carla had given her—the sun and moon entwined as lovers, and she recalled the moment when the now-dead Fish Eyes had yanked it off her neck.

"Did the girl from the kitchen find anything else?"

Colon smiled mischievously. "Check out that little brown envelope."

Sure enough, the envelope was in the purse's inner pocket, with her cherished necklace inside. As she fingered the silver charm, fresh tears sprang to her eyes. "I'm so glad you found my purse and necklace, but why didn't you return them sooner?"

Again Colon blushed. "I am sorry, Ms. Birdsong. The cops in Ponce dismissed your story, but when you told me last night that you had been attacked by our dead man, an American assailant with connections to Martinez, I believed you. I asked the two jackass officers from Ponce to messenger your belongings to me immediately. Now that you have your credit cards, you can book a flight back home."

She stashed her ruined purse into Carmen's backpack, which Ellie had retrieved, minus the gun, and vowed to be grateful for small blessings. Colon was right about one thing: now that she had her credit cards, she could book a flight home to Atlantic City.

"I just might do that, Lieutenant Colon. But first I have some business to attend to..." Turning abruptly, she left him standing in her wake.

CHAPTER FIFTY-NINE

Eyes on the prize...

Like the old spiritual said: *keep your eyes on the prize, hold on*. Every part of Ellie's body cried out in fatigue as she started the Honda, setting its GPS for the Condado Vanderbilt Hotel in San Juan. If she faltered now, she'd fail not only herself, but Carla and Enrique as well.

She waited until Colon disappeared into the hospital, no doubt to check on Carla. She made sure the other police units were not following, and then continued driving.

She took Route 22 all the way, with dawn lifting over her left shoulder above the sparkling Atlantic Ocean. Under better circumstances, the beauty would have enchanted her. As it was, she could barely stay awake and stopped for coffee at Vega Baja.

She wanted to sleep, and dream about Carla, but she had to make a plan. She'd been lucky at the hospital. The police officer from the cave, the one who spoke English, had been exiting Carla's room just as she was being denied entrance. He had vouched for her and gotten her in. She could not expect such a friendly interloper at the hotel. Should she have called ahead to confirm that Joey Arroyo was in residence? If so, should she just go knock on his door? She didn't know, decided to wing it. She did know she would not be welcome.

The imposing, multistoried hotel was white with a red roof. The hotel was right on the beach in the busy Condado District. She'd never convince the parking valets that she was a guest, so she found a garage a block away and walked back.

The grand lobby offered a double spiral staircase and exuded turn-of-the-century elegance. For lack of a better idea, she went directly to the front desk and told the male receptionist, who looked like a leading man from a Telemundo soap opera, that she was staying with Joey Arroyo. "My husband…" she added.

He raised his dark eyebrows and consulted his computer. "Room 407?"

"Yeah, I guess so."

His eyebrows shot higher in suspicion as he looked her up and down. Ellie knew that after her ordeal of the previous night, dressed like a male street urchin, she looked less like a fashion plate, more like a homeless person.

"Look, I missed my flight, so Joey and my son, Enrique, arrived in town first. He was supposed to leave my key here at the front desk."

Glancing at the monitor, he said, "But we've received payment for only two guests."

"Yeah, me and Joey. Kids stay free, right?" The idea of sneaking a child into a room was likely frowned upon in a place like this, but she hoped he wouldn't call her on it.

"Why don't I call Mr. Arroyo's room and confirm?" He frowned.

She figured Mr. Soap Star would soon be calling security, when a young woman, who had been polishing the dark wood paneling behind the counter, spoke up and told him something in excited Spanish.

"Your husband is the tall guy, an American basketball star?" he said with stars in his dreamboat eyes. "I've seen him. The maid said he just left."

"Was our son with him?" she asked.

He translated for the maid. "The maid says he went alone, for McDonald's takeout."

Ellie couldn't believe her good fortune, and forced a laugh. "Right. Our son loves those Happy Meals. But I do need that key. I should be there when the boy wakes up. Surprise him, you know?"

If the handsome gatekeeper was an adversary, the maid was an ally, because after she whispered something in his ear and playfully shoved at him, he relented.

"I like surprises, Mrs. Arroyo. I'll get you a spare key."

Oh my God! Could it have been more perfect? Clutching the keycard in her moist hand, she raced to the elevators before anyone could question her elaborate bluff. Stepping into the first elevator to open, she pushed the button for the fourth floor and said a prayer of silent thanks as it ascended.

CHAPTER SIXTY

A puppy…

The room was large and expensively furnished, with an enormous king-sized bed dead center. The pillows and spread were fashioned of silk, a subtle tapestry pattern, and in the middle of the sumptuous luxury, sleeping like an angel, was a very small boy. One of Enrique's skinny arms was thrown up on the pillow, while the other snuggled a fuzzy blue teddy bear costumed like a basketball player. His face looked pale beneath the shock of black hair, with lips parted like a rosebud.

She quickly spanned the distance between them. In all her twenty-eight years, she had never seen a sight more beautiful, and fought to keep back tears. With infinite care, she sat on the edge of the bed and gazed in wonder at the child. Then very gently, taking care not to startle him, she kissed his rosebud lips and whispered his name.

Enrique's sleeping eyes blinked open, then closed again. Two small fists rubbed the sleep away, and gradually his eyelids, with long black lashes, fluttered open like butterfly wings to reveal the deep dark pools within. "What are you doing here, Señorita Birdsong?" the warm, sleepy lips said.

"My dear Enrique, I promised I wouldn't leave without saying goodbye."

His mouth opened in a wide smile, and she was startled to see the boy was missing a front tooth.

"Look…" He pointed proudly to the gap. "The tooth fairy brought me this bear." He held up the blue stuffed animal for her to pat. "But I wish she gave me a puppy. All I ever wanted was a dog."

She could no longer hold back the tears.

"Why are you crying?" Enrique touched her eyes.

"Because I'm happy to see you. Don't you ever cry when you're happy?"

The child considered, then offered his lopsided smile. "Not me. Big boys never cry."

She laughed and hugged him to her heart. "You *are* a big boy, Enrique. I suppose this has been an adventure, but are you ready to come home now?"

A fleeting worry clouded his face. "Will that man who says he's my father let me go now?"

"I'm sure he won't mind if you leave. Has he been nice to you?"

"I guess. He said he'd bring me a Happy Meal for breakfast."

She laughed again and squeezed him even harder. "Ready to go? You can bring your bear if you want."

The child crawled off the bed and dressed himself very slowly, causing her to wonder if he had been lightly drugged throughout the ordeal. She did not interfere until he got to his shoelaces. "Let me help you tie those…"

As she knelt on the plush carpet, she heard muffled footsteps in the hall outside and was terrified that Joey Arroyo had returned. But the footsteps passed them by, so she dressed Enrique as quickly as possible. Since he had been snatched off the street, he had no belongings to pack.

He was still half-asleep when she took his hand and led him down the hallway, into an elevator, and down to the main lobby. The helpful maid was still at work cleaning, but she looked up to smile at "mother and son," the latter clutching his new blue teddy bear as they stepped outside to Asheford Avenue.

Moving along as quickly as possible, Ellie was terrified when a white Mercedes sedan pulled under the hotel canopy and an exceptionally tall man climbed out and slipped a tip to the valet. Arroyo's head swiveled right and left, his hawk-like eyes scanning for danger, or prey. Seeing neither, he strode into the lobby holding a McDonald's bag in his big hand.

In seconds, the maid would undoubtedly inform him that he'd just missed his family, and he'd be after them in a flash, his long legs easily overtaking them on the street. So although he whined in protest, she made Enrique run like his life depended upon it, because quite likely it did.

She fast-walked him to the parking garage, stashed him in the Honda, and then took the driver's seat. Arroyo did not pursue. By the time her speeding pulse returned to normal, the boy was already yawning and rubbing his eyes. He snuggled against her with the teddy bear in his arms. If he'd been drugged, perhaps it was a blessing, and he'd never know he'd been in danger. Unless someone told him, he'd never know something scary happened.

Children were amazing that way. Too bad adults could not bounce back so easily.

With that thought ricocheting in her amped up brain, she set the GPS for Casa Valdez and got on the road. The ride would take about an hour, and as the excess adrenaline charged through her system, she prayed she wouldn't crash the car.

CHAPTER SIXTY-ONE

Special delivery...

They arrived late morning, with the golden sun climbing high, along with the temperature. Along the way, she'd called the Ponce Police Station and left a message that Enrique Valdez had been found unharmed, and was on his way home. She knew the bulletin would find its way to Lieutenant Colon, eventually.

The landscape of cacti and yellow flamboyan trees stretched out under a blanket of shimmering heat, while in the far distance, the Caribbean was a mysterious mirror that saw all—reflected all. Emerging from the trance, she shifted her gaze to Casa Valdez. It too lay dormant, its white wooden walls bathed in a pastel glow.

It was time to make her special delivery.

The ill-fitting men's clothing she'd borrowed from Sylvie were soiled and wrinkled. Her hands and face looked like she'd been rooting in a pigpen, and she ached from her filthy hair to her toenails. She needed a hot bath, a toothbrush, and a fistful of painkillers. But even had she partaken of those amenities, enabling her to make her grand entrance absolutely presentable, she feared she would still be perceived as the villain.

"Time to wake up, Enrique," she gently kissed the top of his sleeping head. "You are home."

He opened his eyes and grinned through his missing tooth. He took her hand, and they approached the front door.

Too late to turn back now. As the doorbell jingled inside the old house, she held her breath. Would anyone answer? She watched the yellow ball of sun climb higher in the sky, and after an eternity, the door swung open, and she was drowning in the deep brown depths of Filo Castillo's eyes.

"*Gracias Dios!*" she cried. "Thank you, thank you!" She bent over to give Enrique a crushing hug, then ushered them into the foyer, where two men stood in the shadows.

"My dear Señorita Birdsong..." Juan Castillo's voice was hoarse with emotion. "What can I say?" He stepped forward, bowed, and then kissed her hand.

In turn, Ellie touched the clean bandage on his forehead. "I see the medics patched you up, Juan."

"*Sí*, thanks to you. How can we ever repay you?"

He was giving her way too much credit, so she moved away, in case he decided to kiss her hand again.

Juan opened his arms. "I will take Enrique up to his bed. He looks like he's still asleep."

"No, let *me* do it." The second male stepping from the shadows was none other than Manuel Castillo. "You have been injured, Father, so let me tuck him in."

She nearly fainted in surprise. She knew Manuel and Roberto had been cleared of all charges, but she never expected them to be home so soon.

Juan gazed proudly at his son, then stood aside as Manuel swept Enrique up into his arms. "Did they drug this boy?"

"It's quite possible," she answered.

She realized her mouth was hanging open as she gaped at Manuel. "I can't believe you're home."

He laughed. "C'mon, Ellie, they can't keep a rebel like me behind bars for long. Once they realized I'd been framed, they decided enough was enough and let me go. They'll deal with the legal red tape later."

She sensed the same gentle nature in Manuel that she'd come to love in his father and sisters. "I'm glad you're free. What about Roberto?"

Filo smiled, pointed toward the patio. "They are waiting for you, Ellie."

For her? Her courage shriveled and she longed to hide.

As Manuel tiptoed upstairs with the sleeping Enrique, she tried to calm her nerves and keep her heart from pounding out of her chest. If Roberto Valdez was truly waiting for her on the patio, what the hell would she say to him?

As she stepped outside onto the flagstones, the scents of frangipani and oleander accosted her like sad old friends, reminding her of the breakfast Carla and she had shared on this patio. The exotic fragrances forced her to recall how their hands had brushed, how even on their first morning together, Carla's soulful eyes and low, seductive voice put her body in turmoil. She remembered how jealous she'd been to observe Carla's nocturnal rendezvous with Carmen in the garden, and although she now realized Carla's embrace was intended to comfort a distressed sister-in-law, the memory still sparked a need that couldn't be denied.

Now, as history repeated itself, she once again caught Carmen locked in a passionate embrace. This time the kiss she shared rendered both lovers oblivious to all but the fire of one another's lips. Noonday light caressed the couple. It heated the raven blackness of Carmen and Roberto's hair, and seemed to infuse them with an inner glow. Ellie approached reluctantly, hating to disturb them, and then loudly cleared her throat to warn them that a voyeur had come on the scene.

She stared at the flagstones while they untangled themselves, and for a brief moment, Carmen looked right through her, a confused look on her face. Then slowly her dark eyes sparked with recognition, and her lips parted in a smile. Ellie stood frozen to the spot as Carmen opened both arms and walked toward her. She took her hands, and then kissed her cheek. Ellie was speechless as their eyes locked, first in questioning, then understanding.

"Please forgive me, Ellie," Carmen spoke at last. "I should have listened to Carla. She believed in you all along. If Roberto and I had trusted her instincts, maybe this tragedy would never have happened."

Ellie refused to cry. Carmen's forgiveness helped, but it came too late. "Never mind, Carmen. Even if you had trusted me, nothing would have changed. Joey Arroyo would still have kidnapped Enrique, and eventually Roberto would have been cleared."

Carmen wasn't buying it. "Listen, we know what happened, and you're not to blame. In fact, if Colon and the police had not intervened, then Roberto and Manuel would have fought those thugs alone. Likely they would have been killed."

"Please, just forget it."

"No, I won't forget it, and neither will Roberto. The police told me what happened in that cave." She took Ellie's hand and gripped hard. "If you had not used my gun, then Carla would be dead."

"How is Carla now? Please tell me the truth."

Roberto approached, looking exceedingly handsome in a dark sports coat and crisp slacks. She guessed his outfit had hung unused in Casa Valdez for the past two years, because while his body was rangy and strong, he failed to fill out the clothes from his former life. In spite of that, and his pale complexion, he seemed like a new man.

He captured Ellie's other hand. "The hospital called an hour ago. They said Carla tried to check herself out, but they don't think she's ready. They wanted to sedate her, so she wouldn't make trouble. And Ellie, I think you should be there when she wakes up."

"Not a good idea," she answered sadly.

"Why not?" Carmen smiled. "I'm sure Carla will want to thank you."

"I don't think so…" Ellie's mama used to say: *too many tears over the dam*—her version of *too much water under the bridge*. Carla and she had suffered too many misunderstandings, too much mistrust. The last two days had poisoned all hope for a lasting relationship. She pulled away from the happy couple.

"When she wakes up, tell her goodbye for me. Promise?"

But she got no promises from Carmen and Roberto, who kept insisting she should go back to the hospital. They didn't understand that she was scared to death to face Carla. Plus, her body required at least eight hours of sleep before she could function at all.

When she finally pushed through their barricade of helpful hands and leaned against the patio wall, her bruised emotions went into overdrive when she saw a taxi pull into the driveway.

"Did someone call for a cab?" Roberto asked.

A jaunty, dark-skinned man leaped from the driver's seat. *Pablo*! What the hell was he doing at Casa Valdez? She didn't know, didn't care. She only knew he was her white knight, come to rescue her.

"That's *my* taxi driver," she told the startled couple. He's taking me back to San Juan."

Carmen's eyebrows shot up, while Roberto tried to convince her to stay.

She had no strength left to explain, nor did she have the heart to say goodbye to Enrique.

In the end, she made a clean getaway.

CHAPTER SIXTY-TWO

Up to her eyeballs...

Ellie heaved a sigh of relief and nestled into the front seat beside Pablo. Exiting Casa Valdez had been a major challenge. She felt like a linebacker who'd run the entire football field and made a touchdown without the help of a single teammate—except Pablo, who ran interference at the crucial moment.

"Thanks for bailing me out," she told him. "Why did you come?"

"Since I'm practically an honorary member of the Force, Lieutenant Colon suggested you'd wind up here without a ride, so he sent me to collect you." He lifted his red Yankees cap, then carefully replaced it backward.

"Muchas gracias, señor." She smiled.

"De nada, señorita."

She punched his arm. "Tell me the truth, Pablo, why did you come? Don't expect me to believe you're lonesome for my company. I suspect you haven't slept all night. Your wife and little daughter must be frantic with worry."

He shrugged. "Tell you the truth, Colon wants you delivered to San Juan. Said I should check you into the hotel of your choice, then make sure you show up for an Inquest tomorrow morning before you skip to the States."

She slumped deeper into the seat, rubbed her aching eyes. "You're kidding, right? Why do the police need me?"

"How the hell should I know? But the cops are paying me good money to babysit you, and hey, I enjoy working with those guys. Maybe I really will sign up at the Police Academy, change careers?"

"What *Inquest*?"

"Colon claims it's only a formality, but you gotta admit, you're in this up to your eyeballs. The lieutenant assumes you've committed no crime, but maybe you can help clear up the details."

They sped through the tropical afternoon, but she was oblivious to the sights, the sounds and the scents of the magnificent day. They thought she had answers, when in fact, she didn't have a clue what had prompted so many unsavory characters to behave so badly. Dollars to doughnuts, Dyna was orbiting somewhere near the center of that criminal circle, so her association with Dyna put her squarely in the bullseye.

Or more precisely, her boss's greed, stupidity, and desperation had landed Ellie in the middle of a manure pile. She assumed her clothes were still waiting for her at the Hotel San Cristóbal, in the room Dyna had rented for her. Or maybe Dyna had tossed her stuff into the nearest dumpster? After all, she'd stood Dyna up yesterday, left her waiting in the bar at happy hour.

And where was her boss, anyway? Had she escaped on a jet to destinations unknown, or was she cooling her heels in a Puerto Rican jail? Who cared? Not Ellie. When she finally emerged from this nightmare, she'd go back to her apartment in Atlantic City and lick her wounds, but life would never be the same.

"Wake up, Ellie." Pablo's voice jerked her back to consciousness.

Lord, had she really fallen asleep? As she swam back to reality, she decided waking up was too upsetting. Next time anyone tried to pull her out of sweet oblivion, she'd jolly well ignore him.

"Where are we?"

"San Juan. Should I drop you at the Hotel San Cristóbal?"

She sat up, stretched her legs, and made a decision that proved she had finally lost her mind. "No, I'd prefer to stay at El Rincón. Do you know the place?"

Pablo did a double take. "You bet. My parents spent their honeymoon there. Islanders consider it the finest hotel in town, but how did you know about it?"

No one could avoid death or taxes, but she could sure enough avoid Pablo's question. She retrieved Carmen's backpack, which still contained the ruined remains of her purse.

"How much do I owe you, Pablo? I have one credit card, and you're entitled to max it out."

He held up both hands in protest. "Later. We're not done with each other yet, Ellie. I've been hired to drive you again first thing in the morning. To that Inquest, remember? After that, I'll present you with my bill."

"How do you know I won't skip town?"

He laughed. "Hey, you're as curious as I am. You'll want to be at that Inquest to find out how this story ends."

But would this story ever end? Not in Ellie's tortured mind. No matter what happened tomorrow, who was held responsible for this whole depressing mess, she would never forget what happened here in this land of enchantment, where she almost lost her life, where she definitely lost her heart. She knew instinctively that she'd carry those scars forever.

They rode the next few blocks in silence, and then Pablo turned down a quiet side street that dead-ended at ocean's edge. Nothing had changed. El Rincón still looked like a vintage American seaside resort, with its old wooden walls now basking in the sun.

He stopped the car and smiled. "I'll swing by the Hotel San Cristóbal and ask them to forward your luggage here, Ellie."

"Thanks, Pablo. I hope you can find it."

"Don't worry, we cabbies have a nose for that sort of thing. Can I walk you in?"

They gazed at one another for one long moment. She wondered how many more times life would throw them together, for she had truly come to care about her brave new friend.

"No, I'll be fine." She smiled in profound appreciation. "But you must promise me, Pablo, do not tell *anyone* where I'm staying."

"I won't, Scout's honor…long as you promise not to bail on me."

"I'll be right here waiting in the morning."

CHAPTER SIXTY-THREE

Déjà vu…

As they waved goodbye, Ellie doubted Pablo had ever been a Boy Scout, but she trusted him all the same and felt the security blanket of his companionship slip away as she climbed the wide steps and entered the hotel. Suddenly, she was utterly alone, without reservations, and she feared the disagreeable little man who owned El Rincón would turn her away when she showed up without luggage.

She walked through the foyer with marble floors polished to a high sheen, saw the same potted plants set among groupings of antique furniture, and experienced a powerful rush of memory. Dear God, she had made a dreadful mistake. She should never have tried to recapture a past that still bled like an open wound.

"*Buenos días*, Señorita Birdsong." Don Miguel wore the same dark suit he'd worn that first night. "Did Doña Carla forget to make your reservations?"

"Doña Carla isn't coming." She tried to ignore the dirty old man staring at the front of her filthy shirt. "If you have no room, I'll gladly return to Hotel San Cristóbal."

"Oh no, *señorita!*" Miguel cried. "We always have room for a friend of Doña Carla. In fact, I can offer you the same suite you occupied on your first visit."

She hesitated only a moment, fully willing to make another dreadful mistake. "That will be fine. When my bags arrive, will you have them sent up?"

"But of course!" He bowed from the waist, then trailed her all the way upstairs to her door. "Will there be anything else, *señorita?*"

He was waiting for a big, juicy tip, but unless he took credit card gratuities, he'd wait until the cows came home. She told him she could use a bath and a good long sleep, but of course a blind man could see she was filthy and dead on her feet. He could not see, however, that she hadn't eaten in more than twenty-four hours, so she ordered room service for dinner, asking him to choose an authentic Puerto Rican meal.

Miguel continued to hesitate. When it became obvious she wanted him to leave, he reluctantly turned and slipped away. She chuckled and shook her head. Did he take her for a rich American, when in fact, even one night in this room was way above her pay grade? Once she could have put it on DynaCo's expense account, but now she was unemployed. If tonight was a foolish luxury, then so be it. What was money for?

As she entered the suite, she was stricken with a painful sensation of déjà vu. She was violently, mercilessly assaulted by memories of Carla. She felt her standing close behind her, recalled how good it felt to lean against her. She smelled the clean scent of her cologne, relived the smooth feel of her cheek in the prelude to a kiss.

She sighed as she turned on the lights in the room designed for a princess, with its brass bed, Queen Anne chairs, and Oriental rug on the hardwood floor. Was it possible that only a few days ago, Carla had led her into this luxurious space? She glanced uneasily at the doors to the balcony, now closed to the oppressive heat. Tonight, if she summoned the courage, she would venture outside to the site of their rendezvous.

She smiled, remembering how she had found Carla showered and standing barefoot on the moonlit balcony, a bottle of champagne held shyly in her hands. Her dark eyes had betrayed wonder at Ellie's presence. Those eyes had continued to caress her throughout their sweet lovemaking, and no matter what the future might hold, she knew she would never find love like that again.

"Room Service, *señorita…*"

The sound swam upstream against the current of her dreams, and she realized she'd fallen asleep, fully dressed in her filthy clothes, after a supper she barely remembered.

"I brought your champagne, also rolls and cheese," a boyish voice announced.

"But I didn't order champagne, or anything else." She yawned.

The bellhop ignored her protest. "Your luggage is here, too. Some man in a taxi dropped it off. May I come in, *señorita?*"

So the resourceful Pablo had located her stuff, after all. Had he also sent the wine and cheese? She kept the boy waiting while she sorted through the night case he delivered and found her emergency money hidden in the lining. She accepted the bottle and tray of goodies, gave the bellboy a generous tip, and then locked herself in once more. She nibbled the food while her tub filled, and then she lay out the white nightgown and robe she'd worn with Carla. Hugging them to her breast, she fancied she could still smell the intoxicating fragrance of their coupling.

She sank into the bath, scented with floral bubbles, and imagined she heard Carla walking back and forth in the adjacent room. She lazily popped the cork and poured frothy liquid into a tall-stemmed glass and enjoyed a long swallow, just like in the movies. But when would euphoria claim her? The seductive waters caressed her body as she finished a quarter of the bottle, yet the numbing release she desired still eluded her.

When the tub grew cold, and the bubbles wilted to flat scum, she climbed out and punished her skin with the towel. She yanked the white gown over her frizzy hair, and cursed the day she set foot on Puerto Rican soil.

She'd have been better off had she never learned to love the land, the boys, and yes, Carla. Because she would never be able to leave them behind, no matter how far she ran. Bitter, and a bit unsteady on her feet, she approached the balcony doors and flung them open.

When she stepped out into the salt-scented air, she heard the moaning Atlantic sliding onto its lover, the beach, only to pull back and recede. Below, she heard a classical guitar strumming a sadly haunting melody. The refrain penetrated her shell of self-pity. She had heard this music once before, at the meeting of the *Independentistas* at the old church in Lares: The Puerto Rican National Anthem. Tonight a young troubadour sang it in English, for the benefit of the Americans who had gathered:

What will become of Borinquen, my dear God?
What will become of my children, of my home?
Borinquen, land of paradise... pearl of the seas.

Borinquen—the Indian name for Puerto Rico. Carla had explained it, and Ellie remembered. Like the sorrowful poet guitarist, she wondered what would become of this land she'd come to love? And what would become of her when she left, never again to see the pearl of the seas?

CHAPTER SIXTY-FOUR

Adiós...

"This won't take long, Ms. Birdsong," the man from the American Consulate assured her. "The authorities in Ponce have already cleared you of suspicion, but we still need your help. The defendant, Dyna Collins, will be tried in the States. Perhaps you can tell us why a successful woman like that would stoop to blackmail and kidnapping?"

By then she knew the story: Dyna had conspired with Joey Arroyo to "borrow" Enrique. As Arroyo had said on the plane, he met Dyna playing poker in Atlantic City. In the course of the game, they found they shared a common interest: winning negotiations with Carla Valdez. Dyna stood to gain financially, while Arroyo, in his twisted mind, figured that without her land, Carla would have less standing as sole custodian of his sons. Likely the violence would not have escalated, the kidnapping might not have occurred, had Diego Martinez not intruded as competition.

The Consul droned on and on, the interrogation room was hot and airless. Too much champagne and a sleepless night had taken their toll, and even though she now knew her boss had committed these horrendous crimes, she would never understand it.

She should feel sorry for Dyna, for old times' sake, but instead, she felt nothing at all. She stared out to the courtyard, where Pablo leaned against his car, tossing a baseball into the clear blue sky, and then catching it in an ancient mitt.

"What happens to Mr. Arroyo?" she asked the Consul.

"A restraining order, to begin with. It's hard to charge him with a crime, when he claims he only wanted to visit with his son."

"He doesn't care a flying fig about Enrique. The boy didn't even recognize him. What's the point?"

"I suspect it is jealousy, or a male power thing. But I think you are right, Ms. Birdsong, he doesn't care about those boys. I doubt Ms. Valdez needs to worry about him in the future."

She thought about it a moment, remembering Antonio's glorification of Arroyo's basketball career, and his love of all things American. Was it fair, long-term, to completely isolate the boys from their father? It was a tricky balance that Carla would have to deal with, maybe when the boys were older.

The Consul said, "I suspect you're out of a job. What will you do, Ms. Birdsong?"

Good question. She guessed she'd return to Atlantic City, then spend time with her brothers in North Carolina. She had invested years in earning her broker's license and climbing the corporate ladder, but now, none of that mattered.

"Will I have to appear at Dyna's trial?" she asked the man.

"I'm afraid so. Everyone connected with this case will be obliged to testify, and that includes the locals. The Puerto Ricans involved will have to travel to Atlantic City, but what else can we do? The plot originated in the States, so Mrs. Collins must be tried there."

When he finally dismissed her, Ellie escaped into the tropical sunlight.

If Carla and her family came to New Jersey for the trial, could she face them again?

"You okay, Ellie?" Pablo frowned as he tucked his ball gear away, and then opened the front door of the taxi. "You look like a ghost. Are you suffering from a hangover?"

"It was hot as Hades in there," she grumbled as she slid into the car. "Mind your own business, will you?"

He rolled his eyes, exhaled in exasperation. "Hey, don't take it out on me, *chica*. I'm a hero, remember? Did you see me on the evening news? I was right behind Colon at the press conference."

Pablo's good humor lifted her out of her funk as they headed back to El Rincón. She told herself, things could be worse. At least she had her clothes, her credit card, and she'd been cleared of all charges. She felt almost human in her favorite cotton gauze shirt and the colorful skirt she'd bought last year on a vacation in Cancun. With her clean hair done up in a loose braid, Pablo claimed she looked like a *Navajo princess*. Well, she was part Cherokee, so he was close enough.

When they parked outside the old hotel, she realized the time had come to say goodbye to Pablo...forever. Normally, she didn't get emotionally attached to taxi drivers, but her stay on the island had been anything but normal. Here relationships had been telescoped into high intensity. Intimate encounters blossomed in days, rather than months, or years. Maybe the long growing season in Puerto Rico, always fertile, always bearing fruit, was to blame. For surely, all her new friendships had ripened before she could harvest their benefits.

"Hey, don't be sad." Pablo held her hands as he prepared to leave her at the hotel door. "You'll be back, and we'll meet again."

"Promise?"

"Scout's honor!" He repeated a pledge she'd heard before, but she still didn't believe him. He planted a lusty kiss on her cheek, and after a comical curtsey, walked toward his cab. "*Adiós* for now, *señorita*. Who knows, when you return to the island, maybe I'll be a cop...?"

CHAPTER SIXTY-FIVE

No more games…

Ellie quickly retreated into the shady lobby. She'd expected a huge letdown once Pablo was gone, but the reality was much worse. She had never felt so alone. He was her last link to the island, and to all the people she'd grown to love. She thought about the enormous cash tip she'd withdrawn at the ATM before he picked her up that morning, and then she pictured him finding the money in his glove compartment, where she had secretly stashed it.

She visualized a wonderful doll he might buy for his little girl, but the image failed to comfort her. Fact was, she'd be flying home without the usual silly souvenirs—no straw hat or T-shirt painted with palm trees to show off to her friends in the land of snow. She fingered Carla's necklace, her most precious reminder of the island. Indeed, she was leaving behind more than she brought, not the least of which, was her heart.

"Will you be joining us for luncheon in the dining room, *señorita?*" The owner of El Rincón was unusually solicitous. He was also squirrelly, like he was hiding a nut under his tongue. His beady little eyes glittered.

"No thanks, Don Miguel. I'm really tired, and I don't want to be disturbed."

"As you wish, *señorita*."

She ducked past him into the elevator, and as she neared her room, she heard classical guitar, likely coming from someone's cell phone playlist. The sound came from her neighbor's suite. Someone must have checked in while she was at the Inquest. Thank heavens the new guest didn't favor rap or heavy metal, because the sweet, tragic quality of the guitar perfectly orchestrated her mood. She figured she'd get a few hours sleep, then call the airport. With a little luck, she'd get a ticket to Atlantic City for tomorrow.

She unlocked her door, entered, and suddenly all her senses were bombarded. She was smothered in a riot of flowers, and the impact of all that color—bouquets of a dozen mingling fragrances—assailed her with the abundance of their beauty. All were native flowers, ones Carla had taught her to identify: yellow canarias, pink trinitarias and hibiscus, white frangipani, and even an exotic African tulip greeted her like old friends, even though she'd made their acquaintance only days ago.

Someone must have made a mistake, delivered the flowers to the wrong room. An invisible band tightened around her chest, and she dared not speculate. Her heart beat madly as she glanced at the doors to the balcony.

The shutters were open. In the far distance, the blue Atlantic basked in the brilliance of the noonday sun, while beyond the garden, a row of shimmering palms danced in the breeze on the beach. Just outside the balcony door, she saw the edge of a linen cloth, two covered casseroles, and two crystal wine glasses. The table was set for lunch. Like a sleepwalker in a dream, she drifted toward the shutters, floated onto the balcony, and stopped where shadows played across the concrete floor.

Carla stood in the sun, her back partially turned, so that Ellie couldn't see her directly. The brilliant light made a chiseled profile of her elegant face, but her features were unreadable.

Her black hair glistened like the wing of a raven, and to Ellie, she was like a goddess returned from a fierce battle, in search of grace and repose.

"Carla…" She breathed her name.

"Hello, Ellie…" Carla turned to face her. "You look beautiful today."

Carla's eyes were black coals, but her cheeks were pale beneath her tan. Ellie had forgotten how tall and regal she was. Next to her, all the women she'd admired in the past were mere shadows. This afternoon, the mistress of Casa Valdez was casually dressed in a loose-fitting purple hombre blouse and black skinny denims. And she was barefoot, her graceful feet planted firmly on the brick patio floor. She wore a dark Spanish shawl slung carelessly across one shoulder, but the wrap failed to conceal the sling supporting her arm.

She drank Carla in, deciding she looked less like a goddess, more like a pirate. "I'm surprised the hospital released you."

Carla grinned. "I tried to leave yesterday, but they wouldn't cooperate. This morning, I didn't bother asking for permission."

Although they were several feet apart, Ellie felt her heat. She was painfully aware of her aggressive stance and the tense muscles of her upper thighs inside the soft fabric of her jeans. Carla's good hand gripped the neck of a bottle of champagne. And as Ellie stared at that hand, she recalled how her body had yielded to those long, talented fingers.

Carla's expression darkened. "When my family visited the hospital this morning, they said you planned to leave the island. Both my sons warned me about your imminent departure, even before they inquired about my health. They asked me to stop you."

Carla came two steps closer.

Ellie backed up two steps, took hold of a chair to steady herself. "How did you know I was staying at El Rincón?"

"Pablo was especially helpful." She smiled and advanced. "He called me after dropping you here yesterday, so I was able to send the champagne last night. Did you enjoy it?"

She gasped in surprise. So Pablo had betrayed her, after all, so much for his Boy Scout promise.

"Lieutenant Colon assisted, too," Carla continued. "And so did the owner of this hotel. In fact, Miguel couldn't wait until you discovered the flowers and the surprise lunch."

Now she understood why Don Miguel had been acting so weird. "Poor man, he thinks there's something going on between us." Ellie laughed nervously.

"But he's wrong, of course?" Carla's voice was low and unnaturally husky as she carefully placed the champagne on the table, then moved so close Ellie could smell her fresh, unique scent and feel her warm breath on her hair.

"How did you know I would return in time for lunch?" She felt extremely vulnerable.

"I didn't know, but I hoped. If you had not come soon, I'd have drunk the champagne myself, to ease my disappointment."

She noticed an odd, wistful smile on Carla's lips and realized she had just repeated the exact words she'd uttered that night they made love.

"Listen, Ellie, I can't open this bottle with one hand. Will you help me?"

This was Ellie's *now or never* moment. Once she'd opened the wine, she'd be obliged to stay and share it. But how could she accept a drink and a casual lunch, when she lacked the nerve to look Carla in the eye? If she stayed, Carla would see into her heart, as she had always done. It seemed she had guessed the secret Ellie was desperately trying to hide, even from herself.

Carla shifted from foot to foot. "What are you waiting for, Ellie? Must I beg for my drink?"

This was Ellie's *leap of faith* moment. She knew damn well if she turned away, she'd be turning her back on happiness. So like any sane person, she popped the cork and poured a splash of sparkling wine into each goblet, in spite of her trembling hands.

Carla lifted her glass in a toast. "Here's to you, Ellie, and to this day together."

Ellie swallowed the first glass and poured them each another.

But Carla placed her second drink deliberately on the table and seemed to stretch to a taller height, her face clouded.

"You told my boys you would never leave them without saying goodbye. Am I not entitled to the same courtesy?"

"Carla, please…"

"No, I mean it. After all we've been through, after what we've come to mean to one another, how could you leave without a backward glance?"

Suddenly her face was dark with emotion, and in one swift motion, she seized Ellie's wrist, pulling her off-balance. Carla winced when Ellie stumbled against her injured arm, but seemingly ignored the pain. She pinned Ellie against her, locking her in place with her one good arm.

"No more games, Ellie," she whispered against her ear. "We've survived three days of hell, but I think you still want me, like I want you."

"Carla, please don't…"

Before she could protest again, Carla's lips captured her mouth in a desperate, conquering kiss, the kind she had delivered that day at the top of El Yunque. The more she struggled, the more Carla's passion escalated. Ellie breathed the familiar scent of her skin, the clean gauze smell of her bandage. Trapped in an intimate embrace, she endured the teasing pressure of her teeth against her lips, the relentless probing of her tongue into the soft regions of her mouth. Carla meant to prove a point, and that realization sent heat scalding through Ellie's body. When she held her tighter, flattening their breasts together, she felt the furious raging of Carla's heart.

"Please let me love you, Ellie," she murmured.

When Carla's mouth found her again, her resistance crumbled. She melted against Carla's thighs and moaned in surrender. In response, Carla began an infinitely more gentle approach, tracing the ultra-sensitive lining of Ellie's lips with the stiff tip of her tongue. Utterly devastated, she pulled herself up and grasped the back of Carla's neck. She rolled her head back, exposing her throat. Taking her cue, Carla tasted the slope of Ellie's cheekbone and kissed the pulsating valley at the base of her neck.

Ellie freed one hand to explore the sculpted facets of Carla's face, the fevered ridge of her forehead. She touched the soft lids of her closed eyes and discovered tears in each corner, tears matching her own. She covered her beloved's face with kisses, and all remaining barriers between them burned away in the sudden ignition of their mutual need.

Their physical attraction was a wild beast that could not be denied, and although her body ached for Carla, she found herself pulling away. Carla had said she *wanted* her, but did she *love* her? Before drowning in a tidal wave of passion, she should consider the pain and consequences of unconditional surrender. Her shuddering body bitterly resented her caution, but sheer will enabled her to loosen her hold and move away.

"What's wrong?" The black pools of Carla's eyes burned with confusion, but soon softened with concern.

"Please, Carla, after all the mistrust, can we pretend that nothing has changed?"

"Everything has changed, since the moment I met you, Ellie."

She searched Carla's face for traces of mockery, but saw only tenderness, coupled with suppressed desire. "But that night in the cave you truly believed I was responsible for Enrique's kidnapping. You blamed me for your brother's capture. You hated me then..."

"You are wrong, Ellie."

Ellie backed farther away. "I saw disgust in your eyes."

"You are making this very hard."

Ellie took a deep breath. It seemed Carla was telling the truth, maybe she never doubted her. Did Carla now realize she had never betrayed her? Clearly that web would be hard to untangle, but she was convinced Carla's current romantic gestures were not designed to punish her.

"I don't want to make it hard," Ellie told her. "But I don't understand..."

"Listen, Ellie, we can put this behind us. That night in the cave, when I saw you pick up Carmen's knapsack and bring out the gun, I already knew we were playing for the same team. After the police came and the shooting started, I lost track of what happened, but I know you saved my life. And then later, I found out how you rescued Enrique from drowning. I am so very grateful."

"You bought flowers and champagne because I made a lucky shot and know how to swim?"

"Not exactly…" As Carla closed the distance between them, Ellie's legs felt weak and insubstantial. Carla took her hand, held it to her breast. "It's very complicated. In my heart, I never believed you were guilty of any wrongdoing. I knew you were incapable of committing a crime, or even one unkind act, but another part of me needed to distrust you, so I wouldn't get hurt."

She encircled Carla's waist with her arms, careful not to crush the arm bound to her body like a broken wing. "What are you talking about?"

When Carla closed her eyes, Ellie sensed they were at the brink of some truth. And then Carla's voice trembled, charged by powerful emotion.

"You see, Ellie, I'd come to believe dreams were only for children. My sons have grand dreams, and once I had them, too. But I'd also come to believe dreams die with the coming of adulthood, or at least when life reveals the futility and sorrow reserved for grownups."

Ellie remembered how Carla's partner, Maria, had died so young, and felt her pain.

"We always wake up," Carla continued. "All dreams come to an end, and sometimes it's better to stop a fantasy before it becomes too real, before the ending hurts."

"But we are not a fantasy, we are not a dream," she protested.

"No, but think about it, Ellie. What happens when a middle-aged woman meets a much younger woman? The older woman becomes young again, but does the clock really turn backward, or does time simply stop for one brief, exquisite moment?"

"Please, Carla, the age difference doesn't matter."

"No? I was overcome by the sweetness of making love to you, but once the wonder wore off, I realized I was being totally unfair to you."

"I came to you of my own free will."

"Please listen. For your sake, I should step out of your life so you can meet someone your own age. For my sake, I should run before the dream ends, and that's why I tried to convince myself that you had betrayed me."

She leaned against Carla as tears of frustration welled up in her eyes. Carla was holding their future, or lack of one, in her hands, but they had both been running away from commitment. Yet if Carla had already decided to bolt, why was she here now? Her pulse raced with excitement, and for the first time in days, she felt in control of her destiny. She held Carla tighter, determined not to let go without a fight.

"So you never lost faith in me. I believe that now. But you're wrong about me. I don't want to run away."

Carla pressed one finger to her lips. "But this isn't just about you and me. What about my boys?"

"I love Antonio and Enrique. Don't you get that?"

"But what about the land project? I still think the right development would benefit the community…"

"Okay, I agree. You and I have already established the ground rules." She dropped her arms from around Carla's waist and retreated from her magnetic sphere. "You didn't come here today to discuss real estate."

Carla turned crimson, avoided her eyes. "I feel guilty because you are out of a job."

"So you feel sorry for me?"

"No, damn it!" Carla was running out of excuses. She grabbed Ellie roughly by the shoulder with her free hand. "Why are you making this so hard?"

"What do you want from me?"

"God forgive me, but I want it all," she answered desperately. "Against my better judgment, I want you to stay in Puerto Rico, and we'll try to make it work. I want a real relationship. And I'm telling you I love you, Ellie."

Good God in heaven! Ellie collapsed into the nearest chair.

Carla's declaration filled her with joy and unexpected deliverance. Her former life replayed in slow motion as she wondered... Would she miss America, or her family in North Carolina?

She realized Carla wasn't asking her to forsake those things. Loving Carla didn't mean she was giving anything up, because Ellie was sure their love would be rooted in firm ground, a soil connecting both their worlds. They would reach for the sky.

She stood up and took her hand. "I love you, too, Carla."

"My beloved Ellie..." As Carla uttered her name, she gathered her with her good arm and held her close. "Maybe someday we'll adopt more beautiful babies. And I'm sure my sons would agree, they should all be girls, who look just like you."

Ellie tapped her chin, pretending to mull it over. "Sounds pretty good, but I have one more request..." She smiled up into Carla's eager eyes. "If I stay, can Enrique have a puppy...?"

Other books by Kate Merrill

Romance
Northern Lights (as Christie Cole)
Flames of Summer

Diana Rittenhouse Mystery Series
A Lethal Listing
Blood Brothers
Crimes of Commission
Dooley is Dead
Buyer Beware

Amanda Rittenhouse Mystery Series
Murder at Metrolina
Homicide in Hatteras
Murder at Midterm
Assault in Asheville

Art Book
Miss Addie's Gift: Portrait of an American Folk Artist

Poetry Collection (editor):
North Shore by Herbert Merrill

Bella Books, Inc.

Women. Books. Even Better Together.

P.O. Box 10543
Tallahassee, FL 32302

Phone: 800-729-4992
www.bellabooks.com